"A charming love story with plenty of witty dialogue and warmth. Don't miss it."
—*Rendezvous*

"A delightfully original heroine . . . matches wits with a sinfully sexy hero . . . Sweet, frothy, and laughter-laced."
—*Booklist*

RULES OF ENGAGEMENT

"A solid cast . . . a fine read . . . Readers will appreciate this delightful matchmaking story."
—*Midwest Book Review*

"Clever, frothy, and funny—an enthralling read!"
—**Eloisa James, *USA Today* bestselling author**

"With delightfully original . . . beautifully matched protagonists . . . amusing supporting characters . . . and clever, tartly humorous writing, Caskie's debut romance is witty and wonderful."
—*Booklist*

~

Love Is in the Heir

Kathryn Caskie

NEW YORK   BOSTON

Copyright © 2006 by Kathryn Caskie
All rights reserved. No part of this book may be reproduced in any form or by any electronic or mechanical means, including information storage and retrieval systems, without permission in writing from the publisher, except by a reviewer who may quote brief passages in a review.

Warner Forever and the Warner Forever logo are registered trademarks.

Cover art by John Paul
Typography by David Gath
Book design by Giorgetta Bell McRee

Warner Books
1271 Avenue of the Americas
New York, NY 10020

Printed in the United States of America

First Printing: June 2006

10 9 8 7 6 5 4 3 2 1

For Melanie Murray,
who took a chance and made my
grandest dream a reality.

Acknowledgments

This book could not have been written without the sage advice, support, and assistance of:

Jenny Bent, my incredible agent, whose vision and belief in my work transformed my career.

Author and friend Sophia Nash, who came up with the title for this book—one that totally trumped my original "Comedy of Heirs."

The lovely Hannah Heglund, who was my visual inspiration for Miss Hannah Chillton.

Nancy Mayers, whose patience and breadth of Regency-era knowledge is truly amazing.

Deborah Barnhart, Denise McInerney, and Pam Palmer Poulsen, who were always there for me.

And a special thank you to my family, who put up with my writing schedule and didn't take the documentary *Super Size Me* too seriously.

Author's Note

Many works of fiction are inspired by true events and characters, and *Love Is in the Heir* is certainly one of them. I'm not referring to the "ripped from the head-lines" sort of inspiration. I mean the tidbits of historical fact that start an author thinking, *What if . . . ?*

The Comet Encke, the second to have been found to have a periodic orbit, inspired the framework for this novel. The comet was spotted in 1786, 1795, 1805, and 1818, but until twenty-seven-year-old Johann Franz Encke worked out the orbit and correctly predicted the comet's return in 1822, no one knew that all the recorded sightings were of the same comet. The discovery enthralled England's society, which led me to wonder what would happen if a renowned astronomer predicted that a comet was to orbit low, directly over Bath? What would Bath society—and the Featherton sisters—do? Why, anticipate . . . and celebrate, of course. And so the Bath Comet was born.

Now, one might think, while reading this story, that frail Miss Caroline Herschel is likely a work of fiction as well.

After all, I love quirky characters, and she certainly is one. She stood only four feet three inches tall, was a trained performance soprano, a brilliant mathematician and astronomer, and at seventy-two years of age was still sweeping the heavens with her telescopes. Even more unlikely, Miss Caroline Herschel was one of England's foremost authorities on comets. She sounds like fiction, but she was very real.

Yes, authors of fiction tread the line between reality and fantasy in the creation of their worlds, their characters, and their stories. But this blend of research and imagination is what makes writing stories like *Love Is in the Heir*, stories that readers tell us they love, so rewarding.

Love Is in the Heir

Chapter One

Kirkwell Abbey Churchyard
Devon, England

The Earl of Devonsfield was having a bad heir day. And now his eternity looked equally bleak.

He removed his beaver hat, then lifted his freshly curled wig to scratch his bald head with ragged, chewed fingernails. "Well, what say you, Pinkerton, can it be done?"

His manservant, who was as clever as he was shrewd, was a lean, hawkish-looking gent, who at the moment was dangling precariously from a rowan branch high above the mausoleum. "I fear the reverend's man is correct, my lord; there is no way, at least none I can see, to add a second level to the crypt without compromising the existing structure."

This did not please the earl, who had hoped for an altogether more positive answer, but during his long life he'd learned that adaptation was necessary for one's own survival. "Then we have no other choice. We shall have to expand *outward*. Surely, with the right inducement"—the portly lord retrieved the single surname from the quartet of headstones beside him—"*the Anatoles* could be persuaded to move their family plot across the way."

Pinkerton glanced down at the earl. The expression on his long face made it clear that he was dubious about a favorable outcome. Still, he was nothing if not loyal. "I shall contact the family to determine your plan's viability, my lord."

With hat and wig in hand, Lord Devonsfield walked through the dried grass that poked up through the crisp, withered leaves alongside his family's crypt.

He sighed wistfully as he ran his pudgy fingers along its marble wall. This was just his sort of horrid luck—after two hundred years, the Devonsfield mausoleum was full, just when his own time on earth was at an end.

It was his brother's fault, of course. Even after Lord Devonsfield's entire remaining family was killed in a dreadful accident last month—both of his sons—there was still one space left and, damn it all, it had been meant for *him*. But then his brother, Thelonius, nearly ten years his junior, unexplainably expired while sitting atop his chamber pot, thereby claiming the last eternal resting place in the family crypt.

"My lord, may I descend from the tree now?" Pinkerton, habitually dressed from hat to boot in ebony, nervously straddled a thick branch.

"What? Oh, certainly. We're finished here." The earl flicked his wrist dismissively and waved his man down. "Though while we are on the subject of trees, will you explain your concern about my family tree—more specifically the branch where my *heir* might be found?

It has been a month since the accident, and still you have not located the heir to the Devonsfield earldom."

Pinkerton cautiously settled his feet to a lower branch, bouncing a bit to test its soundness. "Oh, no sir, I know exactly where to find your heir. The gentleman resides in Cornwall. He is your late second cousin's son."

The earl's mouth fell open in disbelief. He scurried to the base of the rowan tree and rapped at its trunk with his cane. "Devil take you, Pinkerton. Why haven't you informed me until now?" Lord Devonsfield peered up through the branches. "I must speak with him at once. What is the man's name?"

Pinkerton lowered himself to the ground, then brushed the bark shreds from his breeches. "I do not know . . . *exactly*. For I must inform you that your heir is—"

"What—a Whig? An invalid? A madman?" The earl sucked in a breath. "He's not . . . *a wastrel*?"

"No, my lord. He's a . . . twin."

"A twin? Is that all? What in blazes does that matter?" The earl huffed his frustration. "Determining which twin is heir is not half so difficult. It is simply a matter of knowing which child was born first."

"That's just it, my lord." Pinkerton peered down his hawkish nose at the earl, his eyes clouded with worry. "As preposterous as it might seem, no one knows which boy is firstborn. Even the parish baptismal records are unclear on this point."

"The hell you say." The earl slumped against the tree's trunk.

"From what I've been able to learn, theirs was a difficult birth, with a goodly amount of blood. Their mother did not survive, and since the boys had no hope of inheriting anything of consequence, their distraught father, your cousin, made no effort to name one twin or the other firstborn."

"Oh, good heavens." Lord Devonsfield wrung his pale hands. "Do you know what this means? Why, I dare not think what the House of Lords will do should I die without an heir—which of course I shall within the year, for you yourself heard the physician. I am not a well man."

"Actually, my lord, the physician only said that spending your days obsessing over death will see you to an early grave," Pinkerton muttered, but the earl paid his comment no heed. He knew the truth of it, what his physicians were *really* saying but sought to keep from him.

"One of the twins *must be* acknowledged as firstborn." The earl bit at his thumbnail as he paced back and forth between the tilted and crumbling gravestones. "We simply must find a way to see this oversight corrected."

"Indeed we must, my lord, for if no legal heir can be determined, upon your passing, the Devonsfield earldom will revert to the Crown."

The earl wished he could somehow stuff those blasphemous words back into Pinkerton's mouth and force him to recant ever saying them. But what he stated was true, and there was no way that truth could be ignored.

"I cannot allow the earldom to be lost. You know I cannot." The earl stood upright. His mission was clear. "We've not a moment to lose. Pinkerton, see that my portmanteau is packed. We must away to Cornwall—*tonight!*"

The Lizard
Cornwall, England

Griffin St. Albans adjusted the aperture of his telescope by the golden rays of the setting sun. The cliff above Kennymare Cove was the perfect spot for measuring the constellations on what promised to be the clearest night sky all month.

He bent and eased his eye to the lens, meaning to check his settings, when suddenly a falcon, riding the warm sea air, swooped straight at him and clipped his shoulder. Griffin's feet rolled across the gravel, sending pebbles plunging over the cliff's edge. He slipped and fell hard to the ground, his back slamming down against the short, wind-shorn grass.

A faint feminine voice sailed out from under the cliff's lip. "Is someone up there?"

Griffin sat up, startled. He rose and warily peered over the rocky ledge. There, clinging to the wall, was a young woman stretching out her arm to reach a beribboned hat caught on a protruding root. His foot accidentally sent another bit of gravel her way.

She glanced up with the sharpest look of annoyance in her eyes. "Do take care not to pummel me with pebbles, sir. As you can see, the wind is strong this day, and my foothold is precarious enough as it is."

Good Lord, she could fall to her death at any moment! Griffin flattened himself onto his stomach, inched to the edge of the cliff, and reached out a hand. "Take hold. I can pull you up."

"Take hold? Are you mad? Without my bonnet? Not likely. My brother paid two guineas for it. *Two*. And you can be sure he'll not do that ever again." She stretched out her hand, straining for the hat, but it remained just beyond her fingertips. "Blast!"

"Let the gentleman help you, dear," called an old, twig-thin woman who was looking up at them from the lower cliff trail.

The rounder matron beside her cupped her hand to her brow and looked up at the girl struggling to reach the hat. "Viola is right, dove. Take his hand. Perhaps your bonnet will be easier to reach from above."

The dark-haired young woman peered down at the two women, then turned her pale blue eyes up at Griffin, considering. "It seems I must trust you not to drop me into the sea."

"Take my hand, miss. You have naught to fear. My back is strong."

She glanced down at the waves crashing upon the jagged rocks far below. "That may be, sir, but 'tis not your *back* I worry about." Despite her biting comment, the woman lifted her left hand and clutched his wrist with a grasp so firm that a lesser man might have been put to shame.

Griffin wrapped his fingers tightly around her wrist. "I've got you. Let go of the rock."

"Only if you promise to retrieve my hat before it blows into the ocean." Her eyes conveyed her complete seriousness.

"I vow it," he huffed with frustration. "Now, please, let go!"

With one more cautious look at him, the girl released her hold on the wall. For a moment, she dangled from his arm like a limp rag doll, her momentum sending her swinging back and forth in a pendulum's motion.

All the blood in his body seemed to surge into Griffin's head, and he struggled to raise her to the cliff's lip. Finally, after two perilous minutes, her head appeared level with the ledge.

"We're almost there, miss. Just a moment more and I'll have you by my side."

"Indeed."

Then, with a level of agility Griffin could never have imagined, the woman slapped her free arm over the lip, kicked her right foot up, and swung her body onto the ground beside him.

"Damn me!" While Griffin might have expected such an athletic feat from a performer at a fair, never in all his life would he have guessed it from a young lady such as the one who now gathered her breath beside him.

Griffin leaned back on his heels and stared with amazement at the fearless woman. Her hair was as dark as a starless night, and her skin was pale, save the pink flush that had risen into her cheeks. But it was her eyes that intrigued him most. Inside a ring of vibrant indigo was a burst of a pale silvery blue that made her eyes glimmer like a pair of stars.

"My bonnet, sir." Her voice was still thin and breathy from the exertion. "You promised."

"That I did." Griffin couldn't help but grin at her stubbornness regarding a ridiculous hat. "I just need something to hook it." He glanced around for a stick.

The woman looked around as well, until her gaze fixed firmly on his telescope. A surge of worry shot through Griffin as she rose and started for his most prized possession in all the world.

"Perhaps we can lower part of this contraption over

the edge and catch the brim of my hat." She reached out her hand for the brass instrument.

"No!" Griffin grabbed her wrist, perhaps a bit too roughly, for she whirled around, eyes widened with surprise.

"Not my telescope," he added, softening his voice. "'Tis very expensive, and I do not exaggerate when I tell you there is no other like it."

The woman lifted her chin and twisted her wrist from his grip. "I might claim the same about my hat, sir. Did you see the peacock feather on the band?" She nodded knowingly, as if this comment should make the great value of her hat plain to him.

Griffin knew what a ludicrous notion that was. There was no comparison. His reduced-sized Shuckburgh telescope had been custom-made to his exact specifications by a protégé of Jesse Ramsden, London's premier instrument maker. He doubted there was as fine an astronomical instrument in all of England.

The woman folded her arms across her sprigged gown. "I do not see anything else that might serve as a tool . . . so well as your telescope."

"I-I have a sheep hook at my cottage." Griffin smiled at the lovely woman, deciding that he'd like to know her a bit better. Still, finessing a woman had never come as easily to Griffin as it did his brother, and he knew he'd likely bungle it. But he would try. "Uh . . . if you like, you and your lady friends may take your ease in my home while I return for your bonnet. 'Tis just down the trail to the east. Not far, I assure you."

The young woman suspiciously raked him up and down with her gaze. "I thank you, but no. My bonnet might be caught by a gust of wind and whisked into the sea. I daren't leave it. Besides, I do not even know your name."

"St. Albans . . . Mr. St. Albans." He tipped his head to her. "And you are . . . ?"

Her pink lips formed a smirk. "Not so addled as to follow a man I do not know to his lair."

"*Lair?* My dear lady, I believe you misunderstand my intentions—" Griffin began.

"Oh, sir, please do forgive her. She meant nothing by it," said the heavier of the two old women, who now stood nearby huffing and puffing from the exertion of climbing the steep cliffside path.

"She is Miss Hannah Chillton, our charge." The thinner old woman pinched the girl's arm, eliciting a clumsy curtsy from her.

Just then, the falcon that had struck him earlier spiraled low over the four of them. Griffin watched, with great astonishment, as Miss Chillton withdrew a leather glove from her sash, slipped it onto her hand, and allowed the bird of prey to land on her forearm.

The thinner elderly lady laughed at Griffin's surprise. "And that would be Cupid . . . Hannah's kestrel."

"He is *your* bird?" Griffin stared at the young woman incredulously.

"Yes. Why is that so difficult to believe?" Miss Chillton said rather smugly.

Why, indeed? Griffin thought about it for several moments. Why should he be surprised that a woman he discovered fearlessly climbing a cliff wall, a woman with the strength to propel herself over the rock ledge, might have a hunting falcon as a pet?

"Miss Chillton, in the short time we've been acquainted, I have come to the conclusion that nothing about you should come as a surprise. For, indeed, you are the very definition of the word."

Miss Chillton looked uneasily toward the two old women, as if she had not the faintest notion how to respond to his assertion. Then, she turned her delicately featured face back to him and gestured to her guardians. "Mr. St. Albans, these are my duennas, the Ladies Letitia and Viola Featherton, of London."

"And Bath, of late," the woman she'd referred to as Lady Letitia added. "We reside in the spa city for a few short months each year."

"In fact, our visit to The Lizard was to be the culmination of our grand Cornish excursion." The thinner woman, Lady Viola, smiled brightly up at him. "We are headed back to Bath this very eve."

"Not until we have my hat." Miss Chillton turned toward the sea, took a couple of steps, and peered over the edge of the cliff. She gasped. "Oh, *no*. It's gone!"

Lady Letitia joined her at the cliff's edge and wrapped her arm around the dark-haired beauty. "The wind must have taken it after all, child."

Miss Chillton turned her head around and glared at Griffin. "You, sir, owe me a hat."

"*I?*" Griffin sputtered.

"Yes, for I would have managed to retrieve my bonnet *eventually* had you not interfered." She said something in a low tone to Lady Letitia, who upon hearing the words, reached into her miser bag and retrieved a card. Miss Chillton took it from her and shoved it at Griffin.

"The Oatland Village Hat is available from Mrs. Bell, Twenty-two Upper King Street in London. Ask her to add a peacock feather, please. Can you remember that? Good. When you have acquired it, you may deliver it to Number One Royal Crescent, Bath. The direction is listed on this card."

Her business with him concluded, Miss Chillton took each of the Featherton ladies by an arm and led them up the path to where, Griffin surmised, their carriage must await.

"Good day, Mr. St. Albans," she called back to him, a sentiment echoed by the two elderly women. "I do hope we shall see you soon—for the hat *was* my favorite."

She flashed him an amused smile and, if he was not mistaken, threw him a teasing wink as well.

When the three women disappeared over the rise, Griffin St. Albans absently strolled to the cliff's edge and peered down its steep wall for the missing bonnet. *Gone.*

He patted his head tentatively, wondering if perhaps he'd hit it when the falcon clipped him and he'd fallen—for surely he'd been dreaming.

That was the only possible explanation he could muster, for nothing so outlandish as what had occurred during the past quarter of an hour could have happened to *him*.

Life in lower Cornwall just didn't work that way.

Three days later

Lord Devonsfield and his man of affairs did not knock or even call out their arrival at the home of the St. Albans brothers. There wasn't time enough for that. The earl's hold on this earth was short, and trifling with manners was merely a waste of what few moments he had left.

Smoke trailed up into the cloudless azure sky through the tiny cottage's stone chimney. His heir was at home, or at least someone was, so the earl opened the flimsy plank door, and he and his man stepped inside—to face the barrel end of a hunting rifle.

The earl stared at the two young men before him, who, at first glance, appeared identical in every way . . . save their mode of dress perhaps. They both stood well over six feet and, unlike the earl, their heads were topped with an abundance of slightly curly sable hair.

He supposed their eyes could be called hazel, but in truth they were mostly green, with a flickering of dark amber encircling the pupil. Their shoulders were broad and they had good, strong, square jaws, with a divot in the chin, the sort the ladies so seemed to fancy. Damned if they weren't a pair of the handsomest men he'd ever seen. This pleased the earl on more than one level.

He eyed the one who pressed the rifle, painfully he might add, to his forehead. Now *that* twin had courage, gumption. And, now that the earl had a moment to reflect (for there was no way he was going to make a move with a rifle to his head—he'd leave that to Pinkerton), this twin had a sportsman's build. He was quite strong, his arms well muscled, as though he spent a goodly amount of time studying pugilism, as the earl's own eldest son, God rest his soul, had.

The earl smiled broadly. Yes, his initial impression told him that this twin would make a brilliant heir.

"Sir, I would not be so quick with a grin when my brother has a rifle trained upon your head," said the strikingly handsome but less-muscular twin. "He can take down a bird in flight without effort, so I daresay, he would have no difficulty bagging an intruder at such close range."

The earl lifted an eyebrow. Such a sassy mouth this twin had. Denoted a clever mind. Unlike the other, this man's hands were smooth and his fingernails clean. His clothing was perfectly pressed, and damned if there wasn't something the least bit aristocratic about his stance. *Hmm. Not a bad option either.*

Pinkerton, the bloody coward—for his hands shot into the air the minute he saw the rifle—finally spoke up. "My dear sirs, this gentleman means you no harm . . . nor do I."

Neither twin said a word, didn't move a muscle.

"Er . . . may I . . . lower my hands, young man?" he continued.

The twin with the rifle nodded slowly.

"And . . . uh . . . might you also deign to lower the weapon? We are unarmed, and as you can see, we are hardly in the first bloom of our youth . . . as the both of you are. Even if we wished to challenge you, you could easily subdue us in mere seconds."

The twin paused a moment, then lifted the barrel of the rifle from the earl's forehead. Lord Devonsfield clapped his hand to his brow and felt the ringed indention left behind.

"Fine way to treat your father's cousin," he snapped.

"You are *our* father's cousin?"

The earl turned to see the more refined of the bookend pair of men studying his clothing.

"I am." The earl straightened his spine.

Pinkerton cleared his throat. "May I present the Earl of Devonsfield."

The twins exchanged confused glances before returning their attention to the earl. Then, as if on cue, they honored him with a set of gracious bows.

"Of course we have heard of you, my lord," offered the twin with the soft-looking hands.

"Indeed," said the other. "We just never expected to make your acquaintance. Our lives are so far removed. We work in iron, while your lordship—"

Pinkerton broke in. "His lordship does not labor at all."

The muscular twin raised an eyebrow. *"Exactly."*

The earl pivoted on the heel of his gleaming boot, strode across the small room, and took his ease on a worn chair near the coal fire. "Well, my boys, your days toiling about the iron mines are at an end as of this very day. Come, come. Be seated and let us talk."

"I beg your pardon, my lord, we have so few guests I fear our manners have become somewhat rusty." The aristocratic one snapped his feet together and gave the earl a nod. "I am Garnet St. Albans."

The earl nodded in greeting. *"Garnet.* Refined and polished like the gem itself. How very appropriate." The earl chuckled. He turned his head to the twin with the rifle. "So you must be *Griffin.* Part eagle, part lion." The earl smiled at him. "Yes, indeed you are. How splendid are your names. Perfectly splendid. I shall have no difficulty in discerning between you ever again."

An elderly woman entered through the front door just then, and was so startled to see visitors that she dropped her market basket on the floor, sending two green apples rolling across the stone pavers. "Oh, I beg your pardon. I had no notion you had guests."

Griffin crossed the room in two long strides and helped the woman gather her things. "You need not fret, Mrs. Hopshire. Lord Devonsfield is family. Though perhaps some tea might be in order."

The earl raised his hand. "Pinkerton, trot out to the carriage, will you, and fetch us some brandy, for we must celebrate."

Garnet St. Albans caught Pinkerton's arm as he started for the door. "No need, sir. Mrs. Hopshire, some glasses, please." Near the hearth was a box, a cellarette of sorts, from which Garnet withdrew a bottle of fine brandy. "We are deep in the country, but not without a few luxuries."

Mrs. Hopshire brought a tray laden with several thick, clanking glasses into which Garnet poured the amber liquid. He handed the first glass to Lord Devonsfield.

"Uh . . . you were saying, my lord, something about our days of toil being at an end?"

"Indeed I did." The earl drained his glass and immediately passed it to Garnet to be refilled. "For one of you is to be my heir."

"Your . . . *heir*?" Griffin bent down and added a few more pieces of coal to the smoldering fire. He turned his head up to the earl. "Which of us?"

"My lord, what my brother means is that the law of primogeniture cannot be applied in our situation for we do not know which of us is firstborn. Never had any reason for it to matter . . . at least until now, it seems."

Griffin rose and came to stand beside his brother.

"I am well aware of our predicament." The earl studied both Griffin and Garnet in turn. Each had qualities to recommend him as heir, or at least so it appeared, and the earl had always placed great weight on the importance of first impressions. "Pinkerton, carry on please."

Pinkerton took a step forward. "The predicament, as the earl has put it, is far more dire than you could possibly imagine. Therefore, what I am about to impart to you must be kept in strictest confidence—for the future of the Earldom of Devonsfield depends upon your discretion." Pinkerton's eyebrows migrated toward the bridge of his nose. "Unless it can be agreed upon which of you is the elder, which of you is the *legal* heir, the earldom will revert to the Crown upon the earl's passing."

"Obviously, I will not accept this eventuality." The earl came to his feet and clapped a hand to each twin's shoulder. "And so I have a proposition for you. My time is short. My physicians do not expect me to survive the year."

Pinkerton coughed, then looked up and caught the earl's stern gaze. "Forgive me, my lord. Go on, please."

"As I was saying, I will certainly not survive the year—but I do not intend to allow my family's legacy, the Earldom of Devonsfield, to dissolve."

He gave a nod to Pinkerton then, who withdrew two folded sheets of foolscap from inside his coat and gave one to each of the twins. "For this reason, I will make a secret pact with the two of you. And if you agree to my terms, one of you will become Earl of Devonsfield."

The earl gestured for the papers to be opened. "Read the terms."

Each of the twins opened his paper from its folds and for several minutes read and reread the terms the earl had written inside.

"Do you agree to the terms as set forth?"

Griffin's and Garnet's eyes met, and for a clutch of moments, the earl had the notion that they might be silently conversing, as he'd heard some twins did. A slight feeling of distrust crept into his mind for a moment as the earl wondered if the two men would add some terms of their own. For it was clear they were aware of how desperately he needed their compliance. But, judging from the state of this ramshackle cottage, they needed him as well.

A moment later, he realized that his concerns were all for naught, for the twins agreed to every term, exactly as he'd written them.

"Brilliant, brilliant! Now, since you agree to the terms, cast the papers into the fire, for this discussion must remain a secret for all eternity."

Griffin and Garnet crumpled the papers in their large, capable hands and tossed the damning documents into the coal fire. Together the four men watched in reverent silence as flames fingered the foolscap and eventually reduced to ash the earl's darkest secret.

"We are agreed then. The continuation of the family is paramount. So, per the terms set forth and dually agreed upon, whichever of you marries a woman of quality first will become—"

The twins, as one, intoned a single word.

"*Heir.*"

The earl, greatly relieved, smiled and signaled for another brandy. "Quite right."

For the first time in more than a month, the earl was having a good heir day.

Chapter Two

Two weeks later

Hannah released the tether and watched as Cupid cut upward through the chilly air. *It would work. It had to.* She raised her hand high, and when she was sure the bird had seen the signal, slashed it down to her side. At once the falcon dived from the darkening gray sky and swooped low over the unsuspecting young miss who sat near the pond reading, then turned for the heights once more. The woman never even looked up.

From their vantage point, a half furlong away, the two Featherton sisters exhaled long sighs in unison.

"Oh, such a pity." Lady Letitia slapped her knee. "Your bird missed."

Hannah popped a hothouse strawberry into her mouth, smiling as she chewed. She reached into the bowl for another juicy red berry, and turned her gaze from her falcon to her guardians. "Cupid did not miss his target. 'Twas just a cursory run." She rose from her folding seat, and urged the Featherton sisters to do the same. "Here he comes again. Now watch."

The two old women hurried to their feet to observe the spectacle. The falcon repeated its swoop, flying low over the unsuspecting woman.

"A little lower . . ." Hannah bit her lip with anticipation. "That's it . . . now—*take it!*"

As if hearing her command, Cupid lowered his talons and snatched the ostrich feather cleanly from the lady's straw bonnet. The woman shrieked and leaped up, as the falcon mockingly circled her twice with his plumed bounty.

Cupid turned in the air and started back to Hannah, who waved a finger, directing him to the south. The bird immediately shifted its course.

"'Tis a clever trick, but what is he going to do with the feather?" Lady Viola asked, never once taking her gaze from the falcon.

"You will see soon enough." Hannah felt a little nervous. If this didn't work, she'd soon have one very angry miss heading in her direction. And one disappointed customer as well. "I've worked for nearly a week with Cupid on this maneuver. Do you see the young gentleman fishing from the dock? Give special notice to him."

Cupid dropped low and slowed his speed as he neared the dock, catching the gentleman's attention.

The young woman, her eyes fixed on the falcon, ran along the water's edge shouting for the bird to drop her feather.

Hannah chuckled. Everything was working perfectly.

Just then, Cupid plunged through the air and released the ostrich feather several feet above the gentleman's head. As the plume floated this way and that, it finally sailed within reach of the gentleman's fingers. He snatched it from the air; then, seeing the young lady rushing toward him, held it proudly out to her.

Ah, the gallant knight.

Hannah clapped her hands. "The rest is up to him. Cupid's mission was only to bring the young woman to the gentleman."

Lady Letitia's white brows arched high on her forehead. "You do not mean to tell me that this was all planned? This . . . matchmaking?"

Hannah nodded. "Brilliant, is it not?"

A twittering birdlike laugh burst from Lady Viola's lips. "A new mode of matchmaking. Why, Hannah, we shall have to adopt you, for you are truly a kindred spirit. *Brava!*"

Hannah curtsied. "Why, thank you. That is truly a grand compliment coming from one of England's most creative matchmakers."

Fifteen minutes later, the Feathertons' picnic hamper was packed. Their folding chairs and table were being fastened atop the town carriage when the young man and his new lady friend, both bright with smiles, strolled past.

The gentleman tipped his head at Hannah, then glanced meaningfully toward the dock before drawing his most appreciative young lady farther up the gravel path and out of sight.

"I shall return in a moment," Hannah whispered to

the Feathertons. "Need to collect Cupid . . . and something from the dock." Slipping her long leather glove onto her hand, she rolled it up her forearm and started down the slope toward the water.

As promised, she was back at the carriage a few minutes later with her falcon on her left arm and a gleaming guinea in her right palm. "I shall have to hang out a shingle soon. I already have two more clients and several matchmaking schemes in mind."

Lady Viola, who was about to follow her sister into the carriage, frowned as she glimpsed the coin. She released the coachman's hand and turned back to Hannah. "Dear gel, you are not accepting money for your services, are you?"

Hannah couldn't believe what she was hearing. "Of course I am. But my services are guaranteed. My customers only pay if they deem my matchmaking schemes successful. And in this case, it was, of course. The gentleman and the lady he's fancied from afar are together. Only required one scheme, too. Usually a love match requires three interventions from Fate." She giggled. "I mean *me,* of course."

Having overheard the conversation, Lady Letitia barreled out of the carriage cabin and caught Hannah's shoulders. "Hannah, one does not charge a fee for matchmaking. The ability to match is a gift from the heavens."

"The two of you mightn't ask a fee for your work. But I do. After all, I am performing a sought-after service. You are . . . well, rich, while I depend on my miser of a brother, Arthur, to send a sixpence to me each fortnight."

"Darling, what need have you for money?" Lady

Viola started for Hannah, but abruptly Cupid screeched and flapped his wings, startling the old woman back a double pace. "We do try to provide everything you might need."

"'Tisn't the same. I owe you so much already. Do you not understand? I need to feel as though I am somehow earning my keep. And I shall by generating what money I can—with the assistance of Cupid from time to time."

The heavier of the two elderly sisters shook her head. "I do not fault your desire to earn a few guineas for yourself. My concern is that you do not understand the very basis of matchmaking . . . which is *love*."

"Though I haven't truly experienced the emotion myself, I think I understand love well enough." Hannah leaned inside the carriage cabin and eased Cupid onto the wall perch the Featherton sisters had had installed recently. When she finished, she turned back to Lady Letitia. "Love really isn't my concern anyway. My job is to bring a couple together. To open my target subject's eyes to my client's true potential. The falling in love portion of the equation is entirely their prerogative."

The Featherton sisters' eyes met for a long moment before they turned their attention back to Hannah.

"You make matchmaking sound so logical, like a simple cipher." Lady Viola glanced at her sister, then back to Hannah. "But love is anything but logical."

"Exactly right, Viola. Hannah, I fear your notions about matchmaking are all wrong." Lady Letitia wrapped her thick arm around Hannah's shoulder. "Matchmaking is not simply putting two people together and hoping that they fall in love. Matchmaking is all about seeing the first sparks of love in two people's eyes—before they even realize they are about to give their hearts to one another."

"Matchmaking is recognizing a long-lasting love while it is still in the bud—that is the gift." Lady Viola took Hannah's hand and led her, and Lady Letitia, back toward their conveyance. "One cannot force love, Hannah. This is why a matchmaker cannot take coin for someone desirous of the love of another."

The rising wind nearly blew the three women toward the open carriage door, prompting them momentarily to cease their conversation and hurry inside to take their seats for the hour-long ride home.

"I daresay, I do hope we make Bath before the sky opens," Lady Viola muttered.

"As do I." Hannah glanced out the window at the angry clouds above, then returned her gaze to the gleaming gold guinea in her palm. Just looking upon its sunny color made her happy. Still, she sat quietly for a moment or two, considering what the sisters had told her.

She traced the rim of the guinea with her index finger and sighed softly.

She supposed they could be right. Perhaps it was wrong to charge a fee to help those desperate for affection.

Perhaps.

But then, she did so love the feel of a coin.

"Bloody hell!"

Garnet St. Albans wrenched his traveling gloves

from his hands and yanked his heavy portmanteau from the roof of the toppled post chaise.

A fat drop of rain splattered atop his nose, then dripped down upon his perfectly starched and tied neckcloth, as he stood cursing his foul luck and the pot-shaped hole in the road that had caused it.

Three wheel spokes were fractured, *three,* and here he was, a good eight miles from Bath, with a downpour only moments away. His new clothing, purchased with funds generously provided by the Earl of Devonsfield, would be ruined.

He knelt beside his driver and studied the broken wheel. "There's no way to repair it, is there?"

"No, sir. Not here anyway. All we can do now is wait for help." A heavy droplet hit the coachman in his left eye, causing him to squint and turn his wide, pock-marked nose upward to the low clouds above. "Haven't seen a sky like that in nearly a year. You can wait here with me, Mr. St. Albans, or walk to town. Either way, you're bound for a good washin'."

"Perfect, just perfect." Garnet expelled a long sigh until, quite unexpectedly, he felt a gentle hum beneath the leather soles of his boots.

The vibration grew stronger, until he was almost sure that the tiny stones on the road were about to pop and dance beneath his feet. He turned to the coachman. "Do you feel that?"

"Aye, I do. A wagon, or perhaps a coach, is comin'. Your fancy coat might survive the storm yet, Mr. St. Albans." The driver chuckled merrily.

"Indeed." Garnet did not find the comment half as amusing as the driver, though it did set his heart to beating with anticipation. He came to his feet and fixed his gaze on the point where the road wound around the bend . . . and waited.

Billowing clouds of buff dust preceded the shining town carriage that rounded the bend. Garnet's cheeks pulled up, and he smiled broadly. Not only was he to be rescued from certain drenching, but it would be done in luxury.

But the carriage was coming fast. Too fast, Garnet surmised. It was going to pass him by.

Garnet strode into the center of the road and waved his arms madly, shouting for the carriage to stop.

His eyes locked with those of the driver atop the perch, and for the briefest of moments, he registered the wide-eyed shock in the man's eyes as he yanked back on the leather reins.

Good God. There was no way the carriage was going to be able to stop—and worse yet, no possible way for Garnet to get out of the way in time. None at all.

The horrified driver cried out a warning. The sable horses in the lead seemed to scream, and at that very moment, Garnet St. Albans knew he was a dead man.

"Have you noticed, sister," Lady Viola whispered, "men are often trod upon by horses when our Hannah is near?"

"I had *nothing* to do with this." Hannah hurried toward the injured man, who was lying supine in the very center of the road. "And as for running down my brother in London, well, everyone is quite aware, that was an accident . . . of sorts."

Lady Viola glanced at her sister for a brief, yet

meaningful moment. "'Twas just an observation, dear. Nothing more."

As their coachman argued with his counterpart, the driver of the broken carriage, Hannah and the two Featherton ladies circled around the body of the man, who for some odd reason had not had the sense to get out of the way of an oncoming town carriage.

Hannah knelt over him and laid her hand to his heart. "Sir, can you hear me?"

His eyes opened slightly.

"There, do you see?" she smugly told the Feathertons. "What did I tell you? He's not dead after all."

"Am I not?" the gentleman asked.

Hannah snorted. "What a perfectly ridiculous question, sir. You are speaking with me, are you not? Do I resemble a winged angel?"

He blinked at her then and peered deeply into her eyes. "Actually, yes, miss, you do somewhat."

"Lord above, to make such a comment you must have hit your head when you fell. We must move you from the road and see you to a physician without delay." With great care, she caught up his hand. "Are you able to stand? Pray, let me help you try."

The gentleman squeezed her hand and lifted his head but moved no farther. "Can't." He winced. "I fear I've broken something. A rib or two. Perhaps my leg as well."

Lady Viola glanced up at the blackening clouds, then spoke to the gentleman sternly. "Sir, I do apologize for this wretched accident, but if we do not soon find a way to see you inside our carriage—for clearly the post chaise is entirely disabled—I fear the coming storm will make the road into Bath impassable. So please, do your best to put your pain aside for the moment and stand if you can."

Lady Letitia clapped her hands loudly, effectively silencing the two arguing coachmen, then signaled for their assistance. "A bit of help, please. We cannot lift this gentleman alone."

Not more than five minutes later, the dusty gentleman was ensconced in the Featherton town carriage, and they were all once more headed for Bath.

Hannah could not seem to remove her gaze from the handsome young passenger they'd added to their fold. But she could not seem to ascertain why.

Despite the wash of dirt on his face, and that his features were somewhat contorted by pain each time the carriage wheels dipped into a divot in the road, it was clear he was unusually handsome. But it was something more.

There was something oddly familiar about this man. And then it struck her.

"Lud, you are the gentleman from Cornwall. Mr. St. Albans?"

The gentleman seemed more than a little surprised at her utterance of his name. "Indeed, I am, miss. I do apologize for not introducing myself sooner. I was—"

"Where is my bonnet?" Hannah broke in excitedly. "You have brought it from London, have you not? Is it in your portmanteau? I do hope it isn't crushed."

"Your . . . *hat*?" The gentleman looked thoroughly confused, but then Hannah supposed that was only natural given the fact he had only just been trotted upon by a team of horses.

"Hannah!" Lady Letitia actually sounded angry, though her expression revealed that she was just as dumbstruck that their carriage had run down the very same gentleman they'd met only a few weeks earlier upon a cliff in Cornwall. "Mr. St. Albans is injured. Do allow him to rest during the remainder of our journey. There will be time enough later to speak of your bonnet."

Mr. St. Albans drew his eyebrows close. Confusion was clear in his eyes. "I do not understand; how did you know my name? I did not hear my driver offer it, and I am quite certain I did not."

Hannah gave the poor man a pitying look, then glanced at Lady Viola, who seemed likewise empathetic with the gentleman's predicament.

"How horrible it must be for you, Mr. St. Albans, to have lost your memory in the accident."

"Lost my . . . what?"

"Why, your memory." Lud, Hannah only hoped his affliction was temporary . . . so he could inform her about her hat soon. It had been her favorite, and she did so miss it.

Lady Viola reached a comforting hand across the carriage and patted Mr. St. Albans's forearm. "Dear sir. Do you not recall meeting us at Kennymare Cove? You sought to retrieve Miss Chillton's bonnet from the cliff face."

Hannah broke in. "But you wouldn't allow your telescope to be used to retrieve it, and, as I predicted, the wind swept my bonnet into the sea as a result. You . . . sort of . . . promised to buy another for me."

Mr. St. Albans shook his head slowly, but then his eyes changed, and she knew something she said had resonated with him.

He lifted his chin and turned his head to face Hannah, and he seemed to study her for some moments. And for only half an instant a wicked grin appeared on his lips.

"Perhaps you are remembering our meeting now?" Lady Letitia bobbed her double chin excitedly as if to coax Mr. St. Albans to do the same.

But then, the flicker of recognition that had lit his green eyes only a moment before dimmed. "Sadly, my lady, I cannot recall that day at all. I . . . I thought there was something—that perhaps I was remembering Miss Chillton."

The two Featherton sisters leaned forward on the leather bench and waited expectantly for his next words.

"But then I realized, dear ladies, that the memory I was unearthing was far more recent." He turned his face back to Hannah.

For a moment, Hannah thought she felt his thigh press against her own. Yes, she was sure of it. Her gaze locked with Mr. St. Albans's and hardened.

Mr. St. Albans drew in a breath and gave a long sigh. "It was not our meeting in Cornwall I recalled, but rather the vision of this angel leaning over me in the road."

Hannah felt a flush of warmth race into her cheeks. Heavens, had she not been aware that Mr. St. Albans had only just been injured, she would have marked him a studied and practiced charmer of the first rank. In fact, she still might. She was not some naive miss fresh from school. No, indeed. She'd read *A Lady's Guide to Rakes,* a cautionary guidebook to all manners of rogues and scoundrels, and now knew a true rake when she glimpsed one.

And he was one . . . at least she was fairly certain of it.

"You were headed for Bath, sir," Lady Letitia began, but Hannah knew from the puckering of her withered lips that the old woman had a tastier question waiting on her tongue. "Do you remember for what purpose? I . . . I only ask because there are a goodly number of celebrations and a quartet of celestial balls planned for the next two months."

"Celestial balls?" A flash of recognition sparked in Mr. St. Albans's eyes.

"Why, yes. It is really quite exciting." Lady Viola's face grew animated with excitement. "Miss Caroline Herschel, the famed astronomer, of our acquaintance actually, has returned to Bath despite her advanced age, for the study of a new comet."

"Yes, yes!" Lady Letitia could not seem to contain her own excitement. "If her calculations are correct, and surely they are, the comet will pass low over the city and light up the heavens. Astronomers and scholars from all over the world are already beginning to arrive to witness the marvel . . . as well as to partake in the merriment, of course."

Mr. St. Albans rounded his eyes and leaned toward the Feathertons. "I believe . . . I am an astronomer. Mayhap that is why I have come." He turned his gaze toward Hannah. "But then, after our meeting in Cornwall, mayhap I have come to court Miss Chillton . . . or to find a bride. I-I honestly have no notion, but I am sure I will remember . . . soon enough."

Lady Viola suddenly clasped her sister's hand and drew her close to whisper in her ear. Then, a moment later, they both beamed at Mr. St. Albans.

Hannah's stomach clenched. Oh, dear, they had that special glint in their eyes. The matchmakers had a plan, and this time it involved Mr. St. Albans and herself, she was almost sure of it.

Why, he had no less than set the challenge of a match before them with his ridiculous mention of courting her . . . or finding a bride.

As if she would be at all interested in a rake . . . assuming he was one.

It was Lady Letitia who would ultimately set the scheme in motion with her next words. "Mr. St. Albans, my sister and I feel terrible about the harm that has befallen you owing to our coachman's inattention. Have you lodgings in Bath?"

Hannah had the distinct notion that the two Featherton ladies were actually holding their breath as they awaited his answer. Seeing this had the unnerving effect of making Hannah do the same.

"I do—" he began, but then his eyes took on a sharp focus. "That is to say, I do *not* remember. Quite a problem, isn't it, not knowing."

"Dear sir, it is not a problem in the least. Do not let the thought concern you any further." Lady Viola's eyes were twinkling. "Please, stay with us in Royal Crescent, until your health . . . and memory have been restored."

It was then that Hannah realized both of the Featherton ladies were staring directly at her, waiting, she assumed, for her to assist them in convincing Mr. St. Albans to agree to their plan.

Something in her mind cried out for her to persuade the ladies that their proposition was anything but proper, for he was an unmarried . . . possible rake, and she was a virginal miss. She wanted to tell them that she doubted the man's memory was half as impaired as he pretended.

But what else could she do but as they wished? They took her in when her brother left for India and had promised him that they would find her a proper husband.

She owed them much. And so, Hannah lifted the corners of her mouth and smiled pleasantly.

"Say you will, Mr. St. Albans. Say you will stay until you are well." She swallowed hard, dreading his answer, for she knew that an affirmation of any sort would set the Feathertons' matchmaking machinations into motion. And given their obstinate yet optimistic natures, the ladies would never give up until she and Mr. St. Albans stood before a vicar.

They were stubborn that way.

The roguish grin she'd glimpsed only moments before returned to Mr. St. Albans's mouth. "For you, my dear Miss Chillton, my angel of mercy," he nearly crooned, "anything."

"B-brilliant." Hannah felt as though she was going to be sick. Still, she smiled at the gentleman, then at her duennas, then turned to look out the window at the driving rain.

She hoped the downpour would stop by day's end and not impair the morrow.

After all, first thing in the morn, she planned to make her way to Trim Street and engage a modiste to stitch the wedding gown she would undoubtedly be needing quite soon . . . if the matchmaking Featherton sisters had their way.

Hannah groaned inwardly.

Chapter Three

Queen Square, Bath

Griffin St. Albans sat before a writing desk in his bedchamber on the uppermost floor of the town house he and his brother had let for the duration of their bride-hunt in Bath.

He stared out the small casement window, watching their longtime housekeeper, Mrs. Hopshire, caning her way up the steep incline of Gay Street to post the letter Griffin had so dreaded to write to the Earl of Devonsfield.

Halfheartedly, he glanced down the road toward the square, with meager hopes of catching sight of Garnet, but he held little expectation for that at this point.

His brother should have arrived at least a week earlier, days before Griffin was delivered by the post chaise from London. But there was no evidence that he'd ever set a boot in the spa city. There had not been a letter, or even a message, and this deeply concerned him.

For days he'd tried to convince himself that his brother, who'd always been given to impetuous behavior, had simply targeted a young lady of quality before he arrived in Bath and was too focused on wooing her to send word of his plans.

But too many days had passed for that possibility.

Yes, Griffin knew he had put off the inevitable long enough. He'd written a letter to inform the Earl of Devonsfield that his brother was missing, and now it was time to inform the Bath constables as well.

Griffin had just risen from his chair to do that very thing when his chamber door burst open.

Relief flooded over him when he saw who was standing in the doorway. "*Garnet*, where in hell have you been? I was about to inform the constables that you were missing!"

"Really, brother, with all your worrying you sound like Mrs. Hopshire. Where is she, by the by? Didn't see her below stairs."

Griffin ran his fingers through his tousled hair. "I sent her to catch the post—" He nearly finished his sentence with the words *with a letter to the earl*, but caught himself in time.

It was too late to do anything about the letter anyway. No doubt Mrs. Hopshire had caught the post, and the letter was already on its way to Devonsfield by now.

Bloody hell.

No use worrying Garnet about it. Griffin would just post another letter in the morning, this time assuring the earl that Garnet was safe in Bath, and all was well with the bride-hunting competition after all.

He studied Garnet for a moment. He didn't seem

quite himself. No, something had happened to his brother. Something, for reasons Griffin knew not, Garnet was not eager to confess.

Garnet moved toward the narrow bed to take his ease, but as he did so, Griffin noted a slight limp to his gait.

"You're *injured*." Griffin stood and crossed the room to stand before his brother.

"'Tis but a cracked rib or two, and a bruised leg. I've had a physician see to my injuries, so stop fretting, Griff."

"You could have been dead for all I knew."

"Well, I'm not." Finally seeming to realize the extent of Griffin's distress, Garnet exhaled and began to share his story. "Very well. I fell victim to a carriage accident during my journey to Bath—a most *fortuitous* accident, as it turns out."

"How so?"

Garnet's eyes were twinkling as he relayed the coincidence of being flattened by the Featherton ladies' carriage and the distinct pleasure he had of finally meeting the spirited blue-eyed miss whom Griffin had encountered on the cliffs above Kennymare Cove.

What a lark it was, he admitted, allowing the women to believe he was Griffin, the astronomer, the man they had met that day.

Griffin's own spirits sank. He'd thought, and spoken, of little else other than the amazing Miss Chillton since the day he'd met her. And, since he was to journey to Bath anyway for the study of the comet, he'd hoped to court Miss Chillton. But now Garnet, the Seducer of Cornwall, had her in his sights. Griffin knew he hadn't a chance to win her affections now.

No chance at all, especially when Garnet the

Charmer could simply ring the young lady's finger and claim the earldom he so desired in only a matter of days.

He removed a hatbox from the wardrobe, then turned to Garnet. "I . . . I have her new bonnet. The milliner in London even added a peacock feather, as Miss Chillton had requested." Try as he might, he could not sift the disappointment from his voice. "You might as well give it to her."

Garnet laughed at that. "What sort of brother do you think I am, sir? You, and no other, will present Miss Chillton with the bonnet."

"W-what do you mean? I thought you—"

"Why? Because I pretended I was you?" Garnet shoved a dangling lock of hair back from his eyes. "I am deeply wounded to think you would believe I would ever seek to steal away the lady of your dreams."

"But why did you take up residence with the Featherton ladies if you did not wish to woo Miss Chillton?"

"Well, you are right there. I did wish to woo her. But for you, Griffin. For *you*." Then, as if something had belatedly occurred to him, Garnet stood abruptly and left the chamber to retrieve a parcel he'd evidently left outside the doorway.

When he tossed it upon the bedstead, his eyes held that familiar glint, the sort that always told Griffin his dear brother was deep into no good. "Go on, open it. I know you want to."

"Unless it's a new aperture dial for my telescope, I tell you, I am not interested." Still, Griffin could not prevent his gaze from flitting over the package.

Garnet exhaled. "Then I shall open it for you, for we haven't much time. Damned balls start far too early in

Bath—end early, too. For the good of the attendees' health, they claim. *Bah*."

"A ball?" Now that caught Griffin's attention. "I have no intention of attending a ball. You know I cannot abide the things."

"You only claim as much because you doubt your dancing ability, but you needn't fear. I have seen to all contingencies. A simple waltz, a dance at which even you excel, shall be the only time you must take to the floor." Garnet grinned. "Agreed?"

"Of course, I do *not* agree to something unknown to me!"

Garnet did not say another word as he dutifully unwrapped the large parcel. From it, he withdrew a dark cutaway coat, gray breeches, a silver-shot waistcoat, and a fine pair of ebony shoes.

"Here you are," he said proudly. "I am in possession of an identical ensemble. I had the haberdasher create two of everything, though I had him add more width in the shoulders, sleeves, and thighs—given your . . . less-elegant form." Garnet lifted the coat. "Do try this on. As I said, we have little time. I must still return to Royal Crescent to dress."

Griffin shrugged his shoulders into the coat without so much as a glance into the cheval mirror propped in the corner. "I still do not understand what you have in that wicked mind of yours."

Garnet tugged on Griffin's sleeves and circled around him, checking the fit. "Ah, *perfect*." He turned his gaze to Griffin's. "You still do not understand? Have I not made myself clear?"

"*No,* you have not."

"Well, it's really very simple. I will be escorting the

Featherton ladies, and Miss Chillton, to the Upper Assembly Rooms this eve."

Griffin straightened at the mention of the women. "Miss Chillton will be in attendance?"

"Isn't that what I just said?" Garnet huffed, then continued, "Now, sometime during the first hour, I will dance with her, converse with her . . . and do my damnedest to attract her, make my interest known."

"Your interest?" Griffin felt the blood in his veins grow ever hot.

"How can you not grasp this idea? Your brain is far superior to mine, what with all those numbers rolling around inside." Garnet exhaled hard.

"Explain it to me then. I own it is difficult for me to follow your logic at times . . . especially when you are being illogical."

"'Tis very simple, and it makes a great deal of sense given our differing natural propensities. Follow me now. For one hour, I will do my best to charm Miss Chillton, priming her for you. Then I shall excuse myself to request a waltz. That is when you will take my place with Miss Chillton."

"This is madness."

"Hardly." A broad grin skimmed Garnet's lips. "We are identical. Our clothing will be indistinguishable. She will never realize the switch that has transpired. And you, dear brother, will be free to make the woman of your dreams fall in love with you."

Griffin dropped his gaze to his feet. "This is never going to work."

Garnet laughed at that. "My dear brother, I have lived with the family for a sennight already. I have not spent my time in vain."

"What do you mean? What have you done?"

"Nothing that need concern you, Griff. Nothing to compromise your lady. Suffice it to say, I have a suspicion that Miss Chillton is already falling in love with me . . . er . . . *you*."

Griffin allowed himself a shallow smile. Was it possible this could actually work? He glanced back up at Garnet. "Are you sure of her interest?"

"Of course. I know women. When have I ever misread a miss?"

Griffin nodded slowly. "Never."

Garnet's lips drew up smugly. "Well then. You best don your attire. It wouldn't do to keep the ladies—and your future bride—waiting."

Goose bumps rose on Hannah's arms and she shivered as she stood half-dressed in her chilly bedchamber, being dressed for the ball. Though the sun had already found its resting place, the upstairs maid had not yet come to refill the coal in the grate and to stoke the fire to coax a bit of warmth into the room. Hannah would have done it herself, but at the moment, her ribs seemed to be cracking.

"Let out all of the air in your lungs, Miss Hannah," her lady's maid told her.

Hannah expelled her breath as Annie laced her into a tight silk corset, when her comfortable linen would have done just fine.

Just another indignity she would have to endure this eve to please the matchmaking Featherton sisters.

"Well, they can matchmake all they like, but I will

not dance with him," Hannah told the maid matter-of-factly. "Lud, the man is so ridiculously self-assured, so full of his own imagined worth. I cannot bear to be in a room with him for more than a quarter hour at a time."

Annie clucked at that. "The ladies claim that man you met on the cliffs in Cornwall is your match—and they ain't never wrong, Miss Hannah. Never!"

Hannah hated to be one who ruined the Featherton sisters' successful matchmaking record, but there was no help for it. She was not the least attracted to Mr. St. Albans . . . though she'd recently met someone who was—the lovely Miss Howard. Miss Howard, who was perhaps a few years older than she, but certainly not in her dotage, had approached Hannah with a shiny guinea in hand and had requested an introduction to Mr. St. Albans. And who was Hannah to deny the woman a chance at happiness?

Besides, she'd spent the money already, so she had no choice but to instigate the fateful meeting.

As Annie tied off the corset, Hannah tested her lung capacity. She sucked in a deep breath, or rather it might have been a well-drawn breath had the corset not been so snug. "Annie, it's too binding. Please, will you loosen it a bit? You know I despise tight corsets."

"If I let the ribbon out a bit, your middle will follow suit, and how will you catch Mr. St. Albans's eye?" Annie shook her head. "No, I am sure to hear all about it from the ladies if I allow you another pinkie width." The lady's maid went to retrieve Hannah's ball gown. "Don't tell me that you have never thought about a life with Mr. St. Albans. He's handsome, that one."

"Yes, he is. I do not deny that. And, for but a day after we met, I might have even entertained a courtship.

But now, after seeing the real man, learning his true nature, no more. The man is little more than a rake."

"But the Featherton sisters are so sure Mr. St. Albans is your match, miss—"

Hannah laughed. "Believe me, in this instance, the ladies *are* wrong. Completely in error. Why, I'd be far more likely to marry . . . Edgar, than Mr. St. Albans."

"Mr. Edgar? Fancy him, do you? Never would have guessed that."

"No, no. You've got it all wrong. That's not what I meant at all—"

"Besides, Mr. Edgar is nine-and-seventy, miss, and, well, *he's taken.* For if I'm not out of my place for sayin' so, I know for a fact that Lady Viola has a soft place in her heart for him."

Hannah whirled around at that. "Really? Lady Viola and Edgar? Are you sure?"

"Oh, absolutely. Everyone, I mean everyone below stairs, knows all about it. You only have to look at their eyes when they're in the same room together. Their feelin's are as plain as the sun in the sky."

Hannah giggled at the thought. "How long has this been going on?"

"Oh, forgive me, miss. I shouldn't have said nothin'. I'll just close my lips now. Won't hear another word from me." Annie lifted the silk gown she'd placed on the tester bed earlier and ballooned it over Hannah's head.

When Hannah poked her head out the top of the mass of silk, it was evident that Annie had been impatiently waiting for her to emerge so that she might continue.

" . . . But from what I've seen and heard, they've been in love for *years*."

"*Years?* And they have never proclaimed it? Never acted upon it?"

"No, miss. Wouldn't be right, would it, with him bein' the butler and her bein' a grand lady?"

"Oh, goodness. What has that got to do with the price of bread? Such societal rules carry no weight with the Featherton ladies. You should know that. No, there has to be some other explanation for Lady Viola's reticence. There just has to be."

Then, an idea burst into Hannah's mind and she grew quiet.

Lady Viola and Edgar. Hmm.

She moved to the window and glanced down at the aviary where her falcon resided. As the tall case clock below stairs dinged the six o'clock hour, Hannah made firm her mind.

She would do it.

Noting the movement in the window above, the falcon looked up at Hannah.

"Such a clever bird," she whispered. "You know already, don't you, Cupid? We've got a job to do. Lady Viola and Edgar are in need of our services."

"What was that, Miss Hannah?"

"Oh, nothing, Annie. Nothing at all." Hannah grinned inwardly.

This is the perfect chance to prove to the Feathertons that I do know a thing or two about love and proper matches.

. . . And I won't even charge this time.

Chapter Four

Upper Assembly Rooms, Bath

Mr. St. Albans, the handsome, yet impossibly egotistical buffoon, led the two Featherton sisters through the column-framed entrance of the elegant Upper Assembly Rooms, allowing Hannah to trail behind on her own.

She didn't mind being without an escort this evening. In fact, being a bit of an independent sort anyway (or so her brother, Arthur, had oft claimed when Hannah was growing up), Hannah actually preferred it this way.

Mr. St. Albans was about as close to a rake as a man could be, and she was quite certain that were she to allow him to take her hand, she would feel his other brush her bottom. This, in her opinion, was just the sort of lecherous man he was. Hannah had read all about lechers and oglers in her friend Meredith's guidebook.

As she reached the entrance hall, Hannah passed her silver-and-blue wrap to an awaiting footman, then followed her party through the tight crowd toward the ballroom.

At first, when they seemed to make no progress in their approach, Hannah had thought a rude throng had simply congregated before the doors, blocking entrance to everyone else. But once Mr. St. Albans, with his broad shoulders and commanding presence, had cleared a narrow path, and their small group was able to enter, Hannah realized she had been in error.

The glittering chandeliers above cast an almost magical golden glow on the heaving crowd below.

Though two hundred typically numbered the subscribers and guests who attended the dress balls held each Monday during the Bath season, the ballroom tonight seemed to hold no less than five times that number.

Though the room's ceiling was high to allow for the proper circulation of air, the grand ballroom was stifling this eve. Within minutes the tiny wisps of hair at the back of her neck were sealed to her skin with perspiration.

Hannah plucked at the neckline of her gown, as unobtrusively as possible without being noticed, to separate her already heat-moistened chemise from her skin.

Perhaps she could feign illness. Or begin to swoon. If Hannah could have summoned an adequate reason to leave the Assembly Rooms at that very instant—one the Featherton sisters would accept—she would have done so at once.

But she knew better. No excuse would suffice this eve. The crafty old Featherton ladies knew every trick, she was sure, for they themselves had likely tried them all during their lifetimes.

There was no escape tonight. Besides, Miss Howard had promised she would try to convince her mother to attend the ball with her. Hannah sighed, resigned in the knowledge that there was nothing to do except wait to see if Miss Howard arrived, then fashion a way for her golden-haired beauty to meet and sufficiently charm Mr. St. Albans.

"Do you see? It is as I told you, Mr. St. Albans." Lady Letitia gestured about the expansive room. "Everyone of consequence has come to Bath to see the comet. *Everyone*."

Mr. St. Albans's bored gaze followed the elderly woman's gesturing gloved hand until it happened to pass before Hannah's face. And there his gaze remained.

Hannah looked away, eventually glancing upward, where she noted that the high upper-story windows lining the outer walls were propped open wide for air, though they offered little relief, if any at all, to those below.

"I daresay, Mr. St. Albans." Lady Viola tapped her unfurled cutwork fan on the gentleman's shoulder to snare his attention. "With so many scientific sorts in attendance here this eve, you are sure to encounter someone of your acquaintance. If . . . you are able to remember them."

"Ah, dear lady, even if I do not glimpse a single familiar face, this night would be quite pleasurable. For tonight the three lovely ladies before me are the company I *desire*."

As he intoned the final word in his statement, his gaze dropped almost imperceptibly to Hannah's bosom.

Hannah narrowed her eyes at him, but her silent admonishment did not put a stop to his improper study of her.

No, instead Mr. St. Albans's mouth twitched upward, and his gaze grew ever more focused on her.

Such gall this man had!

Surely the Featherton sisters must recognize a rake when he stood directly before them.

Hannah tilted her head twice in Mr. St. Albans's general direction, for it was not proper to point, and waited silently for one of the ladies to flay him for his roguish behavior.

Instead, Lady Viola and Lady Letitia began to discuss the music with Mr. St. Albans, as if nothing were amiss.

Were the elderly ladies losing their hearing as well as their eyesight? No, both women had seen her gesture to the man. On that point she was perfectly clear.

He had charmed them both. There was no other explanation.

And so, when Hannah was sure Mr. St. Albans was completely occupied by the Feathertons, and his heated gaze was no longer upon her, she took a furtive step backward. Then another, hoping that she might lose herself in the crowd and escape unnoticed into the Octagon or card room.

"Hannah?" She felt a firm grasp on her wrist. Her gaze released the path of her escape and turned to Lady Letitia.

"Dear gel, I think it a marvelous idea. What say you?" Lady Letitia stared hard into Hannah's eyes.

"I am dreadfully sorry, but with the music and the conversations nearby . . . I could not hear—"

Lady Viola caught Mr. St. Albans's arm and directed his attention to the orchestra in the balcony above.

Lady Letitia huffed out her breath and leaned close to Hannah's ear and whispered to her, "I understood your message, dove."

Hannah widened her eyes. "I am sorry. I don't understand. Which message was that?"

Lady Letitia chuckled softly. "I caught your glance, then you nodded at Mr. St. Albans." She smiled broadly, puffing her full chest out like a pigeon. "'Tis all arranged. Mr. St. Albans has requested the pleasure of a dance with you; didn't you hear him?"

"I do apologize. Actually, I did not." Hannah glanced nervously as Lady Viola and Mr. St. Albans turned back around to face her and Lady Letitia once more.

"Aren't you glad then that sister and I both heard him for you? So off you go."

The plumper of the two snowy-haired sisters shoved Hannah forward, sending her stumbling into Mr. St. Albans's eager embrace.

When she regained her footing, Hannah knew there was no possible way to excuse herself from a dance now.

None at all.

So, she reluctantly took Mr. St. Albans's proffered arm and allowed him to lead her through the milling, perspiring guests to the center of the dance floor.

On their way, Hannah met the gaze of Miss Howard, the fine-featured, blonde beauty who lingered at the perimeter of the dance floor with her stout-looking mother. "Oh, Mr. St. Albans, before we dance, I would like to greet a new friend. Will you allow me?"

Mr. St. Albans tipped his head, with no little amount of exasperation exhibited on his face, and followed her to the edge of the floor. His eyes brightened when he saw to whom Hannah was about to introduce him.

As Hannah formally introduced the pair, she could not help but see the attraction between the two . . . the very sort the Featherton sisters had mentioned.

"If you will permit, Miss Howard, I would greatly enjoy a dance—er . . . after Miss Chillton, my dear friend, and I have concluded our turn about the floor."

Miss Howard glanced at her mother, who nodded her assent. "I should like that very much, Mr. St. Albans." She blushed, most becomingly, and at the very same moment, Mr. St. Albans seemed to grow four inches taller.

Perfect.

Well then, the old women could hardly blame her for initiating the match, now could they? Mr. St. Albans and Miss Howard were clearly meant to be together. Just look at them!

If she could just maintain his interest in Miss Howard and discourage any interest in herself, all would be right with her world once more.

With a very pleased curve to his lips, Mr. St. Albans led Hannah to the center of the floor.

"Miss Howard is quite lovely, is she not?" Hannah prodded.

"Indeed she is. Almost as lovely as you, Miss Chillton."

"Why, thank you, Mr. St. Albans." *Hmm.*

As they took their positions, Hannah glanced up at the first-floor gallery and waited for the musicians to begin the country dance that had been called—anything to avoid Mr. St. Albans's gaze.

"You needn't feel uneasy about the dance, Miss Chillton," Mr. St. Albans told her in his usual overconfident manner. "If you are uncertain of a step, I will gladly lead you."

"I beg your pardon, sir." *The lout.*

"I offered to instruct you, if you are unsure of the dance steps."

A glare tightened the skin around Hannah's eyes. He had just initiated a frontal attack on her social training. And he just expected her to accept such rudeness?

"How dare you, Mr. St. Albans." Hannah angrily snapped her head around, ready to thrust forth her own stinging verbal blade, when she noted the clear amusement on his face.

He lifted his eyebrows and took in a deep breath as he dropped his gaze momentarily to the floor. When he looked up at her again, he no longer seemed so merry.

"I do apologize, Miss Chillton. You seemed so solemn this eve, that I had hoped to coax a smile from you with my absurd offer."

Hannah peered deep into his twinkling green eyes. Was he toying with her, or was he being genuine? She never quite knew how to read Mr. St. Albans.

"Oh, come now. You must know I jested. The Featherton ladies advised me to practice my dancing skills before escorting you to the floor. They told me that your grace in dance is unmatched in Bath."

"Did they?" Hannah cast her gaze to the two elderly ladies who were watching them intently through matched mother-of-pearl lorgnettes. "Well, Mr. St. Albans, I fear the Feathertons were having a chuckle at your expense."

The orchestra commenced with their music, startling Hannah's attention back to Mr. St. Albans.

"Allow me to decide that for myself, will you, Miss Chillton?" he told her. "But as I said, do feel free to follow my lead. I am known in The Lizard as the Prancer, you know." The edges of his mouth twitched, and she knew he suppressed a grin.

Hannah raised a single eyebrow. "Somehow, I do not doubt that, sir." Her own lips curved upward.

Mr. St. Albans caught up her gloved hands and twirled Hannah in a tight circle, urging forth from her an unbidden laugh.

As the dance progressed, and the moments as his captive partner passed without her becoming nauseous even once, Hannah began to wonder if her negative assessment of Mr. St. Albans's character was altogether correct.

She was fairly certain it was, but then, he was rather diverting tonight, and that in itself was a desirable quality in any gentleman. Even if it was the only one he possessed.

Hannah had at last begun to allow herself to relax and enjoy the dance when she noticed the Feathertons, watching from the perimeter of the dance floor, exchange one of those knowing glances of theirs.

Oh, good heavens. Was this all part of their matchmaking scheme?

Well, on her oath, it wasn't going to work. And Hannah would prove it this very night.

She was in control of her evening. Not they.

It was simple enough. She would just pay no heed to

Mr. St. Albans for the rest of the eve . . . beginning right after this set.

Or, perhaps after nine, when everyone would move to the Tea Room for refreshments. Or maybe it would be most effective to ignore him during their drive home. Miss Howard was next on his *prancing* list anyway.

Yes, she'd practically ignore the man. That's exactly what she would do.

When was the only question that remained.

At half past nine that evening, Hannah and the Featherton sisters were sitting around a small table in the Tea Room's upper colonnade, sipping weak tea with arrack and lemon.

Lady Letitia, whose robust appetite seemed unaffected by the sweltering heat of the room, happily supped on the sweetmeats, cold ham, and plump biscuits provided for the subscribers.

"I had hoped that we'd have the advantage of air up here, but it seems I was quite wrong." Hannah rose and walked to the gilded-iron railing, and peered down at the tremendous crowd below. I wonder where Mr. St. Albans has gone?" Those words, spoken softly and without thought, were meant only for herself, but Lady Viola's hearing was too keen to allow her comment to pass.

"Miss him already, do you, dear?" Lady Viola's birdish laugh twittered atop the heavy air.

"Mayhap you are a mite concerned about his new lady friend," Lady Letitia added.

Hannah cringed at that comment. "Hardly. Besides which, Miss Howard is just below with her mother. I . . . just think it somewhat inconsiderate for our escort to see to our tea service, then abandon us without so much as a word of pardon."

Lady Letitia grunted at that. "Dear child, Mr. St. Albans is the perfect gentleman. And if you feel you must be apprised of his whereabouts, he has returned to the ballroom to speak with the conductor."

Hannah whirled around and faced the two old women. "The conductor? Good heavens, whatever for?"

After wetting her mouth with a sip of tea, Lady Letitia continued. "I believe he intended to enjoy a second set with you, Hannah, and wished to request a waltz as the opening dance."

"A second dance, with the Prancer?" Hannah was incredulous. "I daresay his intention is quite bold, given that I have not even been asked if I wished to dance again."

Lady Viola flipped open her lavender-and-blond lace fan and waved it before her powdered face, which was already liberally dotted with beads of perspiration. "Well, sweeting, the fault of that would be mine. I assured him you would delight in another set."

Hannah stared incredulously at her.

The old woman's fan paused midway in the stifling air. "I-I was not incorrect in my assumption, was I, Hannah? I caught your earlier message . . . and you did so seem to be enjoying yourself when you were dancing with him earlier."

Hannah exhaled her surrender. "No, Lady Viola. You are not incorrect. I was feeling rather fatigued earlier, but, after taking tea, I believe my vigor is returning." At least that much was true. "I shall dance once more with Mr. St. Albans if it pleases the both of you. But only if it does. Otherwise, I shall be ever so happy to remain by your sides."

"Oh, it does," the Featherton sisters chattered together as one.

"Brilliant." Hannah turned to the railing once more and let out a long sigh. "I can hardly wait for the music to begin again," she muttered, with hardly a tincture of sarcasm flavoring her words.

The musicians struck the first note of the Viennese Waltz thirty minutes later, just after Hannah and the Featherton sisters had returned to the ballroom from taking refreshments.

Hannah surveyed the crowded room but did not see Mr. St. Albans, who should have been easily discernible because of his commanding height.

Her lips curved upward, for she had almost decided that he had left the ballroom owing to the heat. After all, she was damp with perspiration in her silk gown. Mr. St. Albans had to be cooked through in his waistcoat, coat, and that suffocating neckcloth. Yes, she had decided that was exactly the situation. Or so she believed . . . that is, until she felt a large hand cup her elbow from behind.

At that very instant, Mr. St. Albans's mouth was poised just above her ear. "Shall we, Miss Chillton?"

The hum of his low voice tickled her ear, and she instinctively raised her shoulder. She turned around to reply, only to find her chest pressed against Mr. St. Albans's waistcoat. And there wasn't so much as a bead of sweat on his brow. Not a one!

From such a close vantage point, Mr. St. Albans's shoulders seemed much broader, his chest . . . somehow firmer. Indeed, his entire body seemed far more sculpted and muscular. Odd that she had not noticed when they danced earlier that eve.

She turned her face upward and raised her eyes to his.

His breath seemed to hitch the moment their gazes met, and suddenly Hannah could not seem to catch her breath.

Mr. St. Albans raised a hand, gesturing to the center of the dance floor, and again said, "Shall we, Miss Chillton?"

But words seemed quite out of Hannah's mental grasp at that moment, and so she merely nodded.

Mr. St. Albans folded Hannah's hand over his and drew her body close in preparation to pass through the burgeoning crowd.

How queer this all is.

Hannah peered up at Mr. St. Albans as he protectively led her toward the dance floor. There was no question as to the gentleman's identity, and yet, something was different.

Something about his tender touch made her tremble within. But not with fear or dread.

With heart-thumping excitement.

Oh, what had the Feathertons done to bring about such a visceral response in her? It had to be their doing, for there was no other explanation for this sudden fondness for a man she had professed to be the most irritating in all of Bath.

Hannah recalled hearing that the ladies, while in the last shank of a matchmaking scheme, had actually sprinkled some mysterious powder into their own grandniece's cordial. They were shameless when it came to serious matchmaking.

Perhaps they had done something similar to her. She had just taken tea with the two clever spinsters, after all.

Mr. St. Albans turned his green-eyed gaze to her when they reached their place on the floor. He encircled her waist with his muscled arm and gently took her right hand in his. He smiled at her then, and all of her blood seemed to drain into her Turkish slippers.

Hannah's breathing grew thinner still.

Devil take you, Annie, for persuading me to wear this oversnug corset. I do not give a fig how it shapes my form. I need to breathe!

Several times as Mr. St. Albans whirled her around the dance floor, she tried to break the gaze that held her so firmly, but she could not.

What was happening to her? She had danced the waltz a number of times, both in Bath and London, but this time—though there was no accounting for the notion—the proximity to this man seemed all too . . . intimate.

Just then, she felt his fingers trace a small circle upon her back, sending a tingle darting into her middle, and lower as well. She was horrified. Such incredible nerve the man possessed!

"Dear, s-sir," Hannah sputtered, curiously noting

that she did not miss a single step. "I will have you know that I am not as naive as you might believe."

Mr. St. Albans's eyes grew impossibly large and round. "I beg your pardon, Miss Chillton—"

"I admit, I do not know what game you play, Mr. St. Albans"—Hannah leaned close to make sure he heard her next words with total clarity despite the din of music and idle chatter that filled the ballroom—"but I certainly know its nature."

Inexplicably, Mr. St. Albans released her hand and waist, and stilled his step. He stared into her eyes, his mouth opening and closing as if he meant to reply, but could not.

Hannah suddenly felt every pair of eyes in the ballroom upon her. Heat rose into her cheeks and burned the tips of her ears as she turned to see elderly matrons pointing at her and her statuelike dance partner. Young misses giggled at her predicament, and gentlemen grinned.

And they had every right to stare, hadn't they?

Mr. St. Albans had ended their dance abruptly and was creating quite an embarrassing moment for them both. She turned to walk from the floor. Indeed, had walked several steps toward the door when suddenly she stilled her step.

No. No. She'd not give in. She'd not feel shame for this. She had done nothing wrong, after all!

Hannah whirled back around, intending to walk up to Mr. St. Albans and demand he finish the dance—as any polite gentleman would do.

But he was no longer standing where she'd left him. There was only a blatantly unoccupied bit of floor space where the man had once been.

Oh, jolly good. Now her humiliation was nearly complete.

Well, she wasn't going to allow him to do this to her. Not tonight. Not ever!

Hannah's angry gaze swept the ballroom, weaved through the crowd, and even sought out the door.

But he was nowhere to be seen.

Mr. St. Albans was gone.

Chapter Five

Griffin charged through the outer doors of the Upper Assembly Rooms and into the street. At once, a stiff wind ruffled his hair, and in the night air the scent of coming rain became plain to his nose.

Still, it was only a short walk around the stately Circus and down Gay Street to his lodgings. If he hurried, and luck was with him, he might reach Queen Square before the first droplet fell.

But good fortune had not danced with him this eve, and now was no different. Just then, the sky rumbled above him. He glanced down the dark street for a hackney or chairmen but saw neither.

Griffin started around the Circus, his pace quick. A misty curtain, more wind than rain, swept around the curved rows of imposing houses. He raised the collar of his coat. But then wondered why in Hades he bothered.

What did a smattering of water matter anyway? In truth, a little rain might be just what was needed to cool the searing anger he felt for his blasted brother at this moment.

Damn Garnet.

He should have known this brilliant plan of his brother's would not succeed. He was a fool to have ever believed it would have.

"Griff," came his brother's call. "Come on, now, stop! Trying to keep up with your horselike pace is making me perspire. I'll mar my neckcloth."

"I care not." Griffin quickened his strides.

"Please." Garnet sounded breathless. "Ouch—damn it! I've clocked my ankle on the fence. Stop, or slow down for god sakes, just for a moment."

Even from the sound of staggered footfalls on the flagway, Griffin knew that Garnet would catch him at any moment, but he'd be damned if he was going to stop and make it easy for his worthless brother.

"Damn it, this hurts. Hold up—have a little mercy. I'm injured here."

But he kept walking. The so-called injury was likely a ruse anyway to make him stop. That'd be just like his brother.

"Griff, talk to me. I need to know what the hell happened on the dance floor."

As if Garnet didn't know.

Griffin stopped abruptly and jerked himself around. "She *knew*, Garnet. She bloody well knew about the switch."

Garnet's jaw seemed to slacken. He was clearly gobsmacked.

"What do you mean, *exactly*?"

"I mean precisely what I said: Miss Chillton knew I

wasn't *you*." Griffin ground his teeth as he took a step toward his brother.

Obviously seeing the heated look in Griffin's eyes, Garnet raised a palm and double-stepped backward. "Hold off now. Hold off. No need to be angry. I have no doubt that this is all a grand misunderstanding." He shook his head in apparent disbelief. "I assure you, my scheme was foolproof; it could not go wrong. You simply haven't told me enough. There has to be more to it."

"I've had enough of your conniving games, your *schemes*."

"My schemes, dear brother, have never failed."

"Never failed *you* in your conquests." Griffin swallowed deeply. "But Miss Chillton is not a naive milkmaid, a lonely widow . . . or—or a bored shopkeeper's wife from Penzance. She is a respectable woman of Society. And resorting to tricks and plots to win her heart, well, it's disgraceful, that's what it is. And . . . it's beneath honor."

Griffin turned away from his brother and grabbed the wrought-iron fence railing before him with both hands. He squeezed the cool metal until the blood leached from his knuckles, whitening them. Leaning forward, he dropped his chin to his chest in defeat.

"But it doesn't matter anymore, does it?" he said resignedly. "It's too late. I've lost any chance with her. I am sure of it."

Garnet caught Griffin's shoulder and pulled him back into step along the curved flagway of the Circus. "It's not too late. I was watching from the door of the musicians' gallery. I saw the way she looked at you. The way she bent against your chest. Her interest was ever so clear. You must have felt her attraction. You must have. I will not believe you if you tell me otherwise."

Griffin turned his head and looked up at his brother. "I did. We both did. I know it. But then, suddenly, everything changed. She changed. And at that moment, everything I thought I knew, thought I felt, was wiped cleanly away. When I looked into her eyes, saw the betrayal she felt in them, I knew with all certainty that Miss Chillton was aware she'd been deceived."

"Now, now, we don't know that." The fine sprinkles of rain began to bead atop their coats like tiny diamonds.

"There is no other explanation I can fathom."

Garnet pulled up his lapel to protect his starched neckcloth from the rain. "Let us return to the house, with haste, and you can tell me exactly what happened and what was said."

Griffin nodded resignedly, but he knew the coming conversation would be utterly useless.

He had played his brother's deceitful game, and in the process had lost all hope of winning Miss Chillton's affections. Of that, he was quite certain.

Edgar, the ever-efficient butler, opened the door at Number One Royal Crescent before the footman had even turned the handle on the carriage door for the Featherton sisters and Hannah.

By some stroke of fortune, the rain momentarily raised its gray mantle and allowed the women to take the stairs into the house without so much as a single water stain on any of their silk ball gowns.

"My ladies," Edgar said quietly, "I have prepared a fire in the drawing room for your comfort and have taken the liberty of pouring three crystals of cordial."

"Oh, a fire and cordial. How thoughtful of you, Edgar." Lady Letitia passed her fringed shawl to the butler and hurried through the drawing-room door.

As Hannah shrugged off her pelisse, she happened to glance up, and despite the residual sting of humiliation she felt from being abandoned on the dance floor, she did not miss the exchange of warm glances between Edgar and Lady Viola as he took the frail old woman's wrap from her.

Good heavens! Annie had been right. How could she have possibly missed the connection between the two before? Hannah tried very hard not to allow her gaze to linger on the unlikely couple overlong, but the thought of their love for each other, having gone unacknowledged for years, was simply astonishing.

Yes, it was her duty to correct this injustice. In fact, she would begin making her plans the very next morn.

What better way, she decided, to repay Lady Viola for introducing her to Society. Why, she would never have made the matchmaking connections on her own that she had made through the Featherton sisters.

Without them, she would surely have no business or income of her own—save the pittance of a portion she received from her miserly brother, Arthur.

Lady Viola, wearing a fresh smile, glided into the drawing room as light as gossamer and floated into the unoccupied seat beside her sister.

She looked up and frowned, however, when it became evident that Hannah was not following her lead.

"There is a cordial on the salver for you. Do come inside, dear child, and join us by the fire."

"I should be delighted." Hannah raised her pelisse, as if to hand it to Edgar, but when he reached for it, she caught his gloved hand and pulled him away from the drawing-room doorway. "Is *he* here?"

"Do you mean Mr. St. Albans, miss?"

Hannah widened her eyes and nodded wildly. Yes, she mouthed. Is—he—here?

"No, miss, he is not," the butler whispered in a tone so low that Hannah could hardly hear a single word. "He has not yet returned from the ball."

"I beg your pardon?"

"He said, Hannah, that Mr. St. Albans has not yet returned from the ball."

Hannah lurched at the proximity of the voice and whirled around to find Lady Viola standing close behind her.

"Come join us by the hearth, dove. Perhaps a cordial will calm your nerves."

Hannah gave her duenna a smile and dutifully left the entry hall for the drawing room. But a relaxing close to the evening was not precisely what the Featherton sisters had in mind, it seemed. For she had scarcely rested her weight upon the wingback chair when the interrogation began.

"Dear gel, I know you do not wish to discuss it, but I fear we must know what passed between you and Mr. St. Albans on the dance floor. You both are guests in our home, after all, and if something must be done to douse any flaring rumors, sister and I must know at once."

Hannah swallowed the rather large lump that congealed in her throat. "N-nothing happened . . . not really."

The elderly sisters said nothing. Instead, they sat looking at her, not even bothering to blink.

"I swear to you. Nothing happened that should have necessitated Mr. St. Albans's charging from the ballroom floor, leaving *me* the focus of the entire assembly."

Still, the ladies spoke not a word. It was clear they doubted her opinion.

"*I* am the wronged party here. Not *he*!"

"Ah, here it comes now, Viola." Lady Letitia gave her sister a nod, then turned back to Hannah. "How did he wrong you, gel, and what, pray, did you do about it that sent the poor fellow retreating to the street?"

Hannah looked down at her wringing hands. "There was something . . . different about him when we took to the floor after tea. An intensity I had never witnessed in him before. I own, I could feel it." She allowed her gaze to travel slowly across the Aubusson carpet to the settee where the two inquisitors rested.

"But what did he *do*, Hannah, to cause you such worry?"

It took Hannah several seconds to find the words to express his transgression. "He . . . ran his fingers in tight circles on my back as we danced."

Lady Letitia chortled at that. "Well, that is a very egregious offense, to be sure. Viola, I vow we should summon the constables, at once!"

"Letitia, do not mock her. She is a young woman and mightn't have realized that there might have been an alternative reason for his fingers' movements." She focused her faded blue eyes on Hannah once more. "Feeling nervous might be an example."

"Oh." Something seemed to sink inside Hannah. "I had not considered that." In fact, she had been so focused on possible rakish behaviors that it never even occurred to her that there might be any other explanation for his touch.

Hannah lifted the small crystal goblet, allowing the liquid to touch her lips, but she was too absorbed in thought to swallow. She replaced the glass upon the polished tea table.

"No, I don't agree with you. I do not believe Mr. St. Albans was nervous at all," she told the Feathertons. "We had danced the entire first dance together, and not once did he appear the least unnerved. In fact, were I to describe his behavior to anyone earlier in the evening, I would have said that he was his usual supremely confident self."

"Nevertheless, Hannah, you did say he was somehow different when you danced the waltz." Lady Viola leaned forward. "A dance, he requested . . . for *you*."

Hannah shook her head. "If it were simply nerves, he would not have reacted so strongly to my comment about his . . . *touching*."

Now both of the ladies were leaning so far forward that their weight and sudden momentum caused the back feet of the petite settee to buck from the floor.

Lady Letitia's eyes were wide and bright. "What, pray tell, did you say, dear?"

Hannah rose from the chair and walked to stand before the low fire. "I-I told him that I did not know what game he played, but that I knew its purpose . . . or something of that nature. And then, without a word, he bolted from the ballroom."

"Ah, my lovely Miss Chillton," came a deep voice from the doorway.

Good heavens. A twinge of panic pinched at Hannah as she recognized Mr. St. Albans's distinctive voice.

Hannah spun around. She had not even heard the front door open, let alone Mr. St. Albans enter.

"I do apologize. How rude I must have appeared to you at the ball this eve." He tipped a deep bow to the Featherton sisters, then seemed to limp slightly as he moved through the center of the drawing room and made for Hannah.

Lady Letitia tapped the floor as he passed. "Why are you hopping about, young man?"

"'Tis nothing, Lady Letitia. Struck it on a rail while trying to catch a bolting horse."

"How noble of you, Mr. St. Albans. Not many gentlemen would be so gallant as to assist a rider in need."

He smiled in that cocky way of his. "Well, as I said, 'twas nothing really." When Mr. St. Albans reached Hannah, he confidently took her hand in his, then clapped his other hand atop it, assuring she could not pull away no matter how desperately she tried.

Which she did, of course, with all the strength she could muster without arousing the Feathertons' notice.

Still, Hannah's eyes shot to the ladies, and she pleaded with her gaze for assistance. As at the ball, however, they only gazed appreciatively at their handsome houseguest.

Mr. St. Albans looked down into Hannah's eyes and sighed softly. "Please do forgive me, my dear Miss

Chillton," he begged so sincerely that Hannah herself almost believed him.

Almost.

Hannah wrenched her gaze from his and focused her gaze out the window on the sweep of the rain-drenched crescent. "Leaving me on the dance floor was beyond rude . . . sirrah." Her tone was much harsher than she meant it to be, but in truth he deserved nothing less for his behavior.

"Nevertheless, I do wish you would forgive me. Please, Miss Chillton." Mr. St. Albans stroked the top of her hand irritatingly, as if he thought the soothing motion might calm her. "For I assure you, dear lady, there is a good explanation for what appeared to be my most ungentlemanly behavior."

Hannah twisted her captive hand and pulled it from his grip. "And just what, I ask, might that be, Mr. St. Albans?" This she should like to hear.

And so, evidently, did the Featherton sisters, for the room fell silent, and all eyes seized upon the gentleman.

Mr. St. Albans curled his fingers toward his palm and brought his fist to his mouth just as he cleared his throat. Gaming for time, Hannah suspected.

Then he glanced at each woman in turn, as if hoping that at least one of them would release him from his obligation of explanation.

But none of the ladies did so.

"Very well." He cleared his throat again. A flush of color filled the tips of Mr. St. Albans's ears as he hesitantly supplied his excuse for racing from the dance floor.

"I . . . I fear it might have been . . . the ham."

Chapter Six

Queen Square

What in blazes? You send not a word for two full days, and now you tell me that *this* is the explanation you gave Miss Chillton and the Featherton ladies?"

Griffin St. Albans leaped up from his chair, nearly toppling the diminutive tea table Mrs. Hopshire had just set with a selection of cold meats, berries, and cheese. "Please, Garnet, tell me that you truly did not blame my sudden departure on my . . . bowels."

"I'm afraid so, Griff. The moment I mentioned that the ham you devoured in the Tea Room—"

"But I had no ham."

"No, but *I* did." Garnet shook his finger at Griffin. "Do you wish a recounting of what I said on your behalf or not, brother?"

Griffin waved his hand resignedly, and Garnet continued, "Once I explained that the ham had caused a dreadful disturbance in your belly, the ladies were not about to speak another word of the entire incident."

"And how were you so sure of the direction of their reaction?"

"Well, Griff, they are ladies after all, and as such can be counted upon to respond . . . well, gently." Garnet leaned over the table and snatched up a thin slice of pork and popped it into his mouth, seeming to delight in the irony. "So you see, it was the best of all possible explanations."

Griffin set his elbow on his knee and rested his forehead in his hand. "So help me to understand. Miss Chillton now believes that I was playing the rogue on the dance floor until I was compelled to find a chamber pot?"

He looked at Garnet, who was supping on yet another swirl of ham and smiling back at him as he chewed.

"Yes, Garnet, I can see how that is the best possible explanation."

"Glad you agree."

"Are you mad? How could anyone agree with your solution? Damn it all, Garnet, just what the hell were you thinking?"

Garnet chuckled to himself as he polished his signet ring on the lapel of yet another new coat supplied by the earl. "I assure you, I only had your best interests in mind, dear brother." Then he huffed what sounded like a sarcastic laugh. "We both know that the truth was clearly out of the question. This little charade of ours is not only affecting your romance, brother, but mine as well."

"Yours?"

"Your darling Miss Chillton introduced me to the most beautiful miss. Someone I greatly desire to know better. But I could not do so at the ball—for I was being . . . well, *you*."

Griffin exhaled a frustrated sigh as he rose and moved to the drawing-room window, just as a magnificent carriage turned into the square and, surprisingly, drew up before their door.

He gripped the mullion and leaned closer, for surely his eyes deceived him. "Oh, *no*."

A pang of dread pinched at his middle, and Griffin held his breath as he waited to see who would emerge from the carriage, praying it was not who he believed.

The footman opened the cabin door, and who else should step out but the ebony-garbed Pinkerton followed by the squat Earl of Devonsfield himself.

Griffin spun around to warn Garnet, but even as he did so, he heard the click of the lock followed by the whine of rusted hinges as Mrs. Hopshire opened the heavy front door.

It was too late.

"Where is Griffin?" Though he was still standing outside on the front steps, the earl's usual gruff voice sounded thin and distressed.

"Griff?" Garnet's eyes were as wide as his tea saucer. "You failed to tell me that the—" As his words broke off, Garnet's expression shifted from abject shock to absolute delight as his eyes alighted on the earl and his man, Pinkerton. "Dear sir, I had not expected you. How wonderful, though, that you are able to visit . . . and *all* the way from Devonsfield as well. What an honor you pay us."

The earl's beady eyes shifted from Garnet to Griffin. "What is this folly, boy? From your wrenching missive

I was led to believe Garnet was missing and that you feared the worst. Yet here he stands."

Garnet stared at his brother. "Griff? What is this about?"

"I beg your pardon, my lord." Griffin swallowed deeply. "Did you not receive my second missive informing you that my brother had been delayed, but had just arrived in Bath?"

"Do you think I would be standing here in your doorway had I received it? Do you? Think you Devonsfield is just around the corner?"

"No, my lord, I suppose not."

"Of course *not*. Why, I left the very instant Pinkerton apprised me of the dire situation."

Damn me. The day had just sunk from bad to horrid.

Garnet called for Mrs. Hopshire to fetch a decanter of brandy, then managed a jovial smile for the grimacing earl. "But now that you are here, my lord, I must tell you of my brother's progress. Why, I wish I had half the good fortune he has had in finding a potential bride."

The earl turned his head from Griffin to Garnet, then back again, so quickly that his wig did not quite follow in time and now sat slightly askew atop his head.

"A potential bride, you say? Well now, perhaps coming to Bath is not wholly a waste after all. Might stay a while and observe the proceedings. Yes, yes, indeed I shall," the earl muttered to himself before turning an eye to his man. "Pinkerton, be a good man and see what the delay is with the brandy. I own the journey from Devonsfield has left me quite parched."

Pinkerton nodded and, as requested, disappeared silently into the entry hall.

The earl crossed the room to the sofa, flipped up his coattails, and took his ease on the plump cushion. "Now, lad," he said to Griffin, "sit down and tell me all about your young lady."

"He can *tell* you about her, my lord, but if you wish, you may meet her yourself—this very eve." Garnet removed a lavender-edged card from his pocket and waved it teasingly in the air.

Griffin snatched the card from his brother's hand. "'Tis an invitation to the Featherton ladies' house on Royal Crescent—for a precomet soiree."

The earl cleared his throat. "Precomet soiree? What sort of nonsense is this?"

Griffin, who only a moment before had been of like mind with the earl about the nonsensical nature of such a party, read on, and as he did his heart began to pound inside his chest. He lifted his chin and stared directly at Garnet.

"*Miss Caroline Herschel*—why, she's England's foremost authority on comets—will be in attendance? Here, in Bath?"

Garnet nodded in that bored way of his when a topic of discussion did not revolve around him. "Yes, I believe that is right. Some astronomer of note will be the Feathertons' honored guest this eve."

Griffin stuffed the invitation into his own pocket. "Thank you, Garnet, I shall be delighted to attend."

The comment snared his brother's full attention. "No, no, no. 'Tis a *party*, a social gathering—which means . . . my territory. The invitation is clearly inscribed to Mr. St. Albans and guest."

The earl's tiny blue eyes took on a keen focus. "I will be the guest."

"Absolutely, my lord. I would consider no other for such an occasion." Garnet turned from the earl and lifted an eyebrow as he addressed Griffin. "Surely it must be clear to you that only *one* of us may attend the soiree. And you do not wish to jeopardize your budding relationship with Miss Chillton by making some social faux pas, do you?"

"Of course not."

"Well, then, *I* should be the one to attend." Garnet shot a smile to the earl. "We should leave the house before eight o'clock, my lord. Can you dress so quickly?"

"Can you not see that I *am* dressed, boy?" The earl shook his head, which, to his fortune, turned his wig perfectly back into place.

"Yes, eight o'clock. But *I* will be the St. Albans in attendance, Garnet. The house is to be full of astronomers and members of Bath's philosophical society eager to discuss the comet—something you know nothing of. I, on the other hand will be able to attend to such discussions with expertise." Griffin clicked his heels. "Do excuse me, my lord. Garnet will see to your lodgings above stairs. I must dress if we are to depart by eight."

"Did you see what he just did?" Garnet asked the earl with incredulity.

"Yes, I did, boy." The earl leaned back on the settee and considered the exchange he'd just witnessed between the lionhearted Griffin and the highly polished Garnet.

Yes, coming to Bath had been a very good decision indeed.

Hannah followed her duennas and their esteemed guest, the diminutive Miss Caroline Herschel, into the candlelit drawing room. Viewing her from behind, as Hannah was, it was nearly inconceivable that Miss Herschel was a woman grown.

And yet, she was.

Still, at two-and-seventy years, the frail Miss Herschel stood barely over four feet tall. Her impeded growth, she unabashedly had admitted to them at dinner, had been the result of typhus when she was but a girl of ten.

Her ailment did nothing to contain her spirit or her mind, however, for Miss Caroline Herschel was by many accounts the most brilliant astronomer and mathematician of the day—man or woman.

And as their private dinner progressed, Hannah found the elderly woman to possess a singularly wicked sense of humor as well. What a contrary little package this woman was.

An hour later, the expansive candlelit drawing room was filled with members of Bath society and the international scientific world. As cordial, brandy, and sherry were served to the guests, Hannah sat before the fortepiano, regaling the Feathertons' guests with a selection from Haydn.

It was a simple piece for her. One she'd played at least one hundred times before, which now afforded her the freedom to allow her gaze to drift from the music and across the drawing room in search of the rake, Mr. St. Albans.

The Featherton sisters had informed her that evening, several times actually, that he would be in attendance. She was sure he would be, knowing of his interest in astronomy, and yet he had not returned to Number One Royal Crescent all day, which was entirely out of character for the man. If nothing else, he would have wished to dress for the soiree.

In the third time in as many minutes, when Hannah glanced up from her music, she finally saw him. He looked rather dashing, she supposed, in his dark blue coat and buff breeches. Like several other guests, he seemed completely enraptured by what Miss Herschel was saying and, indeed, seemed to be questioning her on several key points.

Still, it seemed clear to Hannah that he was not at ease, for more than once, she caught him glancing her way, absently fingering her aunts' prized Sèvres *seau-à-liqueurs* sitting atop the mahogany table between the high windows.

Suddenly the room went quiet, and Hannah realized that everyone was looking at her.

She turned her gaze from Mr. St. Albans and saw that her fingers were no longer tapping the piano keys, but were instead poised in the air. Heat surged into her cheeks.

"Is something amiss, Hannah?" Lady Viola laid a gentle hand upon her shoulder. "You stopped playing midway through the piece."

"Oh, I-I seemed to be missing a page of music, 'tis all." She forced a twittering laugh. "Dear me. How silly

I am. Here it is after all. It was just turned back to front."

"I . . . I will leave you to your music then if you are certain you are having no difficulty."

"No, none at all. I am perfectly fine." Hannah realized that her reply sounded a little too cheerful to be entirely believable. "Really, please go and enjoy the soiree."

"Very well, then. If you are . . . truly." As Hannah nodded and smiled, Lady Viola hesitantly began to turn and head back in the direction of her sister.

Lord above.

With that embarrassment concluded, Hannah began to play again, bending her back and drawing her face close to the keys to avoid meeting anyone's judging gaze.

Especially *his*.

And then, as if her thoughts had summoned him, suddenly there was a deep voice caressing her ear. "May I turn the pages for you?"

She turned her head a bit to glance up at her all-too-willing assistant. "Do not trouble yourself, Mr. St. Albans. I have played alone for most of my life. And besides, I would not wish you to miss a single word of wisdom Miss Herschel has to impart."

Hannah rolled her eyes. That sounded a bit bitter . . . almost as if she was jealous. Which she wasn't, of course.

Miss Herschel was an elderly woman—and, well, Hannah wasn't the least bit interested in astronomy—or Mr. St. Albans—anyway.

Still, his eyes following the notes across the page, he

reached out to turn the music, his palm sweeping along
her bare arm as he did so.

Sweet tingles of warmth slid down her forearm to
her hand, and before she knew what she was doing,
Hannah had laid her fingers atop his, stilling his movement.

Her gaze turned upward and locked with his own.
For several seconds she stared deep into his eyes, her
hand upon his, her mind hopelessly blank and word-
less.

In the next instant, Hannah caught in her peripheral
vision a glimpse of a plump little man standing beside
Mr. St. Albans. And if she was not mistaken, he was
tugging at the taller gentleman's coat sleeve.

"Well, lad, are you going to introduce me to your
bride, or not?" the impatient little man demanded to
know.

Hannah yanked her hand away from Mr. St. Albans's, accidentally knocking his fingers aside and
sending music sailing in every direction to the floor.

"I-I beg your pardon, sir." Hannah could scarcely
force the words from her mouth. "Did you just refer to
me as . . . Mr. St. Albans's *bride*?"

"Of course I did," the round little man replied. "I
know that no agreement has been made yet, but you are
Miss Chillton, are you not?"

"I . . . well, yes I am, sir, but—"

"*Bride,* did you say?" Lady Letitia suddenly appeared between them as if she'd dropped from the crystal chandelier above.

Lady Viola hurried beside her.

In that moment, other conversations taking place

within the drawing room ceased, and the eyes of Bath society seemed to fix upon the five of them.

Hannah eyed the sole remaining page of music left on the piano and considered lifting it before her face to conceal the fierce red color she felt blossoming on her cheeks.

A mistake had somehow been made, but Hannah knew it was not her place to correct it. She pinned Mr. St. Albans with an imploring gaze. "Mr. St. Albans, I-I do not believe we have had the honor of meeting your guest."

Mr. St. Albans swallowed deeply, as though he felt as much distress as Hannah herself. "Lady Letitia. Lady Viola . . . and Miss Chillton, please allow me to introduce the Earl of Devonsfield."

"Earl of Devonsfield?" Lady Letitia's fluffy white eyebrows drew ever closer.

"Yes." The earl seemed to study Lady Letitia for several moments longer than propriety deemed proper. "I am recently arrived from Devon."

"Devon? Such lovely country. You are perhaps a relation of Mr. St. Albans?" she asked tentatively.

"I'd say so." The portly little man seemed to rise up a bit in his shoes. "Mr. St. Albans is . . . my *heir*."

Chapter Seven

Hannah saw Lady Letitia slip a sly glance at her sister just before flashing a great smile at the two gentlemen.

"Why, Mr. St. Albans. Heir to an *earldom*?" she practically cooed. "Aren't you just a basket of secrets?"

Mr. St. Albans stared at the earl, almost as if he, like Hannah herself, had only just learned he was heir to an earldom.

Lady Viola seemed to catch the congruity, too. "I doubt Mr. St. Albans meant to keep his future a secret from us, Letitia. I suspect, until the earl's recent arrival, he simply did not *remember*—because of—" Lady Viola softened her tone to a whisper. "The . . . carriage accident."

"Oh, you must be right, Viola." Lady Letitia flipped open her purple cutwork fan and swiped it before her face in order to whisper, a smidgen too loudly, to her sister. "He must have not remembered, either, that he has not offered for our Hannah and therefore should not represent her as his bride."

"Sister." Lady Viola's faded blue eyes widened at her sister's shocking words, and even through the dusted coats of white powder upon her cheeks, Hannah could see the rising red evidence of the old woman's embarrassment.

Mr. St. Albans straightened his back. "My dear ladies, I believe the earl has misunderstood the extent of my relationship with Miss Chillton."

The earl's gray eyebrows inched toward his narrow nose. "I do not see how. Was not my purpose here this eve to meet the gel?"

The small laugh that then burst from Mr. St. Albans's mouth was anything but genuine, at least to Hannah's way of thinking.

"Yes, yes, my lord, I did wish for you to make the acquaintance of Miss Chillton—and the Featherton ladies, for without their kindness after my accident, I do not know what I would have done."

Something told Hannah that this was not the truth— not even in the same lane as the truth—but her duennas seemed to accept the explanation well enough.

As the Featherton ladies led the earl across the room for a formal introduction to the famed Miss Caroline Herschel, Hannah trained her eyes on Mr. St. Albans, who trailed behind them, and observed him keenly while pretending to arrange her pages of music.

He may have fooled the Feathertons, for indeed they seemed unable to see past his handsome facade, but Hannah knew that Mr. St. Albans was hiding something, and this notion piqued her curiosity fiercely.

All was not as it appeared with the man, that was for

certain. One moment he was pompous and arrogant, the
next kind and passionate. It was almost as if he were
two different men entirely.

She watched him graciously accept a brandy from a
passing footman. *Just what are you hiding, sir?* she
wondered.

As if he'd heard her thought, Mr. St. Albans turned
and glanced warmly back at Hannah. This initially startled her, but she smiled prettily at him until he grudg-
ingly returned his attention to Miss Herschel and her
learned circle of astronomers.

Hannah's eyes remained fixed on him, however. For
with no matchmaking clients at the present, she had
just decided to devote her unoccupied time entirely to
uncovering the truth about Mr. St. Albans.

And learning how that, possibly, involved her.

Number One Royal Crescent was in an uproar when
Hannah awoke the next morning. She rolled from her
bed and slipped a shawl over her shoulders before hur-
rying to her chamber door and peeking into the passageway.

"No, no! Pick it up." Mr. St. Albans was standing but
a few feet from her chamber, snapping at the footman
who struggled with an oversized portmanteau.

"Yes. Sir."

"Don't run it down the stairway. You'll mar the
leather. I don't wish to see one scratch when you reach
the entry hall. Do you hear me? Not one!"

"Mr. St. Albans?" Hannah pushed a loose lock of
ebony hair from her eyes and tightened the shawl

around her for modesty's sake. "What is the meaning of this? Where are you going?"

Mr. St. Albans exhaled hard through his nostrils. "It *seems* I have taken a house in Queen Square and I am to take up residence there at once."

Now this was a bad turn of luck for Hannah. No sooner had she decided to investigate Mr. St. Albans, to determine the truth about him, than he finally found himself in sufficient health to leave Royal Crescent. "But are you yet well enough to live alone, sir?"

"Well, that's just it, you see. The earl has decided to stay in Bath . . . at least until the comet has passed overhead. Seems he took a sudden fancy to seeing the spectacle after attending the Feathertons' precomet soiree last eve."

Or rather he had taken a sudden fancy to a certain Featherton sister, Hannah mused.

She had not missed seeing the admiring looks or hearing the bouquets of sweet compliments the earl showered upon Lady Letitia throughout the evening.

Hannah sensed an opportunity to do a little matchmaking.

"Mr. St. Albans, if the earl is interested in the comet, he should certainly join us this evening. Miss Herschel will be discussing its path through the sky, and her latest calculations, in the Octagon at the Assembly Rooms. I know Lady Letitia will be in attendance, and I vow she would be most grateful if the earl would deign to escort her to the event."

"Is that so?" Mr. St. Albans flicked a dark eyebrow upward. "I shall mention it to him. I am sure he would be delighted."

Hannah had thought that the mention of Miss Herschel's discussion would intrigue the passionate astronomer in Mr. St. Albans, but instead he appeared almost bored with the subject.

How curious.

Then something else occurred to her. The event at the Octagon would also provide an excellent opportunity to study Mr. St. Albans.

She looked coyly up at Mr. St. Albans. "I admit, I had considered attending Miss Herschel's discussion myself. Though, since my education did not include the study of astronomy, I fear her teachings may be difficult for the laity to understand."

Mr. St. Albans's eyes sparkled quite suddenly. "You are an intelligent woman, Miss Chillton. Surely, if I were to accompany you to the discussion, I could explain anything you do not fully comprehend."

Hannah smiled. He had walked directly into her snare, and she'd caught him. "Is that an invitation?"

"Indeed it is, Miss Chillton."

"Thank you, sir, I gratefully accept." Hannah drew back inside her chamber, but before closing the door, tossed Mr. St. Albans a coquettish smile, just for good measure. "Until tonight then, my dear Mr. St. Albans."

He smiled back at her and returned a decidedly rakish wink. "Until tonight."

Hannah had not been in error when she told Mr. St. Albans that Lady Letitia would be grateful for the company of the earl. Though grateful was hardly the correct superlative for Lady Letitia's maidenlike glee upon receiving the earl's card requesting the honor of escorting her to the Octagon that eve.

At once the excited elderly woman raced off to her chamber, dragging poor Annie to help her dress.

Hannah smiled inwardly at her own ingenuity at facilitating a potential match. Next she focused her clever eye upon Lady Viola.

"Dear lady," Hannah began quite sweetly, as she unfurled the leading edge of her second matchmaking scheme. "I own, Bath society has never seen such a grand affair as the precomet soiree last eve."

Lady Viola, who was resting upon the drawing-room settee with a dampened towel upon her brow, smiled proudly.

"It was lovely and a great success, was it not, Hannah?" she asked, though Hannah knew no answer was required.

It was a lovely evening, and Lady Viola was nearly entirely responsible for it—something of which she was very proud.

"Though I vow, seeing to the arrangements right down to the smallest detail has fully drained me of all strength. I shall need a sennight at the very least before I am myself again."

"You are to be commended for having trained your staff so well to support you. I saw how hard they worked on the preparations for nearly a week, both night and day. And yet this morn, as exhausted as they must be, they rose at dawn to see to their household duties. Truly your training is to be admired."

Lady Viola's mouth rounded, and she drew herself upright. "Dear me, I was so weary, I had not thought to release the staff from their duties this day, though they have certainly earned a respite."

Hannah nodded in agreement. "Indeed they have, Lady Viola."

"Be a dove, would you, Hannah, and summon Edgar for me, please." Lady Viola lowered her feet to the floor and handed Hannah the folded towel. "And . . . do something with this, would you? I am feeling much better now."

"Absolutely." Hannah excused herself from the drawing room and hurried below stairs, where she found Edgar having tea with Mrs. Penny, the housekeeper.

"Miss Chillton." Edgar came to his feet at once. "Is something amiss for you to have ventured below stairs?"

"Oh, no, no. Though I do apologize for intruding upon you and Mrs. Penny, Edgar, but Lady Viola would like to speak with you."

"With me?" A small smile budded on his lips. "I was under the impression she was not to be disturbed this day."

"She is feeling much more herself now." Hannah paused, the way she'd seen actors do to intensify their next words. "Oh, Edgar, I should allow Lady Viola to tell you this, but I am ever so worried . . ."

Mrs. Penny reached out for Hannah's hand and drew her near. "Do sit down, Miss Chillton. You seem overwrought."

"That's just it, you see. Lady Viola wishes to allow the house staff a day off—which is well earned after all of their hard work in preparation for the soiree. But Lady

Letitia and I will be away this eve, and Lady Viola, despite her courage, is far too weak to join us—"

Edgar tipped his head at Hannah, understanding her request before she could make her plea. "I shall be honored to remain in the house to see to Lady Viola's needs. You needn't say any more or worry on it any longer, Miss Chillton."

"Oh, thank you, Edgar. You are a dear, sweet man."

Hannah nearly skipped up the stairs. Her plan was falling perfectly into place.

When she reached the drawing room again, she informed Lady Viola that Edgar was indeed on his way above stairs. But as she turned to leave, she stealthily drew the drawing-room door key from its lock and tucked it beneath the rose-hued ribbon tied around her bodice.

It was difficult not to laugh with delight as she reached her chamber and withdrew the key from its hiding place beneath her belted ribbon.

The simplicity of her matchmaking scheme was perfect.

For tonight, she would employ a tried-and-true Featherton matchmaking maneuver.

And the inducement would work, too; Hannah was sure if it. For in her hand she held the key to unlocking Lady Viola's and Edgar's hearts.

It just happened to fit the drawing-room door as well.

Chapter Eight

Lady Letitia, who was enthusiastically greeting the earl and Mr. St. Albans in the entry hall that evening, was making far too much noise. Hannah was sure the old woman would wake Lady Viola, who was napping in the drawing room, and she could not have that.

It would ruin her plan completely.

"Everyone, please. Shhh." Hannah raised a gloved hand and positioned her index finger before her mouth, then gestured to the drawing room.

Silently, Hannah grasped the brass handle and drew the door closed, and while concealing her doings with her body, she quickly locked it and deposited the key in her reticule.

She turned back around with a smile. "I believe Lady Viola's cordial has set her to sleep in the drawing room. I only just sent Edgar inside with a counterpane for her."

"Aren't you a sweeting, looking out for my Viola?"

Lady Letitia took a step for the door, making Hannah suspect she would wish to bid her sister good eve before they left for the Octagon—and would find the door locked!

She grasped the elder woman's arm. "We must away at once. Miss Herschel's discussion this eve was announced in the *Bath Herald* this morn, and I daresay, if we do not hurry, there will not be an open seat to be had."

Lady Letitia moved toward the drawing-room door once more. "It will take but a moment to—"

"My lord"—Hannah frantically turned to the Earl of Devonsfield for assistance—"your carriage must have passed the Upper Assembly Rooms. No doubt the road was clogged with conveyances." Lud, she only hoped she was right!

The earl, who seemed to quite like being the center of attention, raised his head, making it almost appear that he had a neck. "I fear Miss Chillton is correct, Lady Letitia. We risk standing throughout the eve if we do not away at once."

"Oh." Lady Letitia's eyes grew wide. "With my . . . condition, standing is not my first preference."

The condition her ladyship spoke of, yet did not specify in the company of the two gentlemen, was her gout.

It was also the very reason the Featherton sisters returned to Bath each season, eager to partake of the spa city's famed curative waters.

How fortuitous for Hannah that the earl had led Lady Letitia down that particular avenue of thought.

"Shall we go?" Mr. St. Albans opened the front door, as Lady Viola had graciously allowed the entire staff leave, save Edgar. With a smile to Hannah, Mr. St. Albans indicated the way to the carriage with a grand sweep of his hand.

Lady Letitia snared the earl's proffered arm and caned her way through the door and down the steps to the carriage with all the enthusiasm of a girl first out.

Thank heavens.

Hannah looked back over her shoulder at the drawing-room door. Any moment now, she was sure Edgar would find the door locked and begin pounding upon it for immediate release.

And so, she made for the carriage in such haste that it completely escaped her that Mr. St. Albans had offered his arm to her and was now standing on the top stair of the porch alone, with a despondent expression pulling at his handsome face.

Griffin could not believe his fortune. He was about to hear Miss Caroline Herschel's discourse on the Bath Comet.

Just one month ago, he would never even have dreamed of such an opportunity.

While his gaze reached the heavens, his place on this earth had always been limited by his pocket to the confines of Cornwall's Kennymare Cove. And so he believed it would always be.

Yet here he was, standing inside the door of the Upper Assembly Rooms' famed Octagon, with a stunning beauty on his arm. Griffin doubted there had ever been a moment when he'd felt more content.

Though he might feel more confident that Miss

Chillton truly wished to come to the oration with him had he not strongly suspected that Garnet had somehow used intimidation or trickery to convince her to attend the event.

As the earl and Miss Chillton had predicted, the Octagon was brimful with scholars, scientists, and well-dressed members of Bath society.

Miss Herschel's discussion was not scheduled to begin for a quarter of an hour, yet every bench was more than occupied. If even a hand's width of wood peeked out from beneath a coattail or skirt, someone hurried to squeeze into the space.

Then there was a great commotion in the center of the front row. Griffin edged forward for a better look.

Standing a full head above any other man in the room, Griffin saw quite clearly that the disturbance was being caused by none other than Mr. Pinkerton.

A young man, his less-than-new coat labeling him a student or possibly a scholar, rushed through the burgeoning crowd and straight up to Griffin. "Sir, the gentleman in black asked me to fetch your party. I am to bring the four of you to the seats the man has procured on your behalf. Will you come? I shan't be paid, unless you do at once."

Griffin grinned, and within two minutes they were sitting directly before the lectern in seats the earl had evidently paid dearly for through his man, Mr. Pinkerton.

Almost at once, the diminutive Miss Caroline Herschel appeared in the chamber to a round of roaring applause. Because of her advanced years and short stature, she was assisted up three wooden steps, and a moment later, her rather stern-looking face appeared over the edge of the lectern.

All those who had the privilege to have made their way inside the Octagon before the doors were closed fell silent as the tiny woman opened her mouth to speak.

But Griffin, who had so looked forward to Miss Herschel's oration this eve, could not focus upon a single word. Not a one.

Because of the tight seating arrangements, Miss Chillton's thigh was pressed against his own, and, indeed, her arm was wedged slightly behind his, causing her breast to brush his biceps with her every breath.

He could press the gentleman to his right aside an inch or two for a little more room. He should do just that. *Should.*

But he wouldn't.

No, that feeling of contentment he'd had when they'd first entered the Octagon had transformed into an altogether different sensation, and truth to tell, he wasn't content anymore at all.

Even through the fabric covering his thigh, he could feel the maddening heat of Miss Chillton's body. His heart quickened, and he wanted to feel more.

He leaned his body toward her, ever so slightly, and savored the softness of her breast against his arm.

He knew what he was doing was wrong.

In fact, it was exactly the sort of rakish behavior Miss Chillton had accused him of as they danced at the ball, but he did not draw back. He pressed his thigh harder against hers and savored the sensation.

And suddenly, for the first time in his life, he truly understood his decadent, womanizing brother, Garnet.

They were more alike than he ever would have believed.

More than he ever would have admitted.

Until tonight.

❧

Hannah was quite glad that she didn't give a fig about comets—even the one scheduled to whoosh right overhead, sprinkling glittering dust from the heavens over the whole of Bath.

Yes, she was relieved, because there was no way in the universe that she could possibly concentrate on anything being said about the comet this eve.

How could she, with the wickedly attractive Mr. St. Albans practically sitting in her lap?

Not that she was interested in him. Because she wasn't, a fact she found herself constantly having to remind the Featherton sisters of . . . every day.

She wedged her eyes as far to her right as she might, secretly working to peer up at the gentleman without his being the wiser.

He was striking. She could admit that much, for his manly beauty was not a subject for debate. It was a clear fact. The man was perfectly, indisputably, handsome.

But he was also arrogant and rakish . . . most of the time.

This was *not* one of those times, however, though Hannah wished with all her being that it were. When Mr. St. Albans played the cad, she had no difficulty spurning his advances and spitting bile.

Then there were other times.

Times like this eve, when he looked at her so tenderly, treated her like a lady. And it was those moments Hannah rued. For then, she needed only to look in his eyes, feel his gentle touch, and her heart was set to pounding like rain upon the earth.

She wished, too, that the room was not so stacked with humanity. Though the night was cool, the Octagon seemed void of air. Hannah could not even move without pressing into Lady Letitia on her left or Mr. St. Albans on her right.

At first, she thought she imagined the heat that seemed to radiate between her and Mr. St. Albans, but soon it was evident that wherever their bodies touched, no matter how lightly, a firestorm raged.

He shifted on the bench, then, and now Hannah felt the tip of her breast rubbing against his arm whenever she drew in a breath. Lustful thoughts immediately leaped into her mind, to her private mortification.

She tried to stop breathing, if only for a moment so she could gather her wits about her, but that wasn't going to work. Holding the air in her lungs only made her breathe harder when she released it.

No, there was nothing to do but excuse herself for some cool night air.

When she stood and whispered her apologies to Lady Letitia, Hannah should have realized that retiring from the Octagon would not bring about the result she desired.

She should have anticipated that Mr. St. Albans, feeling gentlemanly this eve, would have her elbow . . . and would be touching her . . . even as they quit the oration.

"Sir, I only wish to take some air." Hannah unobtru-

sively slipped her arm from his and hurried through the
column-framed doors to Bennett Street. "I know what
wonder the study of the comet holds for you, and I do
not wish for you to miss a single word of the oration."

Mr. St. Albans took a step toward her, closing the
distance between them. "I will not leave you alone,
Miss Chillton."

Hannah swallowed and retreated, until her back was
pressed against one of the columns. She gazed into his
smoldering eyes and felt just a little dizzy. "Please, I
will return in but a moment. I am already feeling quite
revived."

"Then I shall wait." He moved closer still, and now
he stood only the span of a hand from her.

She could feel his breath on her face, and her own
breath came faster. This wasn't at all how she had
planned for this evening to progress. She only wanted
to learn more about the man.

Instead, she only learned that Mr. St. Albans, despite
being the arrogant, self-important buffoon . . . could
make her pulse quicken with but a glance.

Oh, her brain was so muddled, and it was all Mr. St.
Albans's fault. The best thing to do, nay, the only thing
to do, was to put some distance between them. Only
then might she regain her senses.

Instantly, Hannah spun to her right, deciding to walk
home to Royal Crescent. But then she realized she
couldn't.

Not yet.

Blast!

Lady Viola and Edgar had not been left alone together nearly long enough.

So, Hannah dug into her mental book of matchmaking trickery until she came upon a solution. *Question him about his passions and reduce the physicality of the moment. Yes. That was it.*

She turned back to face Mr. St. Albans and gazed up through her upper lashes. "Sir, would you care to take a stroll? Walking in the cool air always revives Lady Viola when she has one of her spells. No doubt it will do the same for me."

Without a word, Mr. St. Albans offered his arm, and they set off in the direction of the Circus.

"Are you planning on attending the comet-viewing party on the Royal Crescent lawn? I have heard that the view from there is to be most spectacular."

Mr. St. Albans huffed at that. "For the *ton,* perhaps. I have not yet decided where best to view the comet. I am in the process of conducting sweeps in a list of locales, and only when I have completed my surveys will I select the best vantage for my equipment."

"What can you see through your telescope? Are the stars truly blue and sparkling, as they appear to the naked eye?"

He stopped walking then and stepped in front of Hannah. His eyes were wide with excitement. "Do you really wish to know?"

"Yes. Certainly. Who would not wish to view the stars as if you were one of them?"

Mr. St. Albans looked into the sky, then sighed and returned his gaze to Hannah's. "Too many clouds this eve. But tomorrow eve should be much clearer. Join me after dark. I shall send a card to tell you where I will be."

Hannah gulped. She knew she ought to beg off, but

she could not resist such an offer. And so she excitedly accepted his invitation.

A broad smile broke on Mr. St. Albans's lips. "You will not be disappointed, Miss Chillton. For tomorrow eve, I will show you . . . *heaven.*"

Chapter Nine

Being the gracious hostess she was, when the carriage drew up before Royal Crescent after conveying the quartet from the Octagon, Lady Letitia invited Mr. St. Albans and the earl inside for a glass of her favorite cordial.

A jolt shot through Hannah as she realized where the cordial would be served—in the drawing room—the very place she'd locked Lady Viola and Mr. Edgar.

The footman had not even let down the steps when Hannah flung open the cabin door, leaped from the carriage, and raced up the stairs and into the house.

She fumbled inside her reticule for the key to the drawing room, finally gaining purchase on it and shoving it into the lock. She pressed the latch and pushed open the door just as Lady Letitia's cane tapped the first step outside.

Hannah did not know what she had expected to find when she swung the door open—a smear of red lip paint on Edgar's cheek, or perhaps Lady Viola's hair all a tumble—but the reality was really quite tame. Dignified.

Lady Viola sat upon the settee sipping her nightly crystal of cordial, while Edgar stirred the fire with an iron poker.

Hannah exhaled her disappointment. Her scheme had failed. The two would-be lovers were as tepid as this morn's tea.

Lady Viola glanced up at Hannah and smiled. "Oh, thank heaven you have come home. The door must have blown closed when you left for the Octagon, and I fear Edgar and I have been locked inside all evening."

"I . . . I suspected as much . . . er . . . when I found the key on the floor in the entry hall."

Hannah never was much good at plying falsehoods, but it was not the lie that caused her to stammer. For protruding, just a bit, from Edgar's coat pocket—was Lady Viola's lavender stocking ribbon.

Hannah blinked. No. Impossible. It could not be. They were . . . well, aged.

To be sure, she took a step forward and peered at the satin ribbon. There was no question.

It was a lavender stocking ribbon—Lady Viola's to be sure. Though one would never know anything was amiss by Lady Viola's serene countenance.

Hannah smiled broadly. Success was hers!

Or rather *theirs*, truth to tell, for at long last Lady Viola and Edgar had given in to their true passion for each other—as she knew they would.

Hannah had done her job, perfectly, she might add.

It was just a matter of time now before they admitted their love to the world. It was inevitable.

As Lady Letitia and the two gentlemen entered the room, and the events of the oration were recounted for Lady Viola, cordial was poured and delivered to each of them on a silver salver by Edgar the naughty rascal himself.

Lady Letitia's booming chuckle rattled the crystal chandelier above, seizing Hannah's attention. She eyed the jolly old woman, who at the moment was batting the portly little earl with her unfurled lace fan. The earl smiled adoringly back at the playful plump lady.

Hannah smiled and tipped her glass to her lips. She still had one more Featherton to match to prove her worth as a matchmaker.

But the two elderly ladies were making her task far too easy.

Nearly three-quarters of the next day had passed before the card Mr. St. Albans had promised reached Hannah's hand.

Of course, she hadn't given the matter much thought. It was only that had *she* promised to send a card detailing the location of a meeting, she certainly would have had the good manners to deliver the card early in the day.

That way the person awaiting the card would know how to dress for the occasion. For if one was viewing the stars from atop Bath Abbey, a silk dress, in reverence of the sacred locale, might be appropriate.

Hannah lifted Mr. St. Albans's simple card to her eyes and read the hastily scrawled words one more time.

Beechen Cliff. Follow the trail from west edge of Prior Park. Four hours after dark.

Now if Beechen Cliff was the designated meeting point, which it seemed to be, something less grand would be more suitable . . . such as a smart kerseymere frock with a coordinating pelisse to ward off the chill of the night and the coming rain.

For though the skies were clear at the moment, Lady Viola's bones had told her that rain was soon to be upon them, and the old woman's bones were seldom wrong.

In preparation for her study of the stars, Hannah spent what was left of the afternoon and through the dinner hour reading a clutch of Miss Herschel's pamphlets about the comet.

It was dreadfully dry reading, with far too many formulas and numbers. More than once, Hannah was forced to ring for a reviving cup of steaming tea, just to keep her eyes from closing.

She didn't dare tell the Featherton sisters of her plan to meet with Mr. St. Albans. They would only gloat, sure that they were correct in their assumption that Hannah and Mr. St. Albans were destined to marry.

But they were wrong.

The only reason she was slipping out her back window this very moment and climbing down the ivy vines was that the Featherton sisters would think meeting a bachelor on a dark rise outside town was beyond the bounds of propriety.

And they would be right about that.

But to be perfectly honest, Hannah truly did want to

peer through Mr. St. Albans's telescope at the stars. When would she ever have the chance to do so again?

So she felt justified in climbing down the back wall of the house.

It was a necessity, she told herself—and not just because the two old women were still awake downstairs.

It was five hours after complete darkness when Hannah finally reached the Prior Park gate and made her way across the manicured grounds to the steep cliff trail.

The wind had begun to blow, much more strongly than it had been when she left the house. She looked up, and, before her, the stars were bright and clear. But when she turned and faced the wind, she could see that the skies were naught but a thick blanket of ebony.

A storm was coming. And being so far from Royal Crescent, without a carriage or even a horse, she began to feel worried.

Hannah had all but decided to turn back, for Mr. St. Albans was nowhere to be seen, when suddenly she noticed a flickering light ahead of her—a lantern.

The light was barely visible in the distance, but since it was placed on a rise, a perfect location to situate a telescope, she decided it must be Mr. St. Albans's signal for her, and she headed for the beacon.

Several times she called out for Mr. St. Albans, but the wind was strong upon the bluff, and her voice was lost in the gusts rustling through the trees.

After several minutes of hiking uphill, her breath all

but gone from her lungs, she finally came upon the lantern.

She didn't see Mr. St. Albans right away, for indeed he was not near the lantern at all. Hannah spun and squinted her eyes to look past the glow of the lantern.

There on a level summit, she found Mr. St. Albans peering through a telescope not a half furlong away.

She walked quietly to him, so as not to disturb his study, but it seemed he was aware of her approach.

"'Tis late. I thought you had decided not to come after all." He lifted his eye from the device and turned to look at her.

"Hardly, sir. I was simply delayed." She walked close enough that even in the wind, in the coolness of the eve, she could feel the heat his body was giving off.

She sighed, suddenly feeling comfort in his presence, which made her all too aware of her proximity to a bachelor in the dark of night.

She struggled for something to say. "This . . . this is not the telescope I remember seeing on the cliffs in Cornwall."

He smiled at her as the wind blew his hair back from his handsome face. "No, indeed, it is not. This is a reduced Newtonian sweeper. I have it set to a power of thirty with a field of about one and a half degrees."

Oh, *lovely*. Hannah could already see that this eve, which she had been so excited about, was going to be as arid as Miss Herschel's pamphlets.

Then, everything suddenly changed.

"Miss Chillton, would you like to see the comet?"

She opened her mouth to respond, but before she could, he abruptly took her hand in his and led her to the sweeper.

"But the comet has not yet arrived. Miss Herschel said it shan't for another three weeks." Hannah felt him place his hands on her waist and center her before the eyepiece.

"It is not yet overhead, 'tis true, but the comet is here." His hands felt warm, and a little shiver of pleasure danced on her skin beneath his touch. "Look here and see. Just close one of your eyes and peer inside."

He ran his hand up her back and rested it upon her shoulder, as though it were a most natural gesture between an unmarried miss and a bachelor. Still, she did as he asked, even though her heart pounded.

"There are so many stars, I can't—"

"If you look directly in the center, you will see an object that resembles Mr. Messier's Nebulae. The color and brightness are much the same. Do you see it?"

But the only object Hannah could focus on was the man standing directly behind her, touching her ever so softly, speaking so tenderly into her ear as she stared up into the heavens. "I . . . I don't know," she somehow managed to say.

"It's round and somewhat blurred, like a star out of focus. Here, let me see." His arms looped around her waist and moved her backward a step, giving her a moment to steady her breathing.

He peered into the eyepiece and turned a brass dial the smallest amount. "*There*. There it is. The Bath Comet. Look and see, and you shall be the first of Society to view it."

Hannah brushed the blowing strands of her hair from her face, then hurried her eye to the eyepiece. And there, in the center, she saw it. A teardrop-shaped object. Vivid, round, and white in the center, but blurred behind. "I-I see it! I do! That is the comet? Truly? I-I can't believe it!"

She whirled around so quickly that he hadn't a moment to step away. Their bodies collided, and his arms came around her, to prevent her from disturbing the sweeper . . . or at least she assumed.

"Yes, that's the Bath Comet." He looked down into her eyes with a matching excitement that was palpable. "Amazing, isn't it?"

Hannah looked up at him, and found herself so close that she was barely able to utter anything. *"Amazing."*

It was then that she noticed he was looking at her lips. Her heart thrummed inside her breast so forcefully that she felt light-headed, but even still, she tilted her head back and allowed her lips to part just the smallest amount.

Beckoning him.

Urging him to kiss her.

The way she wanted him to, but dared not ask.

And he did.

Mr. St. Albans ran his tongue lightly over his lips, then bent his head toward hers. He paused then and looked deeply into her eyes.

And then, like the maid she was, she actually felt herself swoon beneath the intensity of his gaze.

She felt somewhat embarrassed at her reaction. For only a woman in love did such a foolish, girlish thing as swoon. And this, of a certain, was not love she was feeling.

No, it was only the excitement of seeing the comet. Yes, that was it. How else was one to react when seeing such a celestial wonder?

But then he drew closer, and, at last, she felt his lips upon hers. Felt them move and urge her lips apart.

And she knew at once that despite her protests, she felt something for Mr. St. Albans. Something she had never experienced before.

But it couldn't be . . . *love*.

That was quite impossible.

Chapter Ten

Hannah slowly opened her eyes, her senses still reeling from his kiss. Even in the coolness of the night, her body and mind felt warm and languid, as if she'd taken a glass of rich sherry too quickly.

His eyes were fixed on hers, but he wasn't smiling. His pupils were dark and wide.

"Miss Chillton," he whispered huskily. "I daresay I should apologize for . . . kissing you. But I cannot. I *will* not."

Something sounding very much like a half laugh punctuated his words. "I will not, because in truth I am not in the least sorry for having kissed you."

Hannah knew a true lady would be appalled at both his action and his audacious declaration. But she was but a simple city miss, and if she were to be honest, it did not take a clever scholar from Oxford to know that she took every bit as much pleasure from the touching of their lips as Mr. St. Albans evidently did.

She had just opened her mouth, realizing she must reply to his bold statement, when an icy raindrop struck her right between her eyes, stunning her.

She hadn't known what to say before, but had thought something would come to mind. Now it was as if the droplet had dissolved any reasonable response, and Hannah found herself merely standing there mutely, mouth fully agape.

Mr. St. Albans had just drawn a handkerchief from inside his coat and dabbed the wetness from her face when another droplet slapped her cheek.

Hannah looked upward at the sky above Mr. St. Albans just as a cloak of blackness obscured the stars above the bluff upon which they stood.

Another droplet splashed her brow, and she returned her gaze to his. "I daresay, I do not think a handkerchief is going to be enough." She gave him a tiny smile, though in the thickening darkness, she doubted he saw the movement of her lips. Indeed, though only moments before her eyes were fully acclimated to the darkness and she could see her surroundings as clearly as any cat—now it was as if someone had suddenly doused a candle. She felt utterly blind.

"The storm. Its timing could not be worse." Mr. St. Albans spun around and stood beside Hannah, and together they watched a heavy, blurred veil of rain race across the dark valley toward them.

"We'll never make it down to the Palladian Bridge." Hannah's gaze locked with Mr. St. Albans's. "And I fear it is the only source of shelter I observed on my ascent."

Mr. St. Albans turned abruptly and snatched up his small Newtonian sweeper, then whirled back to take

Hannah's hand. "Come with me. *Hurry!*" he shouted just as a roar of icy rain showered over them.

Hannah's teeth clacked together as she watched Mr. St. Albans turn the knob on the lantern, raising the flame inside the small military tent where he had taken her for refuge from the storm.

With utmost care, he dried and wrapped his telescope in a length of sailcloth then lashed it to one of the wooden tent poles. From a leather sack, he withdrew a blanket and held it out to Hannah.

"Take off your wet pelisse and wrap yourself in this. You are shivering, and the fire in the brazier won't last long. You are certain to catch a chill if you do not shed your wet clothing now."

His fingers moved to her throat and pulled the ribbon tie of her bonnet loose.

Hannah stared at him as he lifted her bonnet from her head, unable to drag her eyes away from the beautiful man kneeling before her.

Water dripped from his jaw and from the coiled lock of hair at his brow. She swallowed deeply, and at that moment, felt something tighten inside her body.

Lifting her hands outward, Hannah gingerly accepted the blanket from him. "Why is this tent here? You s-seemed well prepared for the s-storm." Already her teeth were chattering with the chill.

His gaze held hers fast and strong, and though he laid not a hand to her, said not a word for several seconds, her every sense seemed intensely attuned to his physical presence.

"The manor house is far from my view site, and I knew from the humidity in the air that a storm might well interrupt my sweeps this eve. I cannot afford to allow my telescopes to be ruined. So I brought the tent as a precaution."

"Yes, of course." Hannah tightened the blanket around her shoulders, suddenly feeling conscious of their proximity. "They are invaluable to you."

He glanced, she was sure without meaning to, at a long narrow box at the back of the tent. "I had them constructed to my specifications. There are no others like them." He quieted then and gazed deep into her eyes, then surprisingly caressed her cheek with the back of his damp hand. "And no other . . . like you, Miss Chillton."

He turned his gaze from her, as if he meant to allow her a moment to take in his words, and shrugged off his soaked overcoat.

As he did so, a rush of heat from his body suffused her, pricking up her senses in a way she could never have imagined. Her heart pounded in her chest, wicking away the blood from her head and making her quite dizzy. Even so, she was more aware of Mr. St. Albans than she'd ever been.

She could hear the heaviness of his breathing over the pelting of rain on the tent walls, see the excitement in his eyes, and her body thrilled.

A warm shiver raced over her skin, and in that moment her instincts became inexplicably crossed. At once, she felt that she should dash from the tent, despite the storm raging outside. But also that she should take refuge in his warm, capable arms and kiss him . . . again.

She truly didn't know what to do.

Oh, that she was more like her brother, Arthur. He was always in control. Always behaving logically. His emotions were at all times tempered by his morals and principles.

Not so for Hannah. At least not when she was near Mr. St. Albans. For when he was near, looking at her so . . . so seductively, her ability to reason seemed to vanish.

Perhaps she just needed a few more moments to tighten her grip on her judgment.

"Please, call me . . . *Hannah*," she told him, before she could snatch the words back. Well, that request certainly purchased her a few more moments. Though she ought not to have ever said such a thing.

It was meant only as a thought, but she had to own that for some reason, as yet unknown to her, it seemed awkward to her ears that the man who touched her and kissed her with such intimacy should refer to her as Miss Chillton.

Her cheeks went hot and pink as the words left her mouth, but at the same time she longed to hear him whisper Hannah in that low, rich voice of his.

At least she didn't say that aloud.

What was it about being alone in the dark with this man that made her want to act on her every impulse, no matter how inappropriate?

"Very well, *Hannah*." Something moved in his eyes then, catching her notice. At first, she thought him wary, cautious, but then she recognized the look of profound uncertainty—something she never expected to observe in a man so confident as Mr. St. Albans. "I am . . . Griffin."

"I overstepped, Mr. St. Albans," Hannah blurted. "Do forgive me."

He shook his head, sending a droplet sailing to her cheek. "No, Hannah, you did not. I've wanted, nay *needed* to tell you who I am—who I *really* am—since I came to Bath." He exhaled, as though a great burden had at last been lifted from his shoulders. "Call me Griffin. *Please*."

Hannah wasn't sure she understood what he was saying, but she knew something had changed within him. It was almost as if he felt a great relief in sharing something so simple as his name with her.

"Griffin." It felt so odd to think of him so.

"That's right . . . I am Griffin. Remember that."

What an odd thing to tell her. Why should she not remember his name?

Griffin leaned toward her, faster than she expected, and in that moment she knew he would kiss her.

Hannah pressed her splayed fingers to his chest, intending to stop him, at least for a minute. But the feel of hard muscles, his strength, beneath her fingertips was her undoing and instead of drawing back, she bowed into his embrace and allowed the strictures of Society to slip out through the fluttering tent flap.

Closing her eyes, she moved her lips gently against his, until he passionately claimed her mouth fully with his own.

Why had she fought these feelings, his advances, for so long?

What a great fool she had been.

She was not like her brother, Arthur. But now, as she felt the heady sensation of Griffin's mouth moving over hers, Hannah wondered why she would ever have wished to be like her ever-proper brother.

It was difficult for Griffin to believe he held Hannah in his arms and that she was kissing him with an ardor that rivaled his own.

He had not resorted to trickery, as his brother would have. He had told her the truth of who he was, and that, somehow, had opened wide the door to Hannah's heart.

Wrapping his arms tightly around her, he lowered Hannah to the homespun pallet he'd laid upon the ground earlier in the night, letting the blanket fall away from her shoulders.

He rested the weight of his upper body on his elbows over her and leaned back, the smallest amount, to look at Hannah . . . this beauty beneath him. Surely this was a dream.

Hannah shivered as she peered intently up at him from heavily lidded eyes, then cupped her hand behind his neck and hungrily drew his mouth back to hers.

Griffin sighed the moment her soft, full lips touched his and began to move.

He felt himself stiffen and his buckskin breeches grew ever tighter as her soft tongue slipped across his lower lip, and her mouth opened to let him explore the fleshy warmth inside.

He rolled to his right and let his finger trail lightly over her hip. Beneath the damp fabric of her gown, he felt the curve of her slender form, the soft give of her body under his fingertips. He skimmed her lower ribs, allowing his hand to drift higher over her body.

Hannah wriggled beneath his seeking touch, and though he knew her to be an innocent, she did not pull away even as his palm brushed over her bodice to the hardened peak of her breast. Instead, she arched passionately against his hand.

Griffin's heart slammed against his ribs, pounding like the rain upon the earth outside the tent. The lustful urges he'd fought so hard to restrain, since the moment his eyes first beheld the beguiling Hannah, broke their bonds.

She stared wide-eyed up at him, her breathing quickening as though with anticipation of his next touch.

Griffin lifted his hand from her breast and ran his fingertip over her full bottom lip and her mouth opened. He expected her to beg him to stop, but instead she astonished him by uttering three simple words.

"Kiss me, Griffin." Though her request was but a whisper, thin and unsure, he did as she asked and pressed his lips to hers.

She moaned as he kissed her, and her arms came up around him, encircling his shoulders.

Never before had he felt like this. Though he'd lain with women many times before, it was never like this. His body was tight and alive with need, his heart full with emotion.

He wanted nothing more than to rip her wet clothing away, and then his own, then press their naked bodies together.

There would be no guilt. Griffin knew this. There would be no shameful regrets, such as the sort he'd always felt after slaking his male needs with an eager miss in the wilds of Cornwall.

No, this time it would be different.

For in the morning, he would procure, with the earl's assistance, a license and take it and Hannah to Bath Abbey without hesitation.

And there, he would make her . . . his wife.

Chapter Eleven

Hannah lifted her fingers to her lips, swollen and still damp from Griffin's heated kisses. She stared up into his eyes, not quite able to reconcile what had just happened.

He lowered his gaze, as if he believed he'd gleaned some unspoken message from her—telling him to stop. But he had it all wrong. So wrong.

"No, Griffin."

Pushing up, he started to rise. *Blood pudding.* She'd done it again!

Her hand shot upward and she caught his loosened neckcloth. Winding the starched fabric around her fingers, she pulled him back to her. "I only meant—" She softened her voice, not wanting to sound needy, the way her mother always did. "When I said 'no,' I meant I did not want you to stop."

Her cheeks flushed hot again with embarrassment,

and now it was her turn to avert her gaze, but somehow she managed one more small word. *"Please."*

She turned her eyes back to his face, hoping with all her being that she would find him smiling and as eager as she to enjoy just a bit more of the secret intimacy they'd shared only a minute or so before.

But he wasn't.

His eyes changed in that instant from an expression of dark seriousness to one of wonder and surprise. She heard him inhale a shaky breath.

Griffin took her hand and pulled her fingers from his neckcloth. He leaned back.

Confusion rioted through Hannah, and suddenly she felt ashamed.

She had acted like a wanton, the very sort of woman her mother had always warned her brother about. The back of her eyes began to heat, and she clapped her palms over her lids.

Then she felt his grip around her wrist.

"Hannah," he said, so softly that she barely heard him above the angry growl of the rain outside the tent.

He pulled her hand from her left eye and she saw that he was untying his neckcloth with his free hand. He let it drop to the ground. His waistcoat followed the same path, and before she knew it, Griffin tugged his shirttail from his buckskins and drew the wet lawn over his head, casting it aside as well.

The pulse of her heart pounded mercilessly in her ears. Lord above, this is not what she had meant, not at all . . . or was it?

Oh, she didn't know anymore.

Her mind this eve was naught but one great tangled mass of contradictions.

Griffin bent his head and kissed her deeply.

Her hands eased up his sides and around to his back. She felt his smooth skin and tight muscles beneath. Her fingers delighted at the sensation, and she slipped her palms around to feel the defined mounds of his chest.

Griffin lifted himself and gazed into her eyes as she wriggled her fingers beneath the crisp mat of hair washing across his chest, until she felt the heavy beating of his heart throbbing against her hands. A sigh of pleasure escaped through her parted lips.

Her gaze sought out his face once more, just in time to see him close his eyes and drag a ragged breath into his lungs.

Within only a heartbeat, he opened them again and rested on his side next to her. He brushed a damp lock of hair from her forehead, then kissed her cheek.

She closed her eyes then, aware that now his fingers pulled at the cinch ribbon at her gown's neckline.

Her own pulse quickened, and heat began to rush lower in her body as she felt Griffin lower her gown from her shoulders, then felt the cups of her stays, and indeed her lace-trimmed chemise as well, drawn back.

She daren't open her lids; the cold air pricked at her nipples, and she thought she would die of mortification at that instant. That is, until she felt Griffin's warm hand supporting the weight of her left breast and his mouth nestle over the hardened nipple of the other.

His tongue alternately suckled her and traced, with aching slowness, the pink skirt surrounding the engorged tip of her nipple.

His left hand gently cupped her breast fully while gently squeezing.

Never before had she imagined anything like this.

Well, maybe the act. On several occasions. But never *this*. Never.

Hannah moaned, lost in heady sensation.

As though hearing her, Griffin raised his mouth from her breast. He leaned over and coaxed her mouth open to his, as he moved atop her, nudging her legs open just enough for his own to move between and support his weight.

She could feel the hardness of him, pressing right against her . . . far too intimately . . . in a place where no miss would ever allow a gentleman to touch her.

She was sure of this, but her body did not seem to mind. And in truth, her body quite seemed to like it.

Without thinking, Hannah bucked her hips, instinctively inching down a little lower, edging him a little firmer between her legs.

Oh, this was so wanton. So, so *wanton*.

Hannah did not know exactly what would happen next. But she knew one thing. She never wanted the rain outside to stop.

Or Griffin, for that matter.

When she wriggled her body downward, he was stunned by the passionate immediacy of her response to him. By the way the curve of her body eased against him, the way her mouth sought his. In all honesty, he had quite expected an altogether more missish reaction when he shed half his clothing and moved over her.

Griffin knew he ought to slow his drive to have her, but that feat was near impossible when he could feel the moist heat of her against him, even through what clothes remained between them.

Bending, he trailed a kiss along her collarbone, then lower to her breast once again. He kissed her nipple, then drew it slightly into his hot mouth, wetting it. Hannah's head thrashed to the side, making him glance up.

Her eyes were tightly closed, and she had drawn half of her full lower lip into her mouth and held the pink flesh between her teeth.

Griffin's own lips curved upward. He was glad his touches tantalized her. He wanted to give her pleasure. So much more.

He prayed the rain would continue to pound the tent above them as he leaned just enough to allow his hand to catch up her skirts and move between her knees.

Her inner thigh was as smooth and soft as fine silk, but he did not linger to savor the sensation. Instead, his palm slipped ever higher, his fingers nudging their way past gatherings of fabric until he found his way to wet heat between her legs.

Watching her face, Griffin eased a finger between her womanly folds and, to his pleasure, found her slick with want. A second finger joined the first, and he eased them higher, moving over the most sensitive part of her in small, circular motions.

Hannah's eyes went wide, and she gasped. He felt the muscles of her thighs pressing against him as she tried desperately to close her legs.

He moved his lips level with hers and kissed her deeply as his fingers stroked her rhythmically below.

His tongue urged her mouth open to him, which she did eagerly as she pressed her lower body hard against his moving hand, making his body ache unbearably for her.

His mind whirled. He wanted her. She wanted him—but did she know what that truly meant?

Griffin stilled his hand. He broke the bond of their kiss and, still positioned between her spread thighs, leaned back on his heels.

"I want you, Hannah."

"I-I want you, too." But her voice shook, and Griffin was not at all sure of her conviction.

"Do you know what I mean, Hannah? What I truly mean?" He stared hard into her eyes. "I want to make you *mine*."

Her eyes were wide and as round as the mirrors in his telescope. She nodded, and leaned up on her elbows. "I know what you mean."

"Do you? Then you know there will be no returning to the way of things before this night." Griffin came up on his knees and bent to take her shoulders in his hands.

Hannah lifted her hand and laid it atop the bulge pressing against his buckskin breeches. "I know, Griffin." She eased her hand along the rise of his shaft, then cut away to catch one of the buttons to the left.

Hannah sat up, causing Griffin to release her shoulders from his grasp and straighten his back. His gaze followed the movement of her hands as she deftly twisted and released each button, then drew away the flap, leaving him fully exposed to her.

Hannah swallowed deeply as the length of him grew and rose up slightly against her bared breasts. That was the only hint of fear or uncertainty he glimpsed. In the next instant, she was easing his buckskin down his hips and thighs.

She looked up at him then, boldly grasping him in her right hand and easing the ring of her fingers higher. She paused just before reaching the tip of him.

He took her delicate hand in his and eased it over his tip. Her expression was sure and confident, but her fingers quivered against his skin as he guided her hand downward again, showing her, teaching her.

When Griffin felt himself begin to grow in her grasp, again he expected her to shy away from him. But once more her passion surprised him by edging his hand away.

Her small hand followed the trail he had shared with her, gently at first, then more firmly, as her confidence in her movements was honed.

His hardness grew until he knew she must stop. Taking her hand in his, he halted her strokes, needing to stop the throbbing. He peered deep into her eyes, and she, this innocent, understood.

Hannah blinked rapidly and inhaled a deep breath, as if what she was about to do took great courage. Then, she leaned back onto the woolen pallet, releasing him just as her back brushed the ground.

Her hand remained poised in the air, as if beckoning to him.

"Make me yours, Griffin."

Hannah did not know what had driven her to this point of no return. But here she balanced oh so precariously on this precipice . . . waiting.

She was a maiden, this was true, but hardly unschooled in the ways of mating. With little else to occupy her time while her brother was about his business, Hannah had spent a goodly amount at the lending libraries studying falconry and ornithology. Which naturally had led her into the realm of animal husbandry. But she didn't remember anything resembling this in those texts.

Clearly, the human male was an altogether different sort of beast.

One she was quite eager to learn more about. Yes, it was wicked of her, but the instinct to mate was entirely natural. She'd read it more than once and from noted authorities on the subject.

Griffin's eyes were smoldering and hot, despite the chill of the air about them. He took her bent knees, one in each hand, and opened her legs wider for him.

Her breathing took flight, for she knew that in the next moment he would claim her.

Reaching beneath her, he clasped both sides of her rear in his hands and raised her just a bit. She felt the heat of his tip press against her, tentatively at first.

"Are you sure, my love?" His voice was breathy and low.

Why was he asking this? she wondered. Why did he wait? She knew he wanted her as much as she wished for him.

Her response was instinctual. She pressed her body down upon him, taking the plum-shaped tip of him inside her.

She gasped at the sensation, wanting more. Wanting all of him. "Yes, I am sure. I know what this means, Griffin. And I want you."

The lids of his eyes closed, and she could have sworn he sighed upon hearing her words. Then he leaned over her and kissed her, easing his tongue into her mouth. At that moment, he filled her.

Her toes dug into the woolen coverlet, and she sucked in a sharp breath at the sting of his entry. She grasped his shoulders, silently begging for a moment.

"Did I hurt you?"

She shook her head, for the twinge of losing her maidenhead was already subsiding, and her womanly muscles relaxed. Hannah brushed her fingers over his cheek and stared up at Griffin as she lifted her hips against him.

He pulled back, and just as she needlessly feared he would stop then, Griffin pressed deep into her.

She exhaled her breath and closed her eyes. There was no pain this time. Only tiny bursts of pleasure, and she knew she wanted more.

Griffin thrust into her again, and yet again. She felt dizzy and exhilarated, and lost count of how many times their bodies came together.

She did not feel the innocent. She did not feel anything but the rhythm of their lovemaking. Hannah felt her muscles contract around him each time he plunged deep into her depths.

From her own lips she heard a whimper, but not one of pain. Of pleasure. And then he moaned, and his breath flowed hotly over her mouth.

Her own breathing grew quicker and more shallow. Their bodies, where they touched, grew hot and slick with perspiration.

She was panting now, her body tightening ever more as he thrust harder and deeper into her core. Something inside of her grew taut, and she raised her hips, meeting him thrust for thrust.

Griffin's eyes were wide and staring down into hers. He sucked what breaths he could gather between his lips as he drove into her, never looking away. Never breaking their gaze.

All at once, she knew what it was she saw in his intent gaze. And it made her heart ache. Hot tears pricked at the back of Hannah's eyes.

"You love me—" The words slipped softly and unbidden from her lips, and she doubted Griffin heard her.

"I do," came his reply.

Then, all of a sudden, Hannah's body convulsed, making her cry out.

Griffin sank deep inside her just then and moaned. He came down on top of her and held her to him, kissing her throat as he gathered her body close.

"I do love you, Hannah. I do."

The sun was bright, and a bluebird chirped merrily from a tree branch outside the dining-room window. Hannah knew exactly how it felt, for indeed, she'd been singing herself since the moment she'd opened her eyes to the new day.

"My, my, you seem quite bright this morn." Lady Letitia sat down at the table across from Hannah and began to fill her cup with Mrs. Penny's fresh pot of tea. "Slept well, did you?" She glanced up at Hannah.

Actually, she hadn't slept well at all. She'd spent nearly the full night in Griffin's arms . . . not sleeping.

The storm had finally shed its last droplet just as the sun peeked over the foothills, providing little time for Griffin to hurriedly escort Hannah to the latticework at the back of the house, her secret stairway to her chamber window.

Yes, she ought be quite weary this morn. Instead she was elated, every fiber of her body charged with a new exhilaration.

She was in love. *Love.*

But what was most astounding was that the object of her affection was in love with her as well.

It was true, though Hannah could hardly believe it.

The dizzying feeling that seemed to course through her every vein, and made her want to dance through the streets of Bath, was altogether new to Hannah. She had never felt this way before, but that, she suspected, was because she had never known love before.

True, as a young child she'd felt affection for her parents.

She remembered being picked up and hugged by her father. It was a warm memory, and one she held in her heart even to this day. But then her father fell from his horse one afternoon and quickly succumbed to fever. She could recall sitting at her mother's knee beside his bed past sunset and through the darkness of night. By morning, her mother was a widow with two young children to care for.

Everything seemed to change after that dark day. Hannah no longer felt affection. Her mother paid little heed to her little girl. Instead, she became more reliant on Hannah's older brother, the new gentleman of the household. Her fondness became focused entirely on Arthur, and Hannah, well, she was all but forgotten.

It was at that point Hannah, hungry to the bone for her mother's attention, began to insert herself into all manner of ill-advised endeavors. She'd wander off to explore the vale, often not returning until late in the night. She'd bring snakes into the house. One day, while pretending to be Shakespeare's Ophelia, she'd accidentally destroyed her mother's favorite opera gown by wearing it into the lake.

While these instances did garner her notice, for her mother had begun to fade into a world walled in by her own mind, it was not the sort of attention Hannah sought. For, instead of gaining her mother's consideration, she found herself packed off to live with Arthur, and then directly to a school for headstrong young misses.

No, Hannah had not felt love in many years, and now, after last eve—a night she would treasure forever—she wondered if she had ever truly known the emotion at all.

"Dear, are you well?" Lady Viola had apparently joined Lady Letitia while Hannah was off gathering wool.

"Oh. Do forgive me, Lady Viola. I am quite well . . . I was just thinking that I might send a card to Mr. St. Albans this morn." Hannah took a sip of her tea to conceal any schoolgirl's grin that might appear on her lips at the mention of her paramour's name.

"Now, this is a change." Lady Viola flashed her sister a quick gaze. "I was under the impression that Mr. St. Albans tested your patience."

"Not so. In truth, we have found a note of common interest—the comet. He is very knowledgeable about the subject, and has even offered to instruct me in the use of telescopes so that I might view the coming comet more closely."

"Offered to show you his telescope, has he?" Lady

Letitia asked, her thick white brows fluttering like gull's wings.

"Oh, he already has."

"Large, was it?" Lady Letitia snickered beneath her breath, earning her a teasing swat from her sister.

"Actually, not so large as you might imagine, but it is very powerful—" Hannah broke off, belatedly understanding her duenna's less-than-ladylike folly. A hot blush burst onto her cheeks.

"Well, dove, I think studying the comet is a fine pastime. It's all the crack this season," Lady Viola told her. "Very fashionable, and I cannot think of a better tutor for you on the subject than our own Mr. St. Albans."

Lady Viola leaned forward over her plate. "Though perhaps this afternoon might be a better time to send a card inviting Mr. St. Albans to call."

Lady Letitia stirred a rather large pinch of sugar into her tea. "Oh, I agree entirely. Sister and I are expecting Lady Ebberly and her granddaughter shortly. The pair have only just returned from the Continent, you know."

"Were you just speaking of Mr. St. Albans?" Mrs. Penny, their housekeeper interjected. She had just entered the dining room balancing a small salver of jam pots. "Saw him only an hour past, I did."

"Did you?" Hannah mentally counted back the hours since dawn when Griffin had helped her climb the latticework into her bedchamber.

Two hours. Not one. Mrs. Penny could not have observed them together. Hannah exhaled the captive breath imprisoned in her lungs.

"Oh, indeed I did. He was taking a stroll in Queen Park with your friend, Miss Hannah. The one with the lovely golden hair." The housekeeper set the tray before Lady Viola and turned to leave.

Hannah leaped to her feet. "Er . . . my friend?" Being new to Bath, Hannah did not possess any true friends. Though she did lay claim to a number of matchmaking clients, one of those being a woman with hair like flax.

The muscles in Hannah's belly began to cinch. "Um . . . Mrs. Penny, might you be referring to Miss Howard?"

Mrs. Penny turned around. "Exactly, miss. She'd be the one. Lovely girl. I can understand why the mister would take a shine to that one."

A biting chill prickled Hannah's skin. No, Mrs. Penny had to be wrong. She just had to be.

Griffin was in love with her. *Her.*

Not Miss Howard. Yes, she'd introduced them, and for a time she thought there might be a match in the couple's future—but certainly not now.

Griffin loved *her*, Hannah told herself again. And she, him.

Mrs. Penny had to be wrong about the woman's identity. More likely she was a new housekeeper or even a cook. After all, Mr. St. Albans had only just taken the house in Queen Square. The man would need to assemble a staff. Surely that was all there was to Mrs. Penny's sighting this morn.

Hannah didn't move for another full minute as she plastered firmly into her mind the perfect explanation for what Mrs. Penny had supposedly seen.

As she sat, as still as a falcon perched high above a mouse-filled field, she busied herself by watching Lady Viola spread gooseberry jam onto a slice of toasted bread, while Lady Letitia pecked the crumbs off her plate with the pudgy tip of her index finger.

Finally, she could endure it no longer. She had to know exactly who was in Griffin's company earlier this day.

Hannah bid the Featherton ladies good morn, then followed Mrs. Penny from the dining room.

She didn't stop when she reached the passageway. Instead she snatched up her pelisse and reticule, then hurried down the front steps.

She had to see Griffin.

Now.

Chapter Twelve

A biting wind cut through Queen Park, gusting into the crux of the hedgerow frame where Hannah stood, hoping that she might remain unobserved.

It had been nearly an hour since she had slipped among the manicured boxwood hedges directly across the street from the home Griffin had taken, and still she had not managed even a glimpse of the man . . . or this mystery woman of whom Mrs. Penny had spoken earlier that morn.

Twenty minutes earlier, she thought she might have solved the question of the woman's identity, when a soot-marred chimney sweep descended from the heights of the town house's rooftop and was ushered inside through the lower kitchen door. It had been an elderly woman who opened the door to him. Not Miss Howard or any other beautiful woman with hair of gold.

This frustrated Hannah. In her hurry to leave Royal

Crescent, she had not dressed warmly enough for the cold weather and now, feeling frozen right down to her bones, she was still no closer to having an answer.

Hannah turned her eyes skyward in her aggravation. The bright cornflower blue sky of morning had already given way to darkening gray yet again, and no doubt the streets would be wet with rain soon enough.

At least that was what Hannah told herself, and the thought was reason enough to put her mission aside for a time, emerge from her hedgerow screen and start back up the hill for home.

The day that had started out so beautifully was growing progressively worse by the hour. She had walked half the steep length of Gay Street when she caught notice of a gentleman heading her way on his way down the hill.

She recognized those shoulders. The towering height. Hannah's gaze widened with panic. Good heavens. 'Twas Griffin!

His eyes were fixed on a folded newspaper in his hand, and it was a godsend that his attention was diverted and he had not yet seen her. She turned her back and gazed down the street. There was nowhere to conceal herself. No place to run. Tightly packed buff-hued houses, each barely distinguishable from the others, ran on both sides of the street, creating what felt to Hannah to be a gauntlet.

At that minute, she knew she had but two choices: up or down the street, and neither choice appealed to Hannah.

And so, when Griffin's footsteps grew loud enough that she knew his approach was but a moment away,

Hannah whirled around and hoisted a manufactured smile onto her lips. "Why, good morn, Mr. St. Albans."

He glanced up from his reading. "Oh, good day, Miss Chillton." He smiled pleasantly enough back at her, but his countenance revealed nothing more.

It did not even hint at the passion and incredible intimacy they had shared only the night before.

It was then that she realized he appeared to be squinting at her. "Have you come to Gay Street for . . . the dentist, perhaps?"

Hannah had not the slightest notion what he was talking about. "The d-dentist?"

"For your tooth."

"I beg your pardon, sir." Hannah felt her eyebrows migrate toward the bridge of her nose. Nothing he was saying seemed to make any sense at all.

He cocked his head to the side and seemed to study her for the briefest of moments. "It's just the peculiar way your mouth is twisted. I thought you must have a toothache."

Hannah tried to relax her mouth, but her lips had gone taut at his ludicrous comment. "I was *smiling* . . . when I saw you, I smiled."

Griffin laughed aloud. "I do apologize, Miss Chillton. Truly, from the bottom of my heart. 'Tis just that I have never seen anyone smile at me with such a pained expression." He clapped her on the shoulder. "So, did you enjoy the Featherton ladies' soiree?"

Did she enjoy the soiree? And why was he referring to her as Miss Chillton? She had given him leave to call her Hannah—which he had last night!

Hannah stared at the man before her, feeling both shock and despair. Was it that he intended to pretend that the intimacy they had shared last eve . . . never occurred?

He glanced down the street and suddenly realized the direction from whence she hailed. "Where are you coming from?"

Hannah didn't know what she should say. So instead she disregarded his question and posed the one her heart demanded she ask. "I came to . . . I wanted to ask you something of great import."

She looked down at her feet momentarily, wishing for a sudden burst of courage in the seconds the brief reprieve took. She turned her eyes up to his. "I wanted to know if you meant, *truly* meant, what you said to me." Her heart slammed against her ribs as she awaited his reply.

His eyes narrowed, and he bit at the corner of his lower lip. "What do you mean? What did I say?"

Tears itched at the back of her eyes, and, God above, she knew that any moment she would begin to cry.

She was such a fool. A complete fool! She'd read Meredith's book, *A Lady's Guide to Rakes*—suspected what the man was capable of, and still she had allowed herself to be . . . *used*.

How could she have believed that the man who turned the pages for her at the precomet soiree, the man who kissed her, caressed her, and made love to her last eve—was the true Mr. St. Albans?

Perdition! Her instincts had been right about him all along. She just hadn't listened to that little voice whispering in her ear.

St. Albans was a rake. A debaucher of women. He had told her that he loved her, and she had been foolish enough to believe him.

And as a result of that trust, she had offered up her heart. That was what hurt most of all.

Why, he might as well have torn her beating heart out of her chest and cast it to the pavers. It would hurt far less.

A lone tear trickled down her cheek, feeling unbearably hot in the chill air.

"Darling, what ever is wrong?" He took both of her shoulders in his hands and squeezed them just a bit. "Have I misbehaved? Tell me, and I shall make it up to you. I promise."

Hannah narrowed her eyes and slammed her palms against his chest, forcing his hands from her shoulders as he stumbled back a double pace.

Pain merged with anger inside Hannah.

She stepped boldly forward, and before she could stop herself, drew back her hand and slapped his cheek with all of her might.

Shocked by her assault, he clapped a hand to his stinging face. "Miss Chillton! I do not understand what has . . ."

But Hannah wasn't listening. Instead, she cut past him and, rising on the toes of her boots, raced up the street, ignoring his frantic calls for her to stop.

Tears were still streaming from her eyes when she pressed open the kitchen door of Number One Royal Crescent and collapsed at the wide bare wood table, where Annie was sitting taking her tea.

"Miss Hannah!" Annie hurried around the table and put her arms around Hannah. "Are you all right?"

Hannah lifted her head and peered out of her reddened eyes at the maid. "No, Annie, I am not." A whimper welled up from within and broke from her lips. "And I doubt I shall ever be all right again."

Griffin St. Albans glanced out the carriage window as he and the earl arrived at the Featherton home on Royal Crescent. The earlier storm still concealed every star, even the glow of the waxing moon . . . and of course the coming Bath Comet.

Somehow, Griffin had imagined this night in an altogether different way, with the heavens alight, as twinkling and bright as the diamond-and-sapphire ring he carried in his coat pocket for his bride.

The cabin door squealed when the footman opened it and let down the steps. Griffin made not the smallest movement toward disembarking from the conveyance.

"Why are you dawdling, lad? Not fretting about this, are you?"

The earl, who had accompanied him that day to assist in accomplishing his most urgent of tasks, pushed at Griffin's shoulder. His eagerness to follow his potential heir inside the house was all too clear.

The earl crossed his arms over his chest, resting his forearms atop his round belly. "The gel is *inside* awaiting your offer. She will accept. Just look at you. Handsome, intelligent . . . and heir to an earldom." The earl chuckled. "You have naught to fear, St. Albans."

Griffin nodded, but still did not rise. "I shall go alone. I must speak with her duennas, then with Miss Chillton herself. But our discussion is a private matter, one I wish to attend to myself."

The earl was surprised by this demand. He huffed and waved Griffin's notion—one he evidently found ridiculous—away. "Your offer to marry Miss Chillton is hardly private. Much is dependent upon the sealing of this union. The future of the Devonsfield earldom is at stake. Hell, boy, the continuance of the family is at risk until you, or your brother, become heir."

"I understand that."

"Do you also understand then that I can take nothing for granted, nothing at all? There can be no error, no oversight. The agreement must be expertly drawn and executed—all without legal or procedural failing." The earl's chest rose and fell rapidly, and his cheeks nearly glowed red. "So you do comprehend why I must join you?"

"No, my lord. I assure you, my wish to marry Miss Chillton has nothing to do with assuming the Devonsfield earldom but rather with love. When I offer for the lady, this is the sentiment I will impart."

Griffin bent as he stood and ducked through the carriage's open door. He descended the steps, then glanced back at the wide-eyed look of astonishment on the earl's round face. "If you will excuse me now, I shall return to Queen Square once I have obtained the Featherton ladies' blessing and Miss Chillton's acceptance of my offer. Good night, my lord."

Griffin closed the door, turned the handle to latch it, then shouted up to the driver to return the earl to his lodgings on Queen Square.

He watched as the well-turned carriage circled around the crescent and disappeared onto Brock Street. Then, straightening his coat, Griffin hurried through the light rain to the front door.

This was it.

Hannah could hear the tinkling of glasses in full toast as she descended the stairs at her duennas' behest that night.

Though it was late in the evening for a caller, Hannah suspected that it was likely Lady Ebberly returning to continue the recounting of her sojourn on the Continent.

There was no way she could shirk her social responsibility to the ladies' bosom friend.

No way either that she could feign happiness for more than a few minutes at best. Any longer and the ladies would know that something was dreadfully wrong.

Her course of action was simple really. She'd just greet the visitors, then plead fatigue and return to her bedchamber. The Feathertons would understand, for Hannah had little doubt that she looked every bit as physically drained as she felt.

She paused a few feet outside the drawing room and lifted the candlestick she found atop the table to peer at her appearance in the wide mirror hanging on the wall. She sighed at her reflection in the silver. Her eyes were puffy and red, and her face had taken on an almost ghostly pale pallor.

There was nothing she could do about her appearance at this moment anyway. And in all truth, she really did not care if she appeared a bit worn. There was no one in all of Bath she wished to impress.

Not anymore.

On account of the sudden turn of the weather, the settee and two wingback chairs had been arranged nearer the hearth for additional warmth. Hannah could not immediately see Lady Ebberly, whose high-backed chair faced away from her.

She gave a quick swipe at a deep wrinkle upon her frock, hoisted the best smile she could manage given the circumstances, and walked quickly into the center of the room with her hand outstretched to greet the Feathertons' esteemed guest.

Except it wasn't Lady Ebberly who rose from a chair.

It was Griffin; the one person in all of Bath she had no desire to see.

The one man she could not see.

Not now.

Not when her heart was shattered in a dozen jagged shards.

Surprisingly, his eyes were bright, his expression almost expectant as he moved toward her and clasped her hand between both his own, as was his way.

From the instant their hands met, a tremble rolled from her fingers, up her arm, and down Hannah's entire body. All strength seemed to leach from her limbs, and for a scattering of moments, Hannah felt dizzy and not at all sure of her ability to remain standing.

"Miss Chillton," Griffin said, his voice as buoyant as his mood seemed to be. "I am so happy to see you. Ecstatic really. I vow, so great was my desire to see you that I could scarce wait the moments for you to descend the stairs and walk the length of the passage."

"Dear gel." Lady Viola stood up from the settee and came to stand next to Hannah. She slipped her frail arm around Hannah's waist. "Mr. St. Albans has something to ask of you . . . and sister and I will have you know that we support his request *fully*."

For an instant, Hannah was more than a little confused. After the incident on the street that afternoon, it was inconceivable that Griffin would—

"Miss Chillton." Griffin came down on one knee before Hannah.

Her stomach clenched. This could not be happening.

"Since the day we first met on the cliffs of Kennymare Cove, I was impressed by your wit, beauty, strength, and intelligence. I knew I wanted to know you, so much so that I followed you to Bath. How could I know the depth of the love that would develop in my heart for you. A love that I believe resides within you for me as well."

Griffin lowered his eyes and said nothing for several seconds. When he raised them again, his green eyes sparkled with emotion.

Hannah's eyes filled with tears upon seeing this, and she struggled to take back her hand, but he held firm and continued.

"My dear Miss Chillton, I know our time together has been short. But I know in my heart there will never be another I will love as deeply as I do you. And so I have asked your duennas for permission to marry you as soon as possible. I-I left early this morn to obtain a marriage license for us. The earl had to use a little influence to expedite matters, I fear, but I was insistent that no impediment lay between us and the altar."

Hannah felt her bottom lip begin to quiver. She pulled her hand weakly one last time, but it was no use.

His gaze held hers fast, preventing her, as surely as his firm grip, from leaving before he made his final plea. "So please, Hannah, say you will. Say you will marry me."

A torrent of unstoppable tears cascaded down Hannah's cheeks for the second time that day.

Her throat was raw; words too hard to grasp. She shook her head violently and jerked away from both Griffin and Lady Viola.

She stumbled closer to the fire and rested her head in her hands, leaning for support against the marble mantel. "How can you do this to me, Griffin?" Her voice was a murmur.

"Hannah?" came Griffin's deep voice.

She lifted her head from her tear-wetted palms and stared into his eyes. *"How?"*

Abruptly, Griffin came to his feet. He made a step toward her, but she raised her palm and halted him before he could reach her. "I do not understand," he said. "Please, what I have I done?"

"You used me. Oh, I do not know what game you play now. Perhaps you mean to salve your conscience for ruining me, or perhaps the earl has some part in this. But *I* shan't."

Hannah drew in a long breath through her nose, then expelled it with her next words. "I will not marry you, Mr. St. Albans. Not today. *Not ever.* I refuse to be a pawn in whatever game you play."

Her words still hanging heavily in the air, Hannah grabbed a fistful of her skirts and ran from the drawing room.

❧

Griffin charged into the house on Queen Square and without a word to his brother or the earl, who were jovially sipping brandy in the parlor, made his way straight to his bedchamber. He flung open his wardrobe and lifted his Newtonian sweeper from the wood-plank floor.

He would head for the bluff where he had shown Hannah the comet. And there he would wait for the skies to clear.

When he turned around to quit the room, he found the doorway blocked by Garnet and the earl.

"Congratulations, Griffin!" Garnet raised his bulbed brandy crystal into the air.

"Yes, yes. I do believe that a grand celebration is in order." The skewed angle of the earl's wig hinted to Griffin that the brandy in his hand was not his first this eve. "Pinkerton has already prepared the documents we shall require, but I see no reason, not one at all, why we should not toast to the future of Devonsfield this very night."

Garnet caught the earl's unsteady hand as he, too, raised his glass upward. His gaze locked with Griffin's, and a look of concern darkened his eyes. "A moment, my lord. I fear something may be amiss."

The earl peered up through his beady dark eyes at Garnet. "What ever are you going on about? Surely the gel accepted the lad's offer. He is to inherit a bleeding earldom after all. She is to become a countess. Why, she'd have to be mad to—"

Griffin hardened his eyes, and the earl quieted immediately.

"Damnation." Garnet released the earl's arm and crossed the room to Griffin. "She refused, didn't she? I knew something had happened when I met her on the street earlier."

Griffin narrowed his gaze. "On the street today? You saw Miss Chillton . . . today?"

"Did I not just say that? She was in a damned odd state of mind, too. Still, you made an offer. Why did she not accept?" Garnet asked, but something moved warily in his brother's eyes and told Griffin that somehow he already knew the answer to that.

An answer to which he himself was not yet privy.

"Will one of you explain to me what is happening?" The earl drained the last of his brandy, then glanced around unsteadily for the decanter.

Griffin lurched forward and seized the twist of his brother's neckcloth. "You know what happened. Tell me now. Tell me what you did to destroy my life."

Chapter Thirteen

A loud rapping at the front door yanked Hannah cleanly from a dreamless sleep. She rolled onto her back and rubbed her eyes.

Who in blazes would be calling so early?

The pounding persisted, and she wondered if the servants were even awake yet.

Her mind was still fogged with sleep, but Hannah crawled from the warmth of her bed, drew back the heavy curtain, and glanced out the front window to the street below.

In the distance to her left, a dark carriage wheeled its way down Brock Street. There was no other movement. Nothing she hadn't seen a hundred times or more.

She pressed her forehead to the cold glass for a better look at the carriage, but it had already disappeared from her line of vision.

The sky above was clear, and a vibrant blue swath of color developed on the horizon, promising a welcome change in the weather. But the day was far too young for visitors to come to the house.

Morning dew still glistened on the expansive lawn edging the grand sweep of the Royal Crescent. The sun could not have risen above the spa city more than an hour prior. Who had come to call?

As Hannah's senses sharpened to wakefulness, she pulled the bell cord to summon Annie to help her dress.

If someone stood at the door at this bleak hour, they had not likely come there to deliver happy news. No, more likely the call was a derivative of the emotional events of last eve.

Hannah set her feet to pacing across the bedchamber while she nervously waited to be summoned before the Feathertons, for if she was correct in her assumptions about the caller, surely the ladies would send for her at any moment.

Her heart tapped in her chest as she passed the door, then turned around and paused to listen for the sound of footfalls on the stairs. Immediately, it seemed, she heard the thud of feet upon the treads. She held her breath and stepped backward several paces as the brass latch sank, and her door opened.

But it was only Annie. Thank heaven. Hannah released her pent breath as the lady's maid hurried inside and secured the door tightly behind her.

"Oh, we've got trouble, Miss Hannah. Grand trouble indeed! I couldn't make out none of what the earl was sayin', but whatever it was, he was sayin' it wickedly loud. I don't think he was just bein' kind, due to the ladies not hearin' so well anymore!"

Hannah sat down on her bed. "The *earl* is here? The Earl of Devonsfield?"

Annie nodded her head. "Aye."

"You are sure the caller is not . . . Mr. St. Albans perhaps, accompanied by the earl?"

"No, miss. 'Tis the earl for certain. His man—you know, the odd one with black-curtained hair and garbed as if he was always in mournin'—he asked Mr. Edgar to bring a chair for him . . . all bold and snooty, like he was the master and not of the serving class like the rest of us. He accompanied the earl."

"But you are sure Mr. St. Albans has not also come?"

Annie huffed her frustration. "I am sure. 'Tis the earl's man in the entry. You can go see for yourself if you like. He's sittin' right outside the drawing room this very minute, like a bleedin' sentry." She clapped her hand to her mouth. "My language. Lady Letitia is always scoldin' me about my choice of words. Beggin' your pardon, Miss Hannah."

Suddenly there was a soft scratch at Hannah's door. Annie's eyes locked with Hannah's, and for a moment neither moved or made a sound.

"Miss Hannah?" It was Mrs. Penny's voice coming from the passage. "Are you in there?"

Hannah gave Annie a nod, and the maid depressed the latch and opened the door a hand's width. Mrs. Penny stood in the passage, her face pinched with agitation.

"Miss Han—" The housekeeper rose on the balls of her feet to see over Annie and to meet Hannah's gaze. "The ladies desire your presence in the drawing room, Miss Hannah. They said you should not tarry, for the matter is of great urgency."

Annie nodded. "Right, I shall give my mistress your message."

Mrs. Penny, suddenly perturbed with Annie's blockade, pushed the maid aside and walked into the room. "Miss Hannah, the ladies did not give me leave to do so, but I feel I should tell you that the Earl of Devonsfield is with the Feathertons, so you will wish to dress."

"My thanks, Mrs. Penny. I will certainly do so."

The housekeeper's gaze shifted to Annie, and she gave a disapproving sigh. "What are you doing standing there with your mouth open, Annie? Make haste, gel, before the earl gets it into his mind to come up the staircase to find Miss Hannah himself!"

Hannah gasped. She could not help herself. For Mrs. Penny was entirely correct in her assessment of the earl's character.

Everyone he encountered learned very quickly that he was not the most patient of men, and coming up the stairs after her, well, it was just the sort of thing he might do if he had a mind to. Society's rules did not seem to apply to his lordship.

Hannah's first inclination, to remain in her room and send her excuses below, was not likely to stop the earl from seeing her if that, and it seemed likely, was what he wished to do. Her only other option, besides doing as the Feathertons requested, was to flee.

Carefully, so the focus of her gaze would not be noticed, Hannah peered across the chamber at the small window facing the back garden.

She could climb down the lattice. It was not the least bit difficult to accomplish. She had scaled the latticework on at least three occasions without so much as snagging her skirt.

"Oh no, Miss Hannah." Annie was already shaking her head, as if she had divined Hannah's thoughts.

"I-I don't know what you mean."

"Oh, nothin' really. I was just thinkin' that I wouldn't leave the Feathertons waiting too long if I was you. Maybe you ain't never seen Lady Letitia angry, but I have. And what good would it do you anyway? You would have to come home eventually, and as soon as you did, you would only be called before the Feathertons to explain yourself. But then you wouldn't have their support, like you'd have now."

Hannah gave Annie a little glare, like the thought of escaping had never even occurred to her. But the maid was quite right, and she'd do well to put the latticework out of her head.

She turned her gaze to Mrs. Penny. "Would you please let the ladies know I am dressing but shall be down presently?"

With an efficient nod, Mrs. Penny left the chamber, closing the door behind her.

Hannah turned her gaze to the two gowns Annie had pulled from the wardrobe and had just spread out upon the bed.

Hannah pointed at the frock on the left. "The blue one, I think. Always imparts a feeling of confidence when I wear it . . . and heaven knows, I will be needing all I can muster this day."

Dressed in her favorite blue cambric frock, her hair twisted, pinned, and magnificently coiffed in the most time-consuming, intricate style Annie could manage,

Hannah slid her hand along the balustrade rail and walked, as if to her death, down the two flights of stairs to the entryway hall.

Her kid slippers were silent on the floor as she approached the drawing room.

She paused before reaching the door, out of sight to grant her a moment or two more in which to gather her courage before facing the earl.

Hannah didn't know why the earl intimidated her so. Very few people in this world did. And she shouldn't allow him to affect her so.

She stood at least a head taller than the squat, physically inconsequential gentleman.

He did not strike her as overly intelligent or skilled in any worthwhile pursuit. In fact, when she considered the qualities to recommend him, she realized, to her shame, that she had allowed his lofty position within the realm to overwhelm her sensibilities. Nothing more.

No longer though. Not after this morn.

Peerage, or lack thereof, had nothing to do with their issue of contention. She was completely in the right when it came to this matter, and she had every reason to decline Mr. St. Albans's offer of marriage.

Hannah raised her chin, and was just about to charge into the room and tell the gentleman so, when she overheard the earl mention her name in a most angry tone.

Her foot froze midstride, and she slowly lowered her slipper to the floor and cowered by the wall in the passage.

Wouldn't do to enter ill prepared, now would it? she told herself. *No indeed.*

Stealthily, she edged along the wall, stopping as

close to the open doorway as she dared. She strained to listen.

"The gel must see the advantage in such a match," the earl was explaining to the Featherton sisters. "She'd be a countess. She'd have standing and influence within society, something, as a mere miss, she does not possess now except . . . by her association with the two of you."

The Feathertons clucked at that.

The earl paused for a moment and lowered his voice, forcing Hannah to draw closer to the door.

"But my dear ladies, what you do not know—and I tell you this only because I know I can trust you implicitly and you will not share what I am about to say with anyone . . . *anyone*—is that the entire future of the Devonsfield earldom rests on the immediate union of Mr. St. Albans and . . . a woman of quality."

The two ladies gasped loudly with surprise at this revelation—as would have Hannah had she not cupped her hand over her mouth.

"His choice, for reasons he does not wish to expound upon," the earl continued, "is your charge, Miss Chillton."

"Um . . . exactly what do you mean by that, my lord?" Lady Letitia asked. "I fear your statement was too oblique for my tea-deprived mind fully to understand this morning."

The earl sighed and dropped his tone to little more than a heavy whisper. "My sons, and recently my brother as well, passed on unexpectedly, leaving Devonsfield without a clear heir for the past few weeks."

"Oh, my." Lady Viola's voice seemed abnormally

high and thin to Hannah's ears. "But Mr. St. Albans is—"

"Yes. Yes, he is." The earl exhaled and for a few seconds he sounded as if he struggled to steady his breathing. "I . . . I will not bore you with the minutiae," he continued a moment later, "but in order for Mr. St. Albans to move from Devonsfield heir presumptive to heir apparent, he must marry before I die."

"But my lord, you appear quite the portrait of health," Hannah heard Lady Viola say. She never spared the sugar when adapting the truth was necessary.

"My physician does not agree with you, my lady. He does not expect that I will survive the year." Several seconds of silence passed before the earl spoke again. "So you see, Mr. St. Albans must marry—immediately."

Hannah heard the hiss of a shoe scraping the floor, and she whirled around.

"Shall I announce you, Miss Chillton? Is that why you are still standing here?" came a deep voice from the deep morning shadows of the passageway.

Goose bumps raced over Hannah's skin. "Who is there?" she asked weakly.

A figure rose from a chair in the corner and walked into the bright wedge of light breaking through the window.

"*Pinkerton.*" Hannah exhaled. She had completely forgotten that Annie had warned her the earl's man was outside the drawing room. "You need not announce me," she said mutedly. "I was just on my way into the drawing room."

Pinkerton said not a word.

"I *was*," she hissed on a rush of breath.

With no other choice, for certainly everyone in the drawing room had heard Mr. Pinkerton's rude prompt, Hannah sucked in a deep breath and strode into the center of her elders' conversation.

The earl came to his feet immediately.

Hannah knew she did not possess the skill, as did Lady Viola, to sprinkle her words with sugar or even to lighten them with tincture of fresh cream.

She had always spoken her mind, for good or ill, and that is what she decided at that instant to do.

"My lord." Her tone was shrill, even to her own ears. "Mr. St. Albans may well need to marry immediately to protect the future of the Devonsfield earldom. I am afraid, however, I will not be that woman."

"Hannah!" Lady Letitia's faded blue eyes shot to the earl. "Do forgive her manners, my lord. Miss Chillton is simply distraught and her sensibilities taxed." She looked to Hannah once more. "Isn't that so, dear?"

"Yes, I am distraught. My every sense is shredded. But the fault of my state is hardly mine. Mr. St. Albans, and his roguish ways, did this to me."

"Hannah . . . you surprise me, child. I know your heart, and I am fair convinced it lies with Mr. St. Albans." Lady Viola started toward her with her arms outstretched. "Tell me what happened, dove."

Hannah shook her head and raised her hand to stop any additional questions.

"Well, no matter what happened between you and our Mr. St. Albans, it can be set to right. Please, only agree to talk to him. I have a strong notion that a misunderstanding is all that separates the two of you."

Lady Letitia pushed up from the settee and sidled up to Hannah as well. "We shall send for him at once to allow the two of you some private time together. I agree with my sister. Grant Mr. St. Albans an interview, and I vow we shall be celebrating a wedding by supper."

The earl flashed Hannah a hopeful smile. "Yes, yes. By supper. He already has the license, you know. The two of you could be married by week's end if you wished. . . ."

Lady Letitia clapped her hands and gazed admirably at the little earl. "I simply adore your way of thinking, my lord. The drawing room is perfect for a wedding breakfast. Why, we only need a few gatherings of hothouse flowers on the table there, and over there some cakes. I shall have Mrs. Penny set Cook to baking right away—"

"No, *no*! There will be no wedding." Hannah shook her head, loosening several hot tears she had not even known had collected in her eyes. "Nor will I grant an interview to Mr. St. Albans. There is no need for that, for I already know the sort of man he truly is. Clearly, all of you do not."

She looked across the room at the earl, who appeared completely dumbfounded.

"I am sorry for you and your family, my lord, but as I told him, I will never marry Mr. St. Albans. *Ever*."

Chapter Fourteen

By the end of that day, having lost all confidence in everlasting love . . . in love at all, at least for herself, Hannah did her best to set aside the pain of loss that still throbbed in her breast and rededicated her life to finding suitable mates for other unfortunates.

By the end of the week, her belief in the good she was doing for others grew ever firm, and Hannah ventured so far as to pay for an advertisement in the *Bath Herald*.

She'd once kidded with the Featherton sisters that she ought to commission a carved shingle to promote her matchmaking service, but only a couple of days past, she'd done just that. And when the sign arrived a day later, she proudly carried it outside and hung it above the kitchen door just below the entry to the Feathertons' grand residence.

Surveying the shingle from the flagway, just beyond

the iron-railed stairway that led down to the outer kitchen door, Hannah allowed herself a pleased smile.

The sign was bright and vividly painted. An emblem of two linked rings of gold gleamed in the center of the shingle. Even Annie, who was always quite critical, admitted that the effect was quite arresting. And it was.

Anyone who visited, or even strolled past Number One Royal Crescent would not be able to avoid noticing it, especially when the sun angled just as it did now, making the rings glitter almost magically.

Still, Hannah did not delude herself into thinking Bath society would support such a venture. Indeed, the fashionable collective would surely gasp at her audacity in establishing a matchmaking business.

But flaunting it in the newspaper and in the street, especially while the Featherton sisters, pillars of the community, were charged with her guidance—well, that was beyond the pale.

Still, Hannah wasn't about to allow the attitudes of others to stop her. No, she had learned that lesson with the earl. She would be true to herself—and in this instance, that meant assisting the lovelorn who had not the skill or nature to secure mates on their own.

It would not be easy, standing up for her service, and especially not at home. The two elderly Featherton sisters would see that her sign was removed the very instant they learned of it, for even the quirky, mischievous old ladies had their standards.

Still, the day or two the shingle would hang in plain sight of anyone who passed would be all that was necessary to start tongues flapping with the news of her venture.

Even if the sign was removed immediately, Hannah

had convinced herself that it really wouldn't affect her business so greatly.

Already her matchmaking services were in high demand—and here it was just nine short days after Mr. St. Albans told her that he loved her, then suddenly could not remember ever having done so.

The wretched rogue.

Surprisingly enough, even the gossipers' retelling of her painful tale of loss, no matter how untruthful or fanciful the story they chose to spread, secured her new business.

Her credibility did not suffer in the least. If anything, her tragic loss of love actually prompted her clients to identify fast and true with her.

This wasn't so with all of her clients certainly, but it didn't matter a smidgen to Hannah that several mamas who dragged their unmarried daughters to her were more interested in learning how she, a simple city miss, had drawn the amorous attention of the heir to an earldom.

It mattered not whether a potential client wished for advice or for Hannah to contrive a meeting with the gentleman or miss of his or her dreams.

Business was business, and her process was always the same, as well as her fee: a single guinea.

And not one customer had quibbled over the cost. Not one.

That proved how vital and valued her matchmaking truly was, didn't it?

Hannah smiled at her shingle, quite proud of her accomplishments that week. She wondered if she ought to write her brother, Arthur, about all the coin she'd been earning, but then decided against it.

Arthur would cease sending what little money he did. And who knew how long her matchmaking service would continue to thrive.

There were only so many eligible, unattached people in Bath. And at this rate, she would have matched them all by May Day.

That evening, Hannah went to bed quite pleased with herself.

She was weary to the bone after meeting with three potential clients that day. But between rising that morn and laying her head to her pillow, she had also taken two new matchmaking projects and planned an "accidental meeting," her specialty, between a scientist visiting the city to attend Miss Herschel's Bath Comet lecture series, and an aging modiste who lived comfortably, yet alone, above her shop on Trim Street.

Yes, Hannah told herself as she closed her eyes and snuggled against her pillow, in no time at all the comet would pass over Bath, and all the city's learned visitors would leave. *All* of them.

And, in no time at all, she would have completely forgotten about Mr. St. Albans.

It would be almost as if they had never met.

That was exactly what would happen.

She was sure of it.

Griffin could not believe what he was hearing. Granted, he had expected as much from the earl, whose remaining days, few as they were, held but a single focus—preservation of the Devonsfield earldom.

But Garnet, too—his own blood?

He never thought he'd see the day when his own twin chose wealth and position over his own brother's happiness. Still, it seemed the situation had come down to exactly that.

"Do not take my warning lightly, lad." The earl walked within a breath of Griffin, peered high up into his eyes, and waved a plump finger before his face. "You cannot inform Miss Chillton, or anyone for that matter, that the earldom is in jeopardy—*owing to a question of birth order.*"

"From what you have said, my lord, it seems you have already confessed as much to the Feathertons and my Hannah." Griffin caught the earl's finger as it swiped rudely past him again and folded it back toward the earl's palm.

"Why must I hold secret," he asked, "one bit of information that could quite possibly return her to me? *I love her.* I have never felt this way for anyone before. Does my life, my happiness, mean nothing to either of you?"

Garnet settled his hand on Griffin's shoulder. "You know it matters to us, brother. Greatly. But the future of the family is at risk."

Griffin shrugged his shoulder, knocking Garnet's hand away.

"I know we can trust her—"

Garnet turned and filled a crystal with brandy. He pressed the short-stemmed goblet into Griffin's hand. "Griffin, Miss Chillton is angry with you . . . or possibly *me* . . . now."

Griffin grimaced. "I am quite sure 'tis *you,* Garnet."

Garnet shook his head. "Well, that is neither here nor there, is it? The point I am trying to impart is that she's hurt, and when a woman is in pain, she is likely to lash out. Think about it. Who knows what Miss Chillton might do if she learns we are twins and that Devonsfield has no clear heir."

The earl started to raise his finger again but seemed to think better of it and folded it back against his palm, then clasped his hands securely behind his back. "She might very well send off a missive straight to the Committee of Privileges—the earldom could be dissolved! We cannot allow the risk. We cannot!"

"More likely Miss Chillton would say nothing, and agree to marry me!" Griffin swallowed his brandy, then angrily pushed past the earl and crossed the parlor in four short strides.

He lifted the decanter of brandy from the tantalus and poured another two-finger measure of amber liquid into his goblet. "For nearly two weeks, Miss Chillton has not agreed to speak to me, or even granted me the honor of leaving my card. However, once she knows that Garnet and I are twins . . . and virtually indistinguishable to her eye, she will realize that whatever it was that upset her so was likely *your fault,* Garnet. Not mine. Her anger, or pain if that is what she suffers, will instantly evaporate, and we will no longer have any cause for worry."

The earl shook his head furiously. "Impossible. We cannot risk it."

Griffin exhaled. How would he ever convince them? "Putting our trust in her will mitigate the risk. She is not a vindictive sort, who would lower herself for revenge." Griffin sank into a chair near the front window. "She is an honest, kind woman, incapable of such craftiness of thought."

The earl's beady eyes took on a suspicious gleam. "Is that so, lad? Are you sure of that?"

"*I am.*"

"Really now. Curious." The earl called for Pinkerton, and when his ebony-clad man entered the room, the earl whispered something in his ear. When his man returned a few moments later, he presented the earl with a newspaper, ironed perfectly flat.

The earl scanned the first page, then reversed it and eyed the columns until he found what he was looking for. "Read this. Go ahead, quickly now."

Griffin hesitantly took the newspaper. He saw that it was the latest issue of the *Bath Herald.*

The earl squeezed up beside him and tapped with his chewed fingernail upon a small advertisement. "Examine this closely, please, then tell me again how certain you are of Miss Chillton's character."

Griffin trained his eyes upon the heading:

Guaranteed Matchmaker Services.

"I-I do not understand. Why are you showing me this? I do not need the services of a matchmaker."

"Read on, lad." The earl tapped the page again.

And so Griffin reluctantly skimmed over the services offered, one after another, until he came to the name of the proprietress.

His heart skipped inside his chest.

Miss Hannah Chillton, matchmaker

"How can this be?" Griffin turned his eyes to his brother. "D-did you know about this?"

Garnet nodded. "Only recently though. I swear. Miss Howard confided that she had hired Miss Chillton a few weeks ago to arrange to meet me . . . *or you.* Cost her a guinea."

"And . . ." Griffin swallowed the ache rising in his throat. "She did it."

"Consider this, brother." Garnet's voice was gentler now. "If she truly loved you, would she accept money to introduce another to you? Could she simply have been using you to further this business venture of hers?"

"I know this is difficult for you to hear, lad, but your brother's comment does give one pause, does it not?" The earl came and rested his pudgy hand on the back of Griffin's chair. "Are you so sure of your Miss Chillton now? Sure enough of her that you will risk your future, your brother's, and mine?"

Griffin set his elbow on his knee and rested his head in hand.

Everything was so different only a few days ago. He would have been able to tell the earl that yes, he believed in Miss Chillton and her love for him with all of his heart. His trust in her was absolute.

But somehow, he and Hannah no longer moved in the same orbit. And now, after learning about her profession, he wondered if they ever had—or if perhaps he had just been so completely enamored with her that he'd only imagined they had shared a path . . . and a future.

Damn it all. He wasn't sure of anything anymore.

Anything at all.

The next morning, the Featherton sisters requested that Hannah join them in their daily medicinal sojourn to partake of the waters in the famed Pump Room.

She wasn't at all certain why they had insisted she come along on this particular day. They knew she could not abide the thick taste of the mineral water and that she never felt comfortable strolling around the Pump Room as though it were crossed by a grid of garden paths. It was all a bit preposterous if you asked her . . . and well, a bit mad, too.

Society loved its traditions though, and each time Hannah trotted through the doors of the Pump Room, she was always amazed that the numbers of well-dressed ladies and gentlemen ambling through the establishment seemed to increase by a dozen or more.

As was her duty, when she visited the Pump Room with the Feathertons, Hannah handed a few coins to the waiter, then turned to distribute the warm, salty water to the ladies.

But they were no longer standing behind her. Instead, they had positioned themselves in the center of the wide room. Their heads were shifting right, then left, as though they searched for someone in particular.

Hannah squinted her eyes and glanced around the room. She had half a notion that they had invited Mr. St. Albans here as part of some planned ambush.

Her eyes shifted along with the motion of the Feathertons' heads. But Griffin was very tall, even for a Cornish gent, and as such would have been immediately discernible to her eye.

But then she saw him through the window, walking

in the abbey courtyard. Her stomach flipped. How had she missed seeing him? He and Miss Howard had to have just left the Pump Room.

Hannah's head began to spin, and she grew unsteady on the heels of her slippers. Lud, she felt like she was going to be ill—and she hadn't even sipped a single glass of the mineral water yet to stir up her belly.

She looked back to the Feathertons, who were standing not far from the quartet of musicians, hoping she could make her excuses and leave the Pump Room that very instant.

Then, suddenly, someone of less-commanding stature came into her view, and their gazes locked. It was the young woman whose feather Cupid had snatched at the lake.

The young woman stared straight at her, obviously recognizing Hannah as well.

She raised her fan and held it before her mouth as she whispered something to the grand matron standing to her left. Now the older woman was staring, too, and lifted her fan to whisper something to the gentleman at her side.

All at once, to Hannah's horror, the two women lowered their fans purposefully, then they and the older gentleman started toward her.

Now she was feeling even more ill at ease. A sensation of worry, not unlike a cold draft in an otherwise warm room, swept over Hannah, raising the fine hairs on the back of her neck.

Who knew what the trio barreling down upon her wanted. After her advertisement in the *Bath Herald*, it was more than likely that the young woman realized she had fallen victim to one of Hannah's matchmaking schemes—and was none too happy about it. Perhaps even humiliated!

Hannah glanced at the door to the abbey courtyard just a few feet away. She could make it out the doors if she hurried. But she looked down at the three cups of mineral water in her hands, then up at the Featherton sisters, who had chosen this moment to beckon her back to them.

Blast!

There was nothing she could do except deliver the water as quickly as possible, then slip through the crowd and out the doors unnoticed.

Hannah threw her duennas a flat smile, then brought her cup to her mouth and downed the water in a single, horrid draught.

She handed the cup back to the dispensing waiter, then hastened to the Feathertons with a single cup in each hand, her arms outstretched to thrust the cups into Lady Letitia's and Lady Viola's hands all the quicker.

Water sloshed over the rims of the cups as she pushed them at the old women. Her task complete, she was about to step past Lady Viola and merge into the milling crowd when Lady Letitia's eyes lit with excitement.

"Look there, Viola, Viscount Titchmarsh comes this way . . . oh, and with her ladyship and Miss Petula O'-Mara as well."

Lady Viola smiled broadly, and Hannah knew the trio was standing just behind her. Slowly she turned, eyes downcast to avoid the snarls that would surely greet her, her smile slipping hopelessly from her mouth despite her best efforts to preserve it.

At once the Featherton ladies began to chat with

Lord and Lady Titchmarsh. It was not until introductions were made to acquaint every member of the party that Hannah was required to lift her eyes as she muttered her greetings.

Except it was not grimaces and snarls that met her gaze, but warm, inviting smiles and outstretched hands.

"We have not formally met until this very moment," Lady Titchmarsh said merrily, "but we are well acquainted with Miss Chillton's talent."

Oh, dear me. Now Hannah understood. Being of the peerage, the family was simply too mannered to curse her and her schemes outright. They would deliver the blade gently, politely, but with a firm upward thrust.

Just then, however, a young man joined their circle of conversation, and he, too, was greeted warmly. Hannah could not believe what was transpiring. For the young man was none other than the merchant's son who had paid Hannah to arrange an accidental meeting between him and a certain nameless miss who read beside the lake each day!

"Lady Letitia, Lady Viola, allow me to introduce Mr. Whitworth. I believe you are acquainted with his father—"

The butcher just off Milsom, Hannah mentally added.

"Baron Taverner," Lady Titchmarsh finished. "I daresay, he and Miss Chillton are already well acquainted, aren't you now? And how fortunate for us all of that, eh?"

Now this *was* a surprise. Hannah stared at the young man as she dropped him a curtsy. "Mr. Whitworth, is it? Son of Baron Taverner?"

Mr. Whitworth laughed. "Forgive me, Miss Chillton.

I happened to be walking behind you and your maid one day and overheard a discussion about your success in matchmaking. I was intrigued, so when I heard the maid mention picking up some mutton for your cook, I raced ahead and convinced the butcher to pretend I was his son."

"Heavens, why would you do such a thing?" Lady Viola's blue eyes were alight with amusement.

"I know it must sound quite mad to you. You see, I was certain my father would be horrified at the prospect of his son, his heir, working with a match-maker to secure a wife. Turned out it wouldn't have mattered to him at all. He met my mother the very same way."

Hannah raised her brows. "So you pretended to be the butcher's son. No wonder you did not know the difference between a portion of mutton and loin."

She could not stifle the chuckle that followed. "For-give me for sharing this, but the situation is most di-verting. Our maid thought that, for a butcher's son, you were cut . . . a bit thick."

Miss Petula O'Mara raised her gloved hand to her mouth to cover a meek giggle.

Mr. Whitworth smiled broadly at her, before turning the conversation back to Hannah. "You must under-stand. To me, anonymity was paramount, which is why I did not share my true identity. I greatly wished to make the acquaintance of Miss Petula O'Mara, but her gentle nature prevented it. You were my only hope."

The corners of Lord Titchmarsh's mouth drew up and he beamed at Hannah. "So that we are not rambling on all morn, allow me to thank you for coming upon a way for my daughter to overcome her shy ways long enough to feel at ease with Mr. Whitworth."

The shy miss was smiling now. "You see, Miss Chillton, Mr. Whitworth and I are to be married. Something my parents and I, because of my quiet nature, never thought an eventuality. But you, dear lady, changed all of that. And for your intervention, I am greatly in your debt." She took a small step toward Hannah and leaned in to kiss her cheek.

The backs of Hannah's eyes grew suddenly hot, and when she turned her head to look at the Featherton sisters she saw tears in their eyes as well.

"My goodness." Lady Titchmarsh glanced around and realized that their story, meant to be private, had been overheard by at least a dozen others standing nearby. She swiped her gloved hand through the air. "Oh, what does it matter? Miss Chillton's ability to see into the hearts of others is extraordinary. She brought about a miracle. An absolute miracle. My daughter is in love and a week hence shall be married."

Suddenly a wave of glove-muffled applause rolled through the Pump Room as word of Hannah's matchmaking miracle spread.

As the clapping grew louder, Lady Letitia slipped her arm around Hannah's shoulder and hugged her, then leaned her mouth close to whisper in her ear. "You did well, child. You have the gift."

From her right, Lady Viola kissed and hugged her as well. "Remember, dove, use your craft only for love, never for coin, and successes like this will always be yours."

Hannah nodded as a tear of happiness rolled down her cheek.

She agreed with Lady Viola's advice.

Completely.

And she would follow the old woman's sage words, too—right after she completed the half dozen projects she had recently accepted . . . a few of which, she had to concede, mightn't *completely* be for the sake of love.

Chapter Fifteen

Miss Chillton." Mrs. Penny rapped at Hannah's chamber door, calling gently from the other side. "You have a caller."

"I?" Hannah tapped pen's nib on the edge of the crystal inkpot, then rested it in its burled-wood niche. Snapping closed her claret-hued leather book of matchmaking strategy notes, she rose from her writing desk and hurriedly crossed the chamber to open the door. "I was expecting no one," she told the housekeeper.

"Nevertheless, miss, there is a gentleman waiting for you in the drawing room. The ladies had just finished taking tea with him when he asked to speak with Miss Chillton, so they sent me to fetch you at once." The housekeeper gave Hannah a quick vertical sweep with her eyes, then shook her head. "Been working hard, I see. But you'll be wantin' to tidy up a bit, for the gentleman is none other than Mr. Hercule Lestrange. Shall I send Annie up to you?"

Hannah shook her head. "No, no. Just a hairpin or two should be all I require. But . . . you mentioned a Mr. Lestrange, and I am quite certain I know no one by that surname." Though for some reason, Hannah had to admit that the name somehow seemed vaguely familiar.

"I don't doubt that. His identity is a well-guarded secret, to most anyway. The Featherton ladies are well acquainted with him certainly, through my daughter Jenny's past connection to him, you know." Mrs. Penny leaned close as if to share a bit of confidential information. When she spoke, her voice was so soft Hannah could barely hear the older woman. "You are as good as family, child, so I will reveal his identity to you before you utter a single word to him. Mr. Hercule Lestrange is the *on dit* columnist for the *Bath Herald*—so pay heed to what you say. Be very careful."

"Good heavens, why would an *on dit* columnist wish an interview?" A dart of worry suddenly shot up Hannah's spine. "Unless he knows about the gaff between Mr. St. Albans and me. You do not think he has heard of it, do you?"

"I couldn't say, miss. Though I do know there is very little he doesn't know about the goings-on with the upper reaches of Bath society. I've heard he has spies everywhere. Pays them a pretty coin, too, for choice bits of gossip. Don't misunderstand me, miss. Lestrange is a good man, but a crafty one as well. His column means everything to him, I've heard tell. So, if there is something he wishes to know, there ain't no preventin' him from findin' out."

"Lovely. Thank you for warning me, Mrs. Penny." Hannah exhaled a long breath, then sat down at her dressing table. "I shall greet him in a moment."

Mrs. Penny nodded.

Hannah did not hear her leave, however. So, she looked into her table mirror, angling her gaze until she caught the reflection of Mrs. Penny lingering just inside the doorway. "Is there something else you wish to add?"

"Oh, I shouldn't say nothing, but . . . well, Lestrange is not nearly as tall as an ordinary man—in truth, there is nothin' ordinary about his appearance at all. I . . . I just thought I would tell you so you are not taken by surprise."

Hannah turned around in her chair to ask what the housekeeper meant by that, but the doorway was empty now. Mrs. Penny had gone.

Letting out a sigh, Hannah turned to the mirror once more. Reaching into the little silver bowl on her table, she snatched up a couple of hairpins and fastened the wispy tendrils that had fallen about her face while she had worked on planning her matchmaking strategies for the coming week.

It seemed that a flock of starlings spiraled in her belly as all of the possibilities for Mr. Lestrange's unexpected visit took their turns in her mind.

Her grip on the hairpin tightened. Bah, why was she allowing her nerves to overtake her senses this way?

After all, she was proud of the matchmaking service she provided.

There was no longer a connection between her and Mr. St. Albans.

In all honesty, she had nothing to hide from Mr. Hercule Lestrange. Nothing at all.

With that thought firmly affixed in her mind, Hannah stood and smoothed her sprigged muslin frock with the flat of her hand, took a deep breath into her lungs, and started for the stairs.

～

Hannah shifted uneasily in her chair, which for some reason as yet unknown to her had been situated in the center of the drawing room, somewhat separated from the center of conversation. The interview had begun gently enough, at least to her way of thinking, but now Mr. Lestrange's questions were veering into the realm of the uncomfortable.

Still, she smiled at Mr. Hercule Lestrange and did her best to reply to his probes without divulging any personal information at all. This, however, was becoming increasingly more difficult as his gentle questions grew ever more pointed.

Miss Penny had been right to prepare her for the astonishing sight of Lestrange. Indeed, had she not, Hannah most certainly would have been startled by his visage.

He was a tiny man, nearly a half foot shorter than even the diminutive Miss Herschel. His head was oddly shaped, too, almost like a turnip tipped to its side, and he was dressed in mismatched tattered clothes.

And yet, there he sat in the grand drawing room of Number One Royal Crescent with the Featherton ladies, chatting about Society events as any well-educated and cultured gentleman might.

But it was his voice that most astounded her, for his was rich and deep, with an almost aristocratic tone. Not what she would have expected from such a small man.

"Your skill as a matchmaker is to be commended,

Miss Chillton. I know of no one else, except perhaps the lovely Featherton sisters here"—he smiled in a charming manner, flattering the ladies—"who might have been able to accomplish the match of one so reserved as Miss Petula O'Mara with Mr. Whitworth."

Hannah felt a blush creep into her cheeks. She opened her mouth to reply, but Mr. Lestrange continued.

"You must have learned your skill at someone's knee." He paused for a moment, and Hannah caught a gleam in his huge blue eyes. "Perhaps . . . your mother was also a matchmaker, informally of course." The tip of his tongue flicked over his lower lip, moistening it, as he anticipated her reply.

"My mother?" Every muscle in Hannah's back stiffened suddenly. She didn't care for this thread of questions one small bit. She had spent years avoiding speaking of her mother entirely, and she was not about to allow Mr. Lestrange to dredge up that painful topic now. "Certainly not."

Clearly her reply was not sufficient enough for Mr. Lestrange, for he pressed harder. "Oh, surely, Miss Chillton, she must have dabbled, at the very least."

The heat rising in Hannah's cheeks eclipsed her blush as anger took over her countenance. She did not wish to discuss her mother. Why her woman had nothing to do with her current life, or choice of profession. Nothing at all! "No, sirrah."

"Come now, didn't she encourage your brother, Arthur, to marry the Feathertons' grandniece, Miss Meredith?" His questions were coming hard and fast now.

"No . . . I mean *yes,* she encouraged him perhaps, but the match was already well on its way—"

"So, Miss Chillton, she did partake in matchmaking."

Hannah leaped to her feet. "No! My mother had no connections. Why do you think I am here, Mr. Lestrange?"

The small man's eyes grew impossibly wide. "Why, indeed, Miss Chillton? Why don't you tell me?"

Hannah's entire body began to shake. This was what he was really after. He didn't care about her own matchmaking successes at all. He wanted to know about her mother—about her condition. About the whispers that she had gone mad.

But she hadn't lost her mind. She had simply become fearful after her husband died. Too frightened to leave the house for even a moment—without Arthur.

Hannah had been a young girl when her father succumbed to fever and died. Before that day, life had been bright for Hannah and her older brother, Arthur.

Her mother loved her then. She woke her in the mornings with a warm kiss to her round cheek. Hannah spent her day at her mother's side as they made calls, planned the family's meals, and called on the crofters who worked the lands bequeathed to their family upon the passing of Grandmother Weston.

Arthur, however, toiled alongside his father, learning the merchant trade. Somehow, even then, Hannah knew that her mother valued Arthur more than her. But still, she felt loved and was happy.

Until her father died. Beginning on that day, Hannah's mother withdrew into herself. She no longer cuddled Hannah, no longer touched her, or even tolerated her presence at her hem. Soon, she no longer left the house, unless accompanied by Arthur when he came each month to visit her from London. She grew forgetful and began to doubt her every decision. Eventually, a woman from the village was engaged to feed her and see to her needs.

Hannah was sent to live with her rigid, frugal brother, Arthur, in London, who promptly sent her to Miss Belbury's School, where she remained until her sixteenth year.

No one needed to know her sad story. No one needed to know about her mother—the woman who was once so vibrant and lovely . . . now confined to her bed, unable to remember her daughter, or even her beloved Arthur.

No one.

Hannah raised her chin. She had been wrong. She knew now that she *did* have something to hide from Lestrange. The truth about her mother.

"I am here, Mr. Lestrange, because . . . because . . . *my mother is dead*!"

"Oh, dear." Lady Letitia's eyes went wide at Hannah's lie. She came to her feet. "Perhaps you ought to leave, Mr. Lestrange." She crossed and pulled the bell cord, and, at once, Edgar appeared in the doorway.

Lady Viola, who now sat stiffly upon the settee, looked up at the butler with the relieved expression of a lady whose knight in shining armor has just arrived to rescue her. "Please, Edgar, do escort Mr. Lestrange to the door. Our dear Hannah is not feeling at all well." She raised the back of her pale hand to her forehead. "And please, do ask Mrs. Penny to bring me a powder, will you? I have the most dreadful pain in my head just now."

Mr. Lestrange slid to the edge of the chair, his legs dangling, until he leaped to the floor. "I beg your pardon, my ladies. I did not wish to cause distress. Do forgive me." He tipped his turnip head then and, without another word, followed the tall, lean butler into the passage.

At the click of the front door closing, the two elderly Featherton sisters caned their way over to Hannah.

Lady Viola hugged her, the way Hannah's mother had so long ago. "Dear, your mother is not dead."

Tears welled in Hannah's eyes but did not breach her lashes. She would not allow this talk of her mother to draw a single tear from her. She had shed enough over the years already.

Hannah pressed her index finger and thumb to the inside edges of her eyes and squeezed just long enough that the hot burning of coming droplets ceased. "The mother I remember is gone. She is ill and will never recover. It is a private sadness Arthur and I bear. Bath society need not know of it."

Lady Letitia's eyebrows cinched at the bridge of her nose, and the wrinkles, more often curved upward to accommodate her frequent smile, fell lax as a look of great concern draped her round face. "It was wrong of Mr. Lestrange to pry. But I fear that is his nature. The city is not so very large, and fresh Society gossip is rare. We should remain on our guard against Mr. Lestrange in the event he attempts to learn more about your family.

"I shall caution the servants—anyone who communicates with Mr. Lestrange in any way will be promptly sacked."

Hannah straightened and walked slowly to the nearest window and gazed out at the sweep of stately homes that was Royal Crescent.

Fury steeled her resolve. She would not allow Mr. Lestrange to expose her mother's frailty. No, she had to divert Lestrange from any possible investigation. Raising her fingers, she tapped out a piano scale upon her lips as she thought.

"I wish there was something more we might do to soothe your mind, dove." Hannah was so lost in thought that Lady Viola's voice was naught but a faint buzzing inside her head.

"What was that?" Hannah turned to give the old woman something that could at least pass for full attention.

"Dear Hannah, I know Mr. Lestrange has upset your mind," Lady Letitia said. "Why don't you join sister and me this afternoon for Miss Herschel's next oration at the Octagon. I vow, a diversion of any sort might help calm you."

Hannah shook her head. "No, Lady Letitia, but I do appreciate your kindness for inviting me. However, I fear—" Outside, Cupid screeched in his aviary, reminding Hannah that he needed to stretch his wings. "I fear—," she began again, but then stopped abruptly as a possible solution stuck her.

Yes. *Yes.* Her lips curved into a devious smile as her plan took shape.

Hannah's spirits bloomed. "No, you are quite correct. A diversion is *exactly* what I require. I should be pleased to attend the oration with you. *Quite* pleased indeed, for there is no one I would rather see this day than Miss Herschel."

As the clock sounded in the passage of the stately Brock Street town house that had become home to Miss Herschel during her Bath sojourn, the old woman looked up from her calculations and directly at Griffin.

"Time for tea, I should think. We've studied the charts long enough." She pushed slowly up from her chair and started across the study for the bellpull.

Griffin came to his feet, strode quickly to the hearth, and grasped the pull before her outstretched fingers could touch it. "Allow me, Miss Herschel."

The old woman chuckled. "You needn't try so hard, Mr. St. Albans. I have already agreed to mentor you." She slowly made her way back toward her chair, breaking into a hearty laugh when she looked up to find Griffin already holding it in place for her. "It was your enlightened calculations and your skill as an astronomer that persuaded me to accept you—not your eagerness to serve me."

Griffin leaned to her side and smiled at her. "Dear Miss Herschel, you mistake my attentiveness for being eager to please, when in all actuality, 'tis merely the behavior of a gentleman in the presence of a lady."

The old woman gave an ingenuous sigh. "Ah, and here I was convinced you were enamored with me. Such a disappointment. But if there is another woman, I suppose I could step aside." She glanced up at him and bobbed her eyebrows good-humoredly.

Something seized in Griffin's chest, and it took him

a moment to reply. He circled around her chair and took his own place once more beside her at the table.

He needn't answer, Griffin knew that. Her question was naught but playfulness. But something inside him made him want to admit his feelings for Hannah. "I . . . thought there was someone. I thought I was in love and that she was as well. I was sure of it, in fact, but"—he drew in a deep breath and exhaled forlornly—"but it seems I was incorrect on that point."

"Now that *is* a pity. You are such a handsome thing, too." Miss Herschel looked up as the parlor maid entered with a tray of tea and biscuits and laid the spread out on the table. "Still, there will be plenty of time for ladies when we go to London—after the Bath Comet has completed its orbit."

Griffin's attention snapped up from the wobbling cup of tea Miss Herschel was passing him. "I beg your pardon, miss?"

"Haven't I mentioned this? Why, Mr. St. Albans, I've decided to take you to London with me, if you are willing. I want to introduce you to some of the members of the Royal Astronomical Society there."

Griffin felt his heart leap. "I?"

"Yes, you, St. Albans. We shall present our findings on the comet *together*."

"I-I do not know what to say—"

"You need not say anything. You only need to devote yourself completely to the study of the comet from this evening until it passes overhead. If your calculations are at the same superior level as the ones I've already reviewed, I can see no reason why I should not recommend you for a post within the Society."

"S-surely, you jest, Miss Herschel." But in his heart,

Griffin hoped she was not. Still, what she was offering was beyond belief.

"I may enjoy a jest now and then, but I assure you, St. Albans, I am entirely serious with regard to your future in astronomy."

"Good Lord!" Griffin shot to his feet. "Thank you, my dear lady. Thank you!"

Miss Herschel waved her pale, thin hand, gesturing for Griffin to be seated. "You need not thank me. You only need to work hard."

"But I must thank you. You—you cannot possibly understand what this means to me. What you are offering . . . well, I've wanted it my entire life. A position within the Society is my grandest dream come true."

"Then do not disappoint me, St. Albans. Bah, I know you will not falter in this task." She thumped her hand to her heart. "I have a feeling about you. You, sir, are destined for greatness in our mutual field."

A little twinkle lit her eyes then. "But, if you *truly* wish to show your appreciation, a peck on the cheek might be nice." Her withered lips drew up into a cheeky smile.

Griffin laughed as he rose and placed a chaste kiss on the old woman's cheek.

"Oh, St. Albans, how you make me wish I was a younger woman," Miss Herschel teased. "If you truly wish, I shall not object if you wish to *thank* me . . . again."

Once again, the Octagon was fair bursting with too many bodies wedged into too few seats.

The Featherton sisters, no doubt owing to boldness

borne of advanced years and heavy purses, walked directly to the front row.

Lady Letitia wasted no time in dribbling gleaming coins into the eager hands of two young scholars, and a moment later she and her sister were seated directly before the podium.

Hannah, however, did not join them, despite their frenetic waves and gestures for her to do so. Instead, she preferred to stand in the back of the octagonal room nearest the doorway. In this position, should she feel the need to quit the room, she would be able to do so without delay. And this was important.

She had no doubt that with the topic of the oration being the coming Bath Comet, Mr. St. Albans would be in attendance.

This disturbed her. But there was no help for it. Miss Herschel was to be the speaker, and that fact was the only reason Hannah had ventured out of the house with the Feathertons that afternoon.

She had a plan—one that might divert Mr. Lestrange from pursuing his investigation of her mother. It would be her greatest matchmaking challenge ever.

In the front of the room, a lean, wigged gentleman tapped a long wooden staff twice upon the floor. The audience fell silent as Miss Herschel made her way to the podium.

As Hannah gazed at the tiny, frail woman, she realized that her plan was destined for immediate failure. Miss Herschel had to be at least twenty years older than Mr. Lestrange. Why had she not considered this fact? What had she been thinking, hoping to match the tiny pair?

There was no use staying a moment longer. Hannah

brought her hand to her forehead and sighed as she slipped through the doorway to leave.

Suddenly there were strong hands on her upper arms, and before she even looked up she knew instinctively that Griffin stood before her, holding tightly.

Warily, she inched her eyes upward until her gaze met St. Albans's shimmering green eyes.

"Hannah." His tone was soft, so as not to disturb those inside the Octagon, and she felt her whispered name sweep warmly over her cheekbones. "My God, 'tis you. 'Tis really you, my love."

Griffin tightened his hold on her arms. He couldn't let Hannah go, not now. This was the closest they had been to one another in weeks. "Hannah, please come with me to the Tea Room. We must speak."

Hannah's eyes glistened as she peered up at him. Her lower lip trembled. "I think not, sir."

Damn it all. She had to come with him. He had to tell her about Garnet. He had to.

To hell with the earldom.

He knew Hannah. She would never reveal the secret, no matter how badly her heart ached.

"Please, Hannah. There is something I must confess. Something that I am sure will mend the break between us."

"Pray, what might that be? I can think of no conceivable confession that could ever make up for the way you treated me." Her voice now trembled with emotion.

"Then consider the *inconceivable*. For that is exactly

what my confession is." Just then, he heard Garnet's voice coming from the Bennett Street entrance. His breath caught in his throat.

Hannah would see him within moments.

No, not this way. He couldn't let her see Garnet. Not yet. He needed time to explain everything to her, to make her understand why he had kept such a great secret from her.

Garnet's voice grew louder. Griffin spun Hannah around so she faced the door to the Octagon.

Then Garnet appeared . . . with Miss Howard on his arm.

Bloody hell.

Griffin flashed an imperious warning with his eyes, hoping that Garnet would see him and recognize Hannah from behind, and would whisk Miss Howard away before they ruined everything for him.

Hannah struggled against his grip, but there was no way he was letting go.

"Mr. St. Albans, *please*. You are hurting me." Anger, not tears now filled her flashing silvery blue eyes. "Release me now, or I shall scream."

He looked up and met his brother's shocked gaze, just as Garnet belatedly recognized the woman in Griffin's arms and the situation at hand.

Garnet whirled and raced back toward the Bennett Street entrance to the Upper Assembly Rooms, dragging a confused Miss Howard along with him.

Griffin let out a sigh of relief and loosened his hold on Hannah. "Please. I only ask for three minutes of your afternoon. Then, if you wish to go, you may, and I will never inconvenience you again."

Please.

In her heart, Hannah wanted to allow Griffin the few minutes he requested.

It truly wasn't so much that he was asking, was it? She could see in his wide green eyes how badly he wanted to speak with her. It was important to him for some reason.

Deep inside, Hannah knew that if she was truthful about her own feelings, she, too, wanted to spend time alone with Griffin—except perhaps more than the few moments he requested. She needed to feel him in her arms once again. Needed to feel his lips pressing warmly against her own.

She needed to love him and to feel his love.

And she knew were she to give him three minutes, he would ease himself back into her life, and she would give him so much more than she ever intended.

But this her pride would not allow her to do.

He was a rake. He had used her, hadn't he? For certain, he would use her again if she allowed him. And maybe next time she would not have the strength to walk away from him.

Griffin seemed to hold his breath as he awaited her reply. His eyes shifted from her eyes to her mouth and back again.

This was so hard. So dreadfully hard, but she had to remember she had been the *victim* of his rakish game.

"I am sorry, sir, but I cannot." She opened her mouth, hoping something polished, controlled, and clever would occur to her, but nothing did. And so, she resorted to the one thing she knew she could do to extricate herself from the painful moment.

In one quick, fluid movement, she twisted from Griffin's hands and ran down the passage for the Bennett Street doors.

He did not follow, though she somehow knew he would not. There was something in his eyes that told her that.

Something, too, that made her want to forgive him for what he had done. Made her want to turn around and go back to him.

But she could not. No matter how much she needed to forgive him, to hold him in her arms again, she could not.

Hannah leaned against one of the pillars at the entrance to the Upper Assembly Rooms, resting her forehead in her hands.

She could not catch her breath. She waited for several minutes, trying her best to calm herself. Trying to forget about Griffin.

Lifting her face from her hands, she looked up into the gold, sun-brightened sky, blinked back the moisture in her eyes, then resolutely lifted her hem and started to walk the short distance back to Royal Crescent.

Hannah began to round the Circus. Her steps were fast, as if a coming storm threatened, but she knew the tempest resided within her, and no matter the distance she put between herself and Griffin, she could never outrun the pain and emptiness that lay within her heart.

Then, suddenly she heard a familiar laugh coming from the direction of Gay Street. She froze midstep and rested against the iron-and-brass rail nearest her for support. Her heart pounded like rain on a carriage top.

It couldn't be. She knew that laugh though. Had

heard it countless times when St. Albans lived with the Feathertons during his recuperation.

Then, at that moment, she saw him.

With *her*.

Less than a quarter of an hour ago, he had begged her to hear him out. And now, here he was with Miss Howard, making merry while she wallowed in heartache. It was too much to bear. Too much.

A biting pain filled her chest, and she clasped her hands to her heart. Dark speckles fluttered like ravens across her vision. With her other hand, she feebly gripped the rail as beads of perspiration erupted on her brow.

Lord help her.

He had not noted her presence yet, however, and so to spare herself yet another humiliation, Hannah hurried down a staircase leading below street level and to someone's kitchen door.

There she stayed, hidden, dabbing away a few errant tears as Mr. St. Albans and Miss Howard walked around the Circus in the direction of Bennett Street.

Once they had gone, Hannah tilted her head back and drew a shallow breath into her lungs.

Why did she allow the man to affect her so?

Why?

Chapter Sixteen

When the Featherton sisters returned home from the Octagon that evening, they immediately summoned Hannah to join them in the drawing room, as she knew they would.

She had not left them word of her sudden departure from the Upper Assembly Rooms, which likely worried them, but she was quite sure that when they learned the reason for her hurried exit, they would not scold her for the transgression. Rather, she was certain they would compassionately hug and coddle her, for indeed she had been through quite a lot that day already.

And so, when prompted, Hannah confessed her ordeal to the elderly ladies. But instead of rushing to hug her as she had expected, they simply sat quietly in their places and eagerly awaited Edgar to circle toward them with their nightly dosing of cordial.

With a childish huff, Hannah threw herself deeper into the cushion of the wing-backed chair nearest the hearth. "As I told you before. There is no longer any connection between me and Mr. St. Albans anyway. At one time, perhaps, I might have held some modicum of hope that there was, I know now that I was merely fooling myself."

A little tingle tickled the back of her throat. That familiar worrisome sort of feeling that came upon her just before a flood of emotion.

Well, she wasn't going to give in to it. She felt nothing for Mr. St. Albans anymore. It was just that she needed to remind her mind—and perhaps her body, too—of that fact once in a while.

Hannah waved a dismissive hand in the air. "It isn't like I have any additional time for romance anyway— not for myself at least. After Mr. Lestrange's mention of my matchmaking in his column yesterday, I have more paying customers than I can service. Why, at this racing horse pace, I shall be as rich—I mean as *comfortable*—as the two of you by summer."

"Yes, dear, it is true that you will have plenty of coin and will no longer need to rely on your brother, Arthur, for pocket money." Lady Viola accepted a cordial from Edgar, pausing before continuing her thought to gaze at him in that loving, heavy-lidded manner of hers. She took a small sip from the crystal glass, then turned her watery blue eyes on Hannah. "You have more than enough business to occupy your days, 'tis true. But you are not happy, Sister and I can see as much . . . even with our aging peepers."

"I was plenty happy . . . that is until I saw Mr. St. Albans walking arm in arm with Miss Howard—directly after he begged me to join him in private for a confession of some sort."

Heavens, just remembering the sight of the two of them together made the back of Hannah's eyes prickle. Just a bit. But that didn't mean anything, such as she still cared for him or anything remotely like that.

It was just as she told the Feathertons. He no longer held a place in her heart. Yes, she was completely over any feelings she might have had for him at one time. Had been for some time, in fact. Only, she just hadn't been entirely certain she no longer loved him until she viewed him with another.

Now she was sure. Quite sure.

Because now . . . she hated him.

Lady Letitia wrinkled her nose. "Why should Mr. St. Albans being with another vex you so, gel? You are acting the ninny. You said yourself that any match between the two of you is an impossibility now."

Hannah straightened herself in the chair and thought about Lady Letitia's sharp question. "Well . . . because Miss Howard is simply not the right match for him. They have nothing in common, except for the fact that they are both more handsome than most, I suppose, but certainly nothing more."

The Featherton ladies both leaned forward at once, as though a puppet string had drawn them toward her.

"Dove, were you not the very person who introduced them as part of one of your 'matchmaking for coin' schemes?" Lady Viola touched her index finger to her lower lip and tapped it twice. "Hmm, I do believe you were. And forgive me if I am incorrect, but Miss Howard paid you for that foreordained introduction, did she not?"

Hannah slid down just a bit in the chair. "It is conceivable that I rushed matters somewhat with the two of them. And mayhap I should have taken more time to acquaint myself with Miss Howard first. I mean, she is beautiful, plump in the reticule, a woman of quality. And yet, she is all of six-and-twenty . . . and still, not married. It should have occurred to me that something was amiss." Hannah lurched upright. "In fact, I believe it is my responsibility to warn Mr. St. Albans of my suspicions. I did, after all, as you have reminded me, introduce them."

"No, you should not!" Lady Letitia scowled at Hannah. "How could you even conceive such an idea? Yes, the gel is advancing in her young years and is not *yet* married. However, that warrants no reason for suspicion. Look at sister and me. Neither of us is married, and yet I do not believe you think either of us dangerous."

Lady Viola nodded and words were shaken from her. "You have the right of it, Letitia. And Hannah, maybe Miss Howard is a tad more beautiful than you would prefer someone in Mr. St. Albans's company to be, but there is nothing, *not one thing,* to indicate anything nefarious with regard to her nature."

Lady Viola settled her cordial glass on the table and jabbed a pointed finger into the air. "Now do you understand the lesson sister and I have been trying to impart for weeks? *It is wrong to match someone with another simply because they wish it and have the coin to make it so.* A matchmaker's gift is seeing love in its earliest form and helping that love to grow."

"Yes, yes. I *do* understand. I do." Hannah nodded slowly at first, then faster as Lady Viola's words infused her mind and heart. "And I vow . . . by next month at the latest, for I have a few matches I am bound to complete—"

Lady Viola's white brows shot upward. "I have heard you make this vow before. Why can you not cease at once?"

Lady Letitia looked impatiently at her sister. "Viola, I suspect Hannah means she has already taken payment for her services and therefore is duty-bound to provide strategy in exchange for the monies she has received."

"Oh, is Letitia correct, Hannah?" As Lady Viola studied her, Hannah's cheeks heated, and she knew they were going red. The thin old woman's eyes widened. "Dear me, she *is* correct! Tsk, tsk, Hannah. Tsk, tsk."

Hannah exhaled her frustration. "Yes, it is true; I have accepted the money already. But that fact is neither here nor there. I will cease to match those who are not suited to one another—very soon. I vow it. I have learned my lesson this time, of that you can be sure."

The persistent tapping at Griffin's elbow grew ever more annoying. Still the earl, who stood beside him, wigless, with his shiny pate glowing in the flickering gold light of the chandelier, said not a word.

Tap, tap, tap.

"My lord, do you wish to speak with me, or are you testing a new code of some sort?" Exasperated, Griffin finally looked up from his pile of star charts and notebooks, and at the earl, who continued rudely to tap a folded letter on the corner of his desk.

"Read it."

"What is it?"

"Your means to win back the affections of Miss Chillton, that's what it is! Read it, I tell you."

Reaching out for the paper, Griffin came to his feet and let his gaze sweep across the page. When he finished, he returned his gaze to the earl. "But this is an invitation to yet *another* ball at the Upper Assembly Rooms." He lowered the paper to his side and sighed. "I haven't time for a frivolous diversion, my lord. I must complete my preparatory calculations before the arrival of the comet. Miss Herschel is counting upon my work being flawless."

The earl made a mouselike whistling sound as he exhaled through his nose. "Bah! You have your priorities muddled. A comet will not keep you warm at night, will it, dear boy? But I reckon a heavenly body like Miss Chillton could." The earl grinned as he flipped his coattails into the air and took his ease in a rickety spindle chair beside Griffin's paper-and-book-strewn desk.

Griffin shook his head. "Why do you worry so about my relationship with Miss Chillton? Garnet and Miss Howard are only days from becoming betrothed. They only wait for her father to return from Dover next week."

"Miss Howard is fair enough, but I fear she may be . . . oh, how should I say this . . . too *mature* to produce an heir. And this, as you must understand, concerns me . . . quite a lot."

Griffin forced a small laugh. "She told Garnet that she has seen six-and-twenty summers. Hardly in her gray-hair years, wouldn't you agree?"

The earl's eyes brightened. "That's just it, boy. If Miss Howard were six-and-twenty, naught would be of worry. But she is not. You see, I had Pinkerton conduct a little investigation on Garnet's behalf."

"Garnet's behalf?" Griffin stared at the earl, unable to comprehend how the little man could possess such a tunneled view of appropriate conduct. "Perhaps you meant to say on *your* behalf?"

"On the behalf of all of us. For what I have learned could affect the entire family. You see, it seems that Miss Howard is somewhat older than she claims. Quite a bit, actually. For only one guinea, a bargain for what we learned, her lady's maid confessed that Miss Howard is actually *three-and-thirty*. Now, tell me that I should not fret over her age."

The earl cleared his throat, then tugged down on the hem of Griffin's coat, forcing him to sit again. "Let us assume that Garnet did marry Miss Howard, and became, upon my passing, Earl of Devonsfield. Let us also suppose that the new countess, nee Miss Howard, was barren. Accidents happen, St. Albans, as I myself can attest! Something could happen to your brother in the swish of a horse's tail. Garnet could be trod upon by a bull, or swept away in a flood. There would be no heir—once again."

"But, my lord, I would likely still be living. The title would fall to me."

"Which would stir up all sorts of investigations, wouldn't it now? Once more the earldom could cascade into jeopardy."

Griffin shook his head. "No, my lord. You fret unnecessarily. There would be no investigation. The title would fall to me."

"Still . . ." The earl lowered his chin toward his chest, then lifted his eyelids to peer up at Griffin.

"There would be nothing for me to worry over if you, Griffin, were to marry Miss Chillton—who is obviously in her childbearing prime."

"Good Lord." Griffin rested his elbow on the edge of his desk, then cupped his chin in his palm. "Assuming I agreed to attend this ball for whatever reason—which, mind you, I have yet to do—how could I be assured that Miss Chillton would actually be in attendance?"

The earl smiled then, and a deep chuckle rose up from inside his throat. "Because the Featherton sisters and I have taken measures to see that Miss Chillton attends."

Griffin sat up straight in his chair, and let his hand fall to the desktop. "What sort of . . . *measures*?" He was almost afraid to hear the answer to that.

The earl chuckled merrily, giddy with pleasure. Too giddy.

"Not two days past, we paid several young gentlemen to engage Miss Chillton as a matchmaker—and had them insist that her match strategies for each of them were put into motion at the same ball—the Grand Celestial Ball at the Upper Assembly Rooms. Brilliant, are we not?"

"B-bloody brilliant," Griffin said beneath his breath. *And bloody mad, too.*

Still, he had to give the matter further thought. Miss Chillton would be in attendance, after all, and though she made her feelings toward him quite clear at the Octagon, her presence alone would be enough to at least consider attending the ridiculous ball.

Even if only to say good-bye to Hannah, the woman he loved, before he left for London with Miss Herschel.

Hannah scratched her head as she flipped through her book of notes. What was so blasted intriguing about the Grand Celestial Ball? It was the last scheduled dance before the comet passed overhead, of course, but nothing else about the ball could be deemed unique in any way.

Certainly not enough to cause such concentrated interest as she was witnessing the past two days.

It was just another addition to the boring string of comet-themed balls given by rich, bored female members of the *ton* during the past two months. Hannah, for one, would be dreadfully glad to see the whole dreary series of balls come to an end.

And yet, four of her latest customers were willing to pay twice Hannah's usual fee if she would agree to arrange a meeting between them and their potential match at this particular event.

Curious.

Still, Hannah wasn't going to question her customers' motives any longer. It mattered to them—enough that they'd pay double, and that was sufficient reason for her.

Hannah drew a grid across the page spread, indicating the dance sets with her pen. She'd just divide her missions among the sets, address each customer's required stratagem one by one, and arrange them in such a way that each meeting felt coincidental . . . or maybe kismet . . . but always as natural as if Fate had planned it herself.

Hannah scrubbed her closed eyes with her palms. This was not going to be a simple matter. She was about to ring for some tea to prepare herself for a dreadfully long night when she heard a solid thump, as if a body had been thrown against her door.

She rubbed her eyes again. "Is someone there?"

Suddenly her chamber door swung open. Hannah lurched in surprise as Lady Letitia backed into the room, her sister Viola following close behind. They were carrying a large parcel between them. Annie bustled in behind them, holding a Lock and Company hatbox from London.

Hannah pushed up from her writing table and stared at the elderly women as they tossed the parcel onto the tester bed.

Two sets of sparkling blue eyes were now riveted on her.

"What are you waiting for, gel?" Lady Letitia was still huffing from the exertion of climbing the stair treads to Hannah's chamber. "Come over and open the package at once."

Lady Viola wrung her hands anxiously as Hannah walked to the bed and opened the linen wrap.

"Good heavens!" Hannah was blessed to have found any words at all, for there was no describing what she found inside—except that it was probably the most beautiful gown she had ever had the fortune to gaze upon. "I-I . . . good heavens!"

It was a confection of deep blue silk, covered by a breath of silver webbing. Tiny crystal brilliants ringed the deep, square-cut neckline and sprinkled the short sleeves vandyked with insets of silver mesh.

"Heavens." Annie chuckled at that. "You got it half right, Miss Hannah. It's your new gown—for the Grand Celestial Ball! Ain't it just the most lovely thing you've ever seen, miss?"

"*Lovely* does not even approach being able to describe this gown . . ." Hannah's mouth fell open as she inched her fingers forward to touch the shimmering silk creation. "It is spectacular, Annie, but my brother would never agree to pay for such an impractical frock—no matter the occasion. And I fear I do not yet have the guineas to pay for it either."

"Dove, the gown is a gift." Lady Viola bent and spread the gown across the bed so that Hannah could take in its beauty more fully.

"Oh, no, I could not accept it. It is too grand."

Lady Letitia set her hands on her bounteous hips. "Nonsense. You must accept it. To decline would simply be ill-mannered, for a good deal of thought and effort went into this gown. And you, gel, have been thoroughly trained in the ways of a lady."

Hannah lowered her head. "I beg your forgiveness. I shall be honored to wear the gown."

Lady Viola's tiny red-painted mouth curved into a pleased smile. "So, you have decided to join us at the ball, after all?"

Hannah nodded and sighed. "I have no choice. None at all, for several of my newest customers are convinced that this ball, this Grand Celestial Ball, is their last opportunity to snare the heart of their intended." She rolled her eyes.

The two elderly sisters shifted their gazes to each other for a brief moment.

Hannah knew that look. They were about to chastise her again. "I am well aware of what the two of you are thinking, but after this ball, I will not agree to match a man and a woman for money ever again."

"Oh, we know, dear." Lady Viola nodded confidently.

Lady Letitia's head started bobbing, too. "We trust you completely, Hannah, and know you will do what is right."

Hannah looked at the two old women quizzically. Something was not as it should be—they should be reminding her of the error of her matchmaking ways. It's what they do. *"Truly,"* Hannah insisted. "I am ever so serious this time. Immediately *after* the ball, I shall cease. But during the dance, lud, I shall have my work laid out before me."

She sighed heavily to make her point, then walked to her writing desk, retrieved her book of notes, and began thumbing through it. "In truth, it is good that I have vowed to stop, for by time the ball concludes, I certainly will have enacted every matchmaking strategy I could possibly imagine."

"Every last one, dear?" Lady Letitia said, giving her sister a sly glance. "Such a pity, but you know, Hannah, 'tis for the best."

The ladies' eyes met yet again, and Hannah was fairly certain she heard them giggling like maids as they descended the staircase.

Annie settled her hands on her hips. "Dear me, Miss Hannah. If you ask me, those ladies are up to one scheme or another—and it involves you."

"You are correct there, Annie." Hannah sat down before her writing desk and wondered what the two strategists might be up to. "Let us hope for my sake that my scheme for the ball will distract the Feathertons from their own machinations."

Taking pen in hand, Hannah lifted the lid to her

inkpot and sank the nib inside. She scribbled a short message, then sprinkled the wet ink with sand to speed its drying. A few moments later, she folded the missive and handed it to the lady's maid. "Annie, would you do me a small service and see that this note is delivered to the Earl of Devonsfield within the hour?"

Annie grinned mischievously. "You can always put your trust in me, Miss Hannah. But . . ." Annie inclined her ear toward Hannah's mouth as if expecting her to whisper something. "What does the note say? You can tell me. Ask anyone below stairs, and they'll tell you. I know how to keep a secret, I do."

Hannah looked slyly at Annie and smiled back at her. "So do I, Annie. So do I."

Chapter Seventeen

Hannah squinted into the mirror atop her dressing table as Annie affixed a dozen or more sapphire-hued brilliants in her ebony hair. "Please, a little more gently, Annie."

Her head throbbed despite the lavender oil Annie had dutifully rubbed into her temples and the powder Mrs. Penny served her along with a suspicious dish of something she termed "black dragon tea."

"I'm bein' as careful as I'm able, I swear it. But I have to use hairpins, Miss Hannah . . . though I suppose I could try to mix up some sort of horse-hoof paste and use it to fasten the sparkles—might have a bit of sour odor though. Still, what with all those fancy folk at the ball, I doubt anyone would know the smell was comin' from you." Annie twisted a coil of Hannah's hair and pinned it securely atop her head.

"Ouch!" Hannah squeezed her eyes tightly shut for a

moment. "The pins will suffice, Annie. Do carry on . . . only perhaps you shouldn't use so many brilliants."

"What? Why, I plan to use every last one. I always say, a lady can never be too sparkly. Men like that sort of thing, they do."

"I am sure you are quite right." Hannah looked into the mirror's reflection at the nearly full bowl of paste-jewel-headed pins and cringed. "Only, the dress is so beautiful I do not wish to draw attention away from it."

Annie looked over her shoulder at the shimmering blue-and-silver dress spread out atop the bed. She nodded then. "I see what you mean, miss. Maybe only a half dozen more. That ought to be just enough." She turned back and looked down at Hannah. "If you don't mind my sayin' so, if your head is still painin' you, perhaps you should to stay home this eve."

"I wish that were an option, Annie. But I have several matches to orchestrate this night, and it matters not how horridly my head pounds." Yes, there was no escape for Hannah. Why, she could be leaking blood from her ears, and still she would be obliged to attend the Grand Celestial Ball that eve.

She only hoped she would not cross orbits with Mr. St. Albans. Or that blasted *on dit* columnist, Mr. Lestrange. She had enough worries on her mind.

Garnet stared at Griffin with marked incredulity. "How could you possibly expect that I would forgo the ball? Why, I had a waistcoat fashioned just for the occasion— midnight blue shot with sterling threads. Spectacular."

"'Tis just a waistcoat, Garnet." Despite his exasperation with his brother, Griffin held the tone of his voice level. Garnet loved a party, and even more, a ball where he could dress in finery and ply his rakish skills on the ladies for amusement. Griffin knew his brother's penchant for entertainment, whatever form it might take, and did not begrudge him this. It was part of who Garnet was.

But this time it was different. This time he needed Garnet to put aside his own pleasure.

"But, Griff, it is the last formal event before your bloody comet streaks through the city and puts an end to all the merriment."

"The earl asked me to attend in an effort to mend Miss Chillton's heart. So I am asking you, please do not attend this eve. I cannot correct her misinformed impressions of me if you and Miss Howard are whirling around the ballroom floor together."

Garnet opened a new bottle of spirits and poured himself a generous crystal of brandy. He glanced back at Griffin, who stood behind him, through narrowed, distrustful eyes.

His stubborn brother was not going to make this an easy task. Griffin knew he had a battle before him.

Before turning around, Garnet held the full glass directly before the candle and checked the color and clarity of the brandy. "Perfect," he murmured. A false smile played at Garnet's lips when he faced Griffin . . . and handed him the glass. "Drink this, for certainly you are not in your right mind."

Griffin waved the crystal away. "I am, brother."

Garnet sighed as he drew back the glass, wasting no time in tipping its rim to his lips and sipping the fine brandy. "I do not agree, for if you were, you would be bent over your charts and scribbles this very moment instead of trying to convince me to disappoint my lady."

He walked to the hearth and leaned his elbow on the mantel. "The comet will arrive in the early hours tomorrow . . . tonight, by my way of thinking. You should be preparing your scopes if you truly wish to leave for London with Miss Herschel—though it is truly Greenwich, is it not? Think of your future, man."

"I am thinking of my future, which is why I am asking you to forgo the ball this eve." Anger seethed through Griffin, and he took a hard step toward his brother. But he stopped short. This wasn't the way to make Garnet understand. "Damn it, Garnet, do you not see? This is very likely my last chance with Miss Chillton—to help her believe that my love for her is true."

"Love? *Love?*" Garnet forced a sharp laugh, one that sent a chill coursing over Griffin's skin. "Is that your *real* reason, brother? Or have you been conversing with the earl? Perhaps he has made you believe that *you* are far more deserving and should be named heir." Garnet's voice grew thinner, and his features hardened in a way Griffin had never seen before. "I already know he does not care for Miss Howard. He has not kept his feelings a secret. Even came up with some nonsensical tale that she is much older than she pretends."

Griffin grabbed his brother's shoulders. "How could you ask me such a thing? I have no interest in becoming earl—never have. I came to Bath, on this supposed quest for a bride, for two reasons only: because Miss Chillton was here and because of the comet. A chance to become an earl holds no allure for me. It is not my dream. But Miss Herschel's offer for a position with the Royal Society is."

Garnet pulled away and refilled his glass to the brim. Trickles of brandy spilled over the side and onto the polished tabletop, but he didn't seem to notice. "Then why are you willing to risk your dream, risk it all, by attending the ball this eve?"

Griffin dragged a thin breath through his teeth. "Because there is one thing in this world that is more important to me than the appointment—*Hannah*. I cannot leave Bath, even for the sake of a royal appointment, without knowing that I did everything in my power to win back her heart." Griffin cast his gaze to the wooden floor. "Garnet, I am asking you this as my brother. Do this for me."

Garnet straightened and silently walked past Griffin as he headed for the passage. He stopped at the doorway, rested his hand on the doorjamb, and looked over his shoulder at Griffin. "Last week, Miss Howard sent word to her father of my intentions to marry her. He left Dover at once and should arrive this eve after the tea interval at the ball. I have arranged with Miss Howard to be there to greet him and her mother."

"What are you saying, Garnet?"

"Just that I will do as you ask—in part. I will attend only the second half of the Grand Celestial Ball. But I must warn you, Griffin, if you are still present at the ball after the tea interval, there will be *two* Mr. St. Albans at the Upper Assembly Rooms—and both of our futures, as the earl so enjoys putting it, will be in jeopardy."

"Lady Letitia!" came a gentleman's voice from across the ballroom, startling the two Featherton sisters and, indeed, Hannah as well.

The dancers had just aligned themselves for the first set, when the Earl of Devonsfield's plump, squat body barreled through their midst in order to reach Lady Letitia.

Miss Herschel, who stood between the two elderly sisters, leaned close to Lady Viola. "Is that . . . ? No, my eyes must fail me."

Lady Viola dug into her reticule and withdrew her mother-of-pearl lorgnette.

She snapped it open with a skilled flick of the wrist and peered through it at the gentleman charging toward them, followed by a lean man all dressed in black. "No, no, they do not. 'Tis the Earl of Devonsfield . . . and his man, Pinkerton, headed our way."

"Though I resided here a good many years, until this very visit, I had always thought Bath a most dull and dreary city." Miss Herschel, who was dressed in a gown as somber as her statement, chuckled. "I wonder now if I was merely traveling in the wrong circles."

Hannah cupped her gloved hand over her mouth to suppress a grin, for it was she who had supplied Miss Herschel's recent amusement.

The crowd at the perimeter of the floor stared, and some chuckled at the unseemly outburst from the country lord—but Lady Letitia only smiled as the earl trotted up before her.

"Lady Letitia," he practically gasped, the air in his lungs obviously depleted after his jog across the expansive ballroom floor. "I am dreadfully sorry that I am late."

"Late?" Confusion was clear on Lady Letitia's round face, sending her brows migrating toward the bridge of her nose like two plump white caterpillars. "What ever do you mean? My lord, you are perfectly punctual. The first set is about to begin."

The earl's expression brightened. "Then, might I have this dance?"

"Oh . . . well, I only meant . . . heavens, I haven't truly danced in years."

Hannah could only smile when she saw a deep blush crest the old woman's powdered and rouged cheeks, as the earl led Letitia to the floor and took her hand in preparation for the dance.

Opening her reticule, Hannah removed her miniature book of notes and pencil nub and drew a thick line through the third stratagem listed beneath Lady Letitia's name.

First was her pairing of her with the earl at the gathering in honor of Miss Herschel. Second was joining the two for the oration at the Octagon. Third was the note Hannah had had delivered to the earl, professing Lady Letitia's deep affection.

Forging the missive had been wicked, she knew, but it had had the desired effect. Lady Letitia and the earl were gazing lovingly into each other's eyes as they danced—albeit a little wobbly—the first set at the Grand Celestial Ball.

Hannah felt rather proud of herself at the moment, and if she wasn't mistaken, the pain in her head was subsiding just a little.

At least she thought so, until she saw Griffin near the doorway, standing shoulders above all, scanning the ballroom. With a gasp, she whirled around, only to find herself peering down at Mr. Hercule Lestrange.

Her head began to throb mightily.

"Miss Chillton. Such a pleasure meeting you this eve." The little man drew back his leg and graced her with a regal bow.

This time, he was dressed like a lord of the realm. His neckcloth was expertly tied, and his coat and waistcoat were of the finest dark blue kerseymere, simply yet elegantly cut.

He wore no watch, or any metal at all. Even his buttons were covered smartly with cloth. Were it not for his unique stature, Mr. Hercule Lestrange would have simply blended in among the other guests . . . which Hannah guessed was his purpose this eve.

Hannah dropped Mr. Lestrange a distracted curtsy as she caught sight of Miss Herschel standing with Lady Viola just to her left. True, they were years apart, but Miss Herschel was most intelligent and diverting. And besides, she had no other option, had she?

And so, Hannah stepped quickly to the side, placing her hand on Mr. Lestrange's shoulder and turning him so he was nearly face-to- face with the diminutive Miss Herschel.

Lady Viola flashed Hannah a warning glance, but being the well-mannered woman she was, formally introduced Miss Herschel to Mr. Lestrange.

"My dear Miss Herschel. I must confess, I have sought to make your acquaintance since the moment I first heard you speak at the Octagon."

Miss Herschel tipped her head graciously. She stepped closer to him. "And I have become an avid reader of your column, sir, since I have come to Bath most recently."

Mr. Lestrange's already large eyes seemed to double in size.

Miss Herschel laughed, then lowered her voice farther. "Do not be so surprised that your secret identity is known to me. I do have my own connections, you know."

Mr. Lestrange looked immediately to Lady Viola, who feigned a sudden coughing fit and excused herself from the circle of conversation.

This was just the sort of moment Hannah had been waiting for. She raised her hand in the direction Lady Viola had headed and excused herself to see to the old woman's well-being.

Hannah merged with a passing collective of matrons, and within a few ticks of a minute hand, she had escaped Mr. Lestrange entirely.

The second dance of the set was about to begin. A dart of uneasiness scraped over her skin. She had strategy to put into motion, and her delay with Mr. Lestrange had cost her vital time.

Hannah drew open the cinch of her reticule and had just touched her book of notes with the tips of her fingers when a large hand grasped her upper arm.

Her lids shot open, and she turned her eyes upward, knowing already who she would see.

Griffin.

"Hannah."

At once she tried to pull away, but he drew her closer still. He took her hand and placed it around his arm, then he pinioned her own arm against him.

"I will not let go. Not this time. Not until you hear what I have to say."

"I shall scream." Hannah raised her chin as he pulled her toward the center of the ballroom. "Then you will free me."

"I seriously doubt you would do that. Everyone would look, and you would no longer be able to hide."

"Mayhap, I was hiding from *you*, Mr. St. Albans."

Griffin smiled down at her. "Had that been your intent, you certainly would have detected my approach. And yet, you did not." As his last words left his mouth, he turned Hannah into the line of dancers awaiting the start of the next dance. "Now, I need you to listen to me."

Hannah shook her head furiously and broke from his grip. She had not taken two steps when she was confronted by Lady Viola, who, for such a bone-thin old woman, possessed a surprisingly strong grip herself.

"Hannah, listen to Mr. St. Albans." Something in Lady Viola's eyes conveyed her seriousness in this matter. "There is something you must know."

"But I cannot," Hannah objected. "I have no less than four strategies to begin."

"No, you do not." Griffin had moved beside her. "Does, she, Lady Viola?"

A grand flush crept up from the old woman's bodice and up her wrinkled neck. Only the thick coating of powder and rouge prevented the fierce red color from extending to her thin face.

"Lady Viola? What does he mean? What have you done?" Hannah looked from the old woman's downcast gaze to Griffin's vibrant green eyes. "Well, will someone please explain?"

Lady Viola cleared her throat softly, then raised her eyes to Hannah. "The earl, sister, and I thought it imperative that you hear out young Mr. St. Albans. For you, I fear, are judging him most unfairly."

Hannah turned her narrowed gaze up to Griffin. "I might have considered that once—but no more."

Lady Viola released her hold on Hannah's arm. "Dove, you have no clients this eve. 'Twas—"

"The *earl's* doing, I fear. He hired several gentlemen to engage you so you would have to attend the ball this eve."

Lady Viola waved her furled fan in the air. "'Twas not just the earl. Sister and I were in league with the earl at every step."

Hannah exhaled. This was unbelievable! "You know how long and hard I worked on these matchmaking strategies—and it was all for naught?"

"Yes." Lady Viola tried to look sympathetic. "But Sister and I had a strategy of our own . . . and, well, dove, we have been at this game far longer than you." The old woman snatched up Hannah's hand and placed it into Mr. St. Albans's. "*Dance*. Listen . . . and above all else, *believe* what he tells you, for I have it on excellent authority that he speaks the truth."

Hannah peered up into his eyes as Griffin positioned her on the dance floor, and despite her intent to remain cool and detached, her heart was sent pounding.

Just what would he say that might actually cause her to forget everything that had passed between them and forgive him?

The orchestra began to play—a slow, soothing melody. Griffin uttered not a single word, but rather gazed down upon her, his eyes glistening with deep emotion as they began to move. Her own heart swelled, and she looked away, feeling all too unable to endure this intimacy much longer.

"Sir, if you wish to speak with me, I should like to hear what is so all-important that you must involve the Feathertons and the earl as well in order to achieve your objective."

"I did not involve them. They involved themselves, for it was clear to everyone that you would not listen to me otherwise."

"Well, Mr. St. Albans, you have my undivided attention now. What say you?"

Hannah felt his arm tighten around her waist, as though he feared that whatever he was about to say would cause her to flee.

"After the comet passes, I am to leave with Miss Herschel for London. She has recommended to the Royal Astronomical Society that I receive a royal appointment." He stared into her eyes then, and she knew he awaited her reaction. She fastened her gaze on Lady Letitia and the earl in the distance, who had collapsed upon a plump cushioned bench along the floor's perimeter and were laughing as they took turns fanning each other with Lady Letitia's lavender-lace fan.

So, he was leaving for London. What did that fact have to do with her? It made little sense to Hannah. "I am very pleased for you, Mr. St. Albans. I know your passion is wed to the study of the stars." Hannah looked up at him through her lashes.

"No, my passion is wed to you, Hannah. From the moment we first met on the cliffs in Cornwall, I knew that *you* were my future . . . and I believe you felt the

same." The pupils in his eyes had grown incredibly
dark. There was more to come.

"Dear God, I do not know what I might have done to
vex you so, but I love you, Hannah, with all my heart."

Hannah felt his hand, the one that held her waist,
tremble.

How she wanted to believe him. Had she not had it
proved to her not once, but twice, that the gentleman
could not be trusted, she would have read the emotion
in his eyes, his face, his body—and taken his words for
the truth.

But she knew better this time. She would not be
taken in by his words of love, only to see him galli-
vanting off with Miss Howard in the very next instant.

Thankfully, the set ended with that dance, and a tea
interval was announced. As the crowd bustled their way
into the Tea Room, Hannah and Griffin were left standing in the center of the dance floor alone.

As he belatedly lowered his hands from her waist
and gloved fingers, Hannah steeled herself for the
harsh reply she was to deliver. "Griffin, you tell me you
love me, then in the next moment, you share your affections with another. How can I possibly believe you
now?"

Hannah stepped past him, ignoring his pleas for her
to stop, and hurried to join the Featherton sisters in the
Tea Room. She pressed through a throng of elegantly
dressed ladies and gentlemen who congregated just inside the open Tea Room doors, and made her way to the
core of the room, a vantage from which she hoped to
spy the Feathertons.

"Hannah." Griffin was only steps from her now and
was gaining on her with amazing speed as people prac-

tically leaped from the huge gent's path as if to avoid being crushed. "Hannah, there is something more— something you must hear."

Keeping her gaze on Griffin behind her, Hannah struggled to slice her way through the gathering.

Then, suddenly, Griffin stopped midstride for no apparent reason. His eyes rounded, and an oath fell from his lips.

This was her moment, the few seconds she required to put distance between them. Lifting the hem of her gown and overdress, she made to run. She glanced once more behind her, and in that instant made a fatal mistake, for she ran headlong into a gentleman.

"I beg your pardon—," she began. But then all the blood seemed to drain from her head. For when she looked up, she met those familiar green eyes.

Heaven help her, somehow it was Mr. St. Albans she had careened into! Then she noticed the flaxen-haired beauty at his side, glaring at her.

"*Griffin*—how . . . ?" Hannah stammered. This could not be happening. It was impossible.

She felt a firm grip upon her wrist and turned her head only to see . . . Griffin—*again*.

She didn't understand how this could be. But there was no denying her own eyes.

"Hannah," the man who held her wrist began, "allow me to introduce my twin brother, Garnet . . . but then, you already know one another, don't you?"

Good heavens. Hannah swallowed deeply.

There are . . . two of them.

Chapter Eighteen

Mind-reeling confusion quickly matured into an overwhelming sense of betrayal. Hannah's body began to tremble uncontrollably.

She looked from Griffin to his more-polished brother, Garnet. How could she not have seen how different they were?

Griffin's shoulders were broader, his waist trimmer, and his body quite a bit more muscled than his leaner, more-aristocratic-looking brother.

His clothing was well cut, but devoid of sparkle and ornamentation . . . and for goodness' sake, he had worn Hessians to a ball!

Garnet, however, was dressed in the height of fashion, every detail of his appearance was studied, perfect, right down to the silver-shot dancing slippers that coordinated precisely with his gleaming waistcoat.

She must have been blind to have let these details slip beneath her notice. The twin brothers, though they occupied the same space, were as different as the sun and the moon.

Hannah rubbed her temples with the tips of her gloved fingers.

Or had she noticed but been too naive to realize it? For now she could recall moments when cocky, rakish Garnet had posed as his brother. She struggled to remember if *that* incarnation of Mr. St. Albans had kissed her . . . or more.

No, no. 'Twas Garnet who vexed her, who taxed her patience at every turn.

And 'twas Griffin, the kind and gentle soul, whom she loved.

Now, knowing the two halves of Mr. St. Albans, she didn't know what to do next. Instead of feeling joy that the man she loved had not forsaken her for another, her heart ached—for both had lied to her. Both had betrayed her trust.

They had made a fool of her.

She just didn't know why.

Her lips quivered. Words were beyond her grasp, and it took everything within Hannah to find a way to express the pain she was feeling.

Drawing back her hand, she landed a stinging palm across Garnet's cheek. The shock of her action had barely registered on Garnet's face when she whirled around to Griffin.

Hot tears were already streaming down her cheeks. She curled her fingers into fists, but at that very moment Griffin moved against her, and she collapsed against his chest.

She felt his arms come up around her, felt him kiss the top of her head.

"Hannah," he whispered into her hair. "I am sorry. If you will just listen . . . Damn it all, I know there is no excuse for not telling you, but—"

Hannah pulled back and peered up at him through her wet lashes. "On that, Mr. St. Albans, we agree."

She twisted in his embrace until she broke it.

A hush fell over the Tea Room. All conversation seemed to stop at that exact second. Even the tinkle of spoons swirling in china cups ceased.

Save a few gasps from the balcony above, the only sound Hannah registered now was the beating of her own heart as the upper reaches of Bath society witnessed her humiliation.

Slamming her palms against Griffin's chest, she pushed away and, near blind from her tears, ran for the doors.

Griffin's eyes met Garnet's, and the two stared at each other for several seconds in stunned silence.

"Griffin . . . I-I'm sorry." Garnet reached out a hand to his brother, but Griffin stepped backward, avoiding his touch.

"No, *I* am sorry. Sorry that I did not confess everything to Hannah sooner. For now, it may be too late."

Pushing past his brother, Griffin raced out into the cool night after Hannah. But there was no sign of her anywhere.

The moonlit street was empty, save for a few chairmen lined up along the flagway, smoking pipes and conversing to pass the time until the ball adjourned and the attendees sought conveyances to transport them to the Crescent Field to await the coming comet.

Damn it. Damn it all! He'd bungled his last chance with Hannah.

Griffin leaned his head back against the outer columns of the Upper Assembly Rooms and closed his eyes.

"Bloody hell, lad! What have you and your thick-headed brother done?"

Griffin opened his eyelids slowly to find the earl standing not a breath away from him. "Did you not witness it? Everyone else did."

"Of course I saw what occurred! At least one member of the House of Commons did as well." The earl began to pace, wringing his hands as he stalked back and forth before Griffin. "The earldom is done for. It will not take long for the *ton* to discover I have no clear heir. If there is one notion I have discovered during my stay, it is that no secret can survive for long in Bath."

Griffin pushed up from the column. "There is a clear heir to the title—Garnet."

"No, he had his heart set on Miss Howard, and I cannot risk the chance that she is barren."

"My lord, should anyone investigate, I will tell them that Garnet is firstborn. He is your heir. I shall never contest the line. Your course of action is simple. Name Garnet your heir, and the earldom will be preserved."

The earl grimaced. "This does not please me. Not one bit. You are my choice. I-I . . . can assist you with Miss Chillton, if you would only—"

"Do you not understand, my lord?" Griffin raised both palms in the air. "Had it not been for the damnable earldom, there would have been no secrets, and in all likelihood, Miss Chillton would already be my wife!"

Even in the thin blue light of the moon, Griffin could see the color rise into the earl's cheeks. "It would seem, then, that I have been left no choice in the matter."

"It would seem so." Griffin lifted his fob and turned the round face of his watch to the moonlight to read the time. He straightened his back and tipped his head to the earl. "Now then, if you will excuse me, my lord, I have only three hours to make my way to the Beechen Cliff summit and prepare my telescopes for the comet."

"I, for one, shall cheer once the bloody comet passes." The earl snorted, then tipped his head back to peer up at the sky. His wig slid off his bald head and fell onto the flagway. "Too much fuss over a little fizz in the heavens, if you ask me." The earl hoisted the waistband of his breeches, then bent to retrieve the wig. When he righted himself, he was surprised to find Griffin St. Albans . . . gone.

Hmmph. Perhaps Garnet was the right choice for heir after all. He, though perhaps lacking the correct choice in brides, did at least have proper manners.

Pinkerton stepped out of the shadows just then, startling the earl so that he choked on his own swallowing. "Damn me, Pinkerton. Announce yourself!"

"I beg your pardon, my lord." Pinkerton tipped his head, sending several spider legs of black hair tumbling about his pale forehead. "I only wished to inform you that the Feathertons have departed through another door moments ago."

"Really?" The earl cleared his throat. "Well, I suppose I would have taken the same route were my charge just humiliated before the *ton*. Dreadful incident to befall such a pretty young gel as Miss Chillton. Just dreadful."

Pinkerton cocked an eyebrow at that comment. "Yes, my lord. Were the Messrs. St. Albans humiliated in the Tea Room, I do not doubt you would also make a rapid departure."

The earl nodded in agreement. "Now that Lady Letitia has left the ball, I have no further interest in attending."

Straightening his wig on his round head, the earl snapped his fingers and summoned a pair of chairmen. "I am in need of a freshly curled wig, however, Pinkerton. Want to look my best at the comet viewing later."

"Yes, my lord."

"The viewing parties are to commence in the Crescent Field just outside Lady Letitia's home. No doubt she will attend the festivities, despite her charge's embarrassment this eve."

"Yes, my lord."

Pinkerton opened the door to the sedan chair and waited for the earl to climb inside before securing the latch.

The earl leaned out the open window. "It's not far back to the house. You can run alongside the chair so we may arrive together." The earl tugged at his neckcloth and cleared his throat yet again. "I believe I shall be requiring a brandy when we arrive. Feeling a bit parched, you know."

Pinkerton exhaled and removed his hat and loosened his own neckcloth in preparation for the exertion ahead of him. "Yes, my lord."

Below stairs, Hannah sat silently at the scrubbed kitchen table with Annie and Mrs. Penny. She was taking a much-needed cup of tea—along with a generous dose of powder for her pounding head.

Annie laid a comforting hand on Hannah's shoulder. "Your eyes are still red as bloomin' poppies, Miss Hannah, but at least you ain't cryin' no more."

"Her tear ducts are dry, Annie." Mrs. Penny filled Hannah's teacup again. "Drink this down, child. Don't want you to go all light in the head."

Hannah smiled weakly in reply.

There had been no consoling her, though the Feathertons had tried for two full hours after she left the ball, until Hannah sought refuge in the kitchen away from their pitying gazes.

The ladies had assured her that there was a good and true reason for the two Messrs. St. Albans to conceal the truth of their identities. They assured her, yes, but neither could tell Hannah what that reason might be.

Hannah sipped her tea until Mrs. Penny stopped gesturing for her to take more of the liquid, then she settled her teacup on the table. She rested her head in her hands.

"Twins. Lud, it all makes so much sense now, doesn't it, Mrs. Penny?" Annie snatched a sugar biscuit off Hannah's saucer and began to munch on it. "So the cocky one was Mr. Garnet, was it?"

Hannah nodded, not bothering to look up.

"Well, the Mr. St. Albans who resided here was certainly cocky, proud . . . and rude."

"It was *Mr. Garnet*, wasn't it?"

Hannah placed her hands on her lap and raised her head. "I am sure of it. Griffin is so different. He is kind, and quiet. So intelligent . . . and passionate. I could have never fallen in love with such a pompous fool as Garnet."

"But you loved Mr. Griffin."

Hannah felt her cheeks color. She diverted her gaze to the popping fire in the cooking hearth.

"You *do*!" Annie leaned close. "I bet he is far more handsome than his brother, ain't he?"

"They are *identical*." Hannah felt the edges of her mouth lift a little. "Though they are formed differently. Griffin is somewhat . . . larger."

"*Larger*. Oh, I get it." Annie's eyes went wide. "Oooo . . . how do you know that, Miss Hannah?"

Mrs. Penny slapped her hand to the table. "Annie!"

"Well, I saw her climb in her window early one morn. It weren't even light yet. And one of those Mr. St. Albans was standin' below making sure she didn't fall or nothin'." Annie peered into Hannah's widened eyes.

Hannah was not going to comment on Annie's observation, though it did make her wonder what Annie was also doing outside the house at such an early hour.

"Which one was it, Miss Hannah? The one with the larger . . . well, you know." Annie was almost salivating in her anticipation.

A small twitter slipped through Hannah's teeth. "No, no, Annie. You misunderstood me. I meant Griffin's body is larger . . . more muscular, while Garnet's is slimmer and lean."

"Well, dear gel," Mrs. Penny said in a confident

tone, "it certainly sounds as though you snared the better of the two Messrs. St. Albans."

The smile on Hannah's lips fell away. She quickly reached for her teacup and brought it to her mouth.

Annie and Mrs. Penny exchanged concerned glances.

"Miss Hannah, you did forgive Mr. Griffin, didn't you?" Annie asked gently.

But Hannah did not reply.

"Miss Hannah, if you love him, then you *must* forgive him."

"I cannot!" Hannah blurted. "Don't you see, he and his brother purposely made a fool of me."

"Are you sure of that, gel?" Mrs. Penny asked. "He must have had a very good reason for keeping such a large secret. Perhaps you should give him another chance to redeem himself. Life is short, dear. Too brief to waste your days simmering over a misunderstanding. Forgive him, and give yourself a chance at happiness." Mrs. Penny was now wearing that same pitying expression the Feathertons had donned earlier.

She couldn't endure it. She just couldn't.

"I am not like my mother. Why does everyone assume we are the same?" Something began to ache inside Hannah, and she leaped from the stool. "I do not need a *man* in my life to be happy."

"No, Miss Hannah, you don't need a man for your life to be full and happy," Annie agreed. "But you might need *Griffin*."

The backs of Hannah's eyes began to sting. Turning, she lifted her hem and raced back up the servants' staircase.

❧

Hannah ran for the front door and swung it open, thinking that a walk in the cool night air might help her clear her mind . . . and to sort out her jumbled emotions.

She lifted her foot to step outside, when she saw several hundred people milling about on the Crescent Field.

The yellow light of lanterns dotted the hillside sloping down from Royal Crescent and the flat field below. In the soft glow of the moon, she could just make out scores of ladies, gentlemen, and even children, stretched out on blankets spread all about the sweeping lawn. They were laughing, supping on sweets, and clinking glasses of drink in celebration of the coming comet.

Hannah turned her gaze upward to the star-strewn sky, then stepped back inside the house and snatched up a candlestick from the table in the passage to check the time on the tall case clock.

Thirty minutes. That was all, according to Griffin's earlier calculations, until the comet would swoop low over the city.

She wondered if the Featherton sisters had already found their places on the field, or if owing to her own drama in the ballroom, they had entirely forgotten about the much-lauded event.

Whirling around, Hannah headed quickly for the drawing room and pressed the door open. It was dark inside the room, but she could hear Lady Viola's voice whispering something, then a heavy thump.

"Lady Viola? Are you in here?"

Hannah raised the candle outward before her and walked toward the settee. The old woman could be napping from the effects of her nightly cordial. When she reached the back of the settee, she lowered the candlestick, allowing its circle of golden light to illuminate the cushion.

"Oh, good evening, Hannah." Lady Viola, who was stretched out across the settee, squinted up at her. The paint on the old woman's lips smeared off the side and down her chin.

"Good heavens, are you well?"

She lifted a frail, withered hand to block the light. "Do lower the candle, dove. My eyes have not adjusted."

"Certainly." Hannah rushed around to the other side of the settee, but she tripped on something on the floor and fell to the carpet.

Something dark and heavy crawled up from the floor and righted the candle immediately. Hannah saw the flickering light rise in the air, as if transported by a ghost, and settle on the tea table beside her.

Then, she felt a hand on her arm, helping her to stand.

"Do let me assist you, Miss Chillton."

Hannah gulped. "Edgar?" Once she was on her feet, she reached down for the candlestick and lifted it toward the manservant. "It *is* you!"

Smudges of red lip paint were smeared across the elderly man's face. Hannah raised the candle higher, and saw three lip-shaped impressions dotting his cheeks. She brought her free hand to her lips to quiet the giggle welling up inside her.

"I shall fetch a few more candles," the manservant said, and quickly disappeared into the darkness.

"Lady Viola, just what was happening in here?" Hannah lifted her brow playfully as she helped the old woman sit up on the settee.

Instead of going all coy, as Hannah expected Lady Viola to do, the old woman actually beamed. "Mr. Edgar and I have decided to marry."

"I beg your pardon." Hannah could not have heard correctly. After all of these years, according to Annie, of Lady Viola and Edgar being in love, what would prompt them to finally proclaim it to all?

"We are to be married. We already told Sister, and at once she rushed to the study to locate her notes on our grandnieces' weddings. She could not be more thrilled than if she herself were marrying the man she loved."

Hannah reached out and took Lady Viola's thin hand. "But why now, after all this time?"

"Because of you, dear."

Hannah blinked at that. *"I?"*

"You showed me how fragile and fleeting love can be."

"I don't understand."

"You and Mr. St. Albans, Griffin St. Albans, are in love. You are meant to be together. Sister and I realized that from the moment the two of you met on the cliffs of Kennymare Cove."

"But what has that to do with you and Mr. Edgar?"

"I watched as the two of you let the wishes of the earl, the impressions of the *ton,* your pride—even your own mother's faults come between you . . . threatening your love. Threatening your own chance at happiness."

The downy hairs on Hannah's forearms prickled as

they rose beneath her sleeves. Lady Viola spoke the truth. There was no denying it.

"After what happened in the Tea Room this eve, after seeing how your stubborn pride would not allow you even to listen to Mr. St. Albans—even if it might cost you your happiness—I knew I had been a fool all of these years." A small whimper fell from Lady Viola's lips. "I had let what others thought, what others told me was correct, prevent me from acknowledging my feelings for the gentleman I loved . . . simply because we are from different classes."

"No longer. At last I will follow my heart. I will marry Mr. Edgar." Lady Viola came unsteadily to her feet. "True love is rare in this world. Do not forsake it, Hannah. If you love Mr. St. Albans, go to him and tell him now. Before it's too late. Come morning, you may not have another chance."

Hannah rose slowly from the settee. For several seconds, she did not move. Did not speak.

In her heart she knew Lady Viola was right. She had to find Griffin. Had to set things to rights.

Now. Before it was too late.

Whirling around, she raced into the passage and tore her pelisse off a hook nearest the door.

At that very moment, Lady Letitia entered the passage from the study and observed Hannah's haste. "Dear gel, where are you going in such a flutter?"

Hannah threw the door open, then cast a glance over her shoulder. "To Beechen Cliff to find Griffin—and tell him that I love him."

Chapter Nineteen

Hannah lifted her hem and raced down from the heights of Royal Crescent, through the huge crowd that congregated on the gently sloping field of grass, and on to Bristol Road.

The moonlight could not reach the ground on the narrow branch streets upon which she turned and ran. The buildings, buff-hued and bright during the day, were dark and menacing in the dimness, and rose up on either side of her, making Hannah feel as though she could not breathe until she was free of them.

Still she ran, finally making her way to the Horse Street crossing over the River Avon.

Instead of passing through the Prior Park gate down the road to her left, she decided to head for Well Road, where the climb to Beechen Cliff would be steep, but a shorter distance.

She paused before beginning her ascent up the vertical path to the cliff and peered upward at its pinnacle.

There, she could just make out a single flickering lantern. Her heart began to pound with excitement.

She had found Griffin.

He would be alone at this vantage, she knew, despite its being the highest point from which to view the coming comet.

All of the other astronomers would no doubt have positioned themselves at Mount Breacon on the complete opposite side of the city. There the Royal Astronomical Society had erected a forty-foot telescope for the sole purpose of observing the Bath Comet. Even Miss Herschel would have taken her position at the lens at the Mount. There was no question that the viewing of the Bath Comet from the Mount would be far superior to Griffin's.

But that fact had obviously not dissuaded him from positioning his telescopes on Beechen Cliff—for as Hannah at last neared the cliff's ledge, there he was, dutifully bent over the eyepiece of his Newtonian sweeper.

Slowly, she walked up behind him, not quite knowing what to say or how to begin.

He heard her, though, for his shoulders suddenly tensed, and he lifted his eyes from the telescope's lens.

Yet, he did not turn. Instead he called out. "So you've decided to join me after all, Garnet." He turned a bit and looked up then, a smile on his handsome face . . . until he saw her.

"Hannah." His countenance became expressionless, and he simply stared at her for several seconds before venturing to speak another word. "What are you doing here?"

Before she realized it, Hannah was running toward

him, hands outstretched. When she reached him, she
threw herself against his hard chest and hugged him to
her. She closed her eyes and held tight, wanting the moment to last yet fearing it would not.

His hands moved over her shoulders, then slid down
her arms until he could pull her back from him. His
hands grasped her upper arms as he leaned closer to
peer into her eyes. "Why are you here, Hannah? After
what happened in the Tea Room—"

Hannah raised a finger and laid it vertically over his
lips. "Shhh," she whispered. "Do not speak. None of
that matters anymore. Do you hear me? It no longer
matters to me."

Griffin released one of her arms in order to catch up
her hand and draw it away from his mouth. "But Hannah, I *must* explain why—"

"Not now. *Please*."

He opened his mouth again, but Hannah covered his
lips with her own and kissed him softly. She drew back
her mouth, then looked up into his amazing eyes again.
"All that matters, Griffin," she said in no more than a
breath against his lips, "is that I love you."

A deep sigh poured from Griffin, and she felt the
tension in his body relax. He stared down at her beneath half-lidded eyes. "And I love you, Hannah. I always have . . . since the moment I first saw you . . . on
another cliff, far, far away."

Neither spoke for several breaths. Then Griffin bent
and caught her in a heated kiss, slipping his fingers
through her hair, sending a twinkling of bejeweled hairpins tumbling down her back to the ground.

She opened her mouth to his, and he eased his
tongue inside, teasing her with its probing tip. Where

their bodies touched lower, she felt him harden against her, and at once she became aware of a tightness building between her legs.

Hannah hesitated for moment and cast her eyes demurely to the one hand that still gripped her arm. She had been here before. Knew what her body was telling her. Knew, too, what his own might offer.

Griffin opened his hand at once and released her.

He would not touch her again, she knew this, unless she let him know she wished it. And she did. Oh, God, she did.

There was no reason to waver. What a goose she was to falter. Griffin St. Albans loved her, and she loved him.

And just now, her body wanted to show him how much.

Rising on her toes, she unhurriedly brushed her lips along his, savoring the feel of his warm breath on her mouth, feeling her own breathing quicken.

Griffin ran his tongue slowly over her full bottom lip, drawing forth a small sigh from her mouth. Hannah drew her head back to look up at him. His eyes burned, even in the darkness, and she felt all apprehension melt away.

She loved him, and nothing else mattered.

Gazing up at him through the fringe of her lashes, she fingered his neckcloth and let it fall to the wind-shaven grass atop the cliff. Then she slipped her hands to his shoulders and, knowing what she desired, shrugged off his greatcoat and laid it out like a pallet on the ground.

"Have you no shame, Griffin?" Hannah smiled.

"None at all." He slanted his dark eyebrows, in that

way of his and kissed her, harder this time. "Sadly, that is one trait my brother and I share."

Hannah caught the sides of his linen shirt and tugged the tails from his breeches before easing her fingers up beneath the soft fabric to his chest. "And thankfully, one my brother and I do not." She smiled saucily up at him, as she felt the pleasurable warmth of smooth skin against her palms.

His mouth trailed along her throat, making her moan as the wetness of his kisses cooled in the night air.

Vaguely, she became aware of her nipples tightening in the chill breeze, and she looked down to see that Griffin had parted her pelisse, pulled the silk ribbon that cinched her bodice closed and had lowered her stays so that her breasts were poised atop them, supported by the light boning.

Her nipples throbbed beneath her thin chemise as Griffin smiled wickedly and kissed her again. He cupped a hot palm over the top of her right breast while settling his other hand in the small of her back and pulling her tight against him.

As he fondled her soft breast, heat flowed through her body, settling in the most wanton of places, making her squirm.

This was taking too long. She wanted to feel him inside her. She did not wish to wait any longer.

With a boldness that surprised even her, Hannah lowered her hand and ran it over the swelling in his breeches.

The moon behind her illuminated Griffin in a pale blue light, and she could see that he had closed his eyes. As quickly as she could, Hannah opened his frontfall. His shirt fell over him, tenting his body's excitement. She lifted it away and took him into her hand, running her fingers along his hardness.

"*Hannah.*" His voice was husky and deep, barely controlled. "You have to stop."

"And so I shall." She released him from her grip and saw him open his eyes. Hannah smiled then. She wanted him to watch her now. Wanted him to see her kneel before him . . . wanted him to watch as she did the sinful thing the scullery maids had once whispered of when they did not know she had come into the kitchen to fetch some powder for Lady Viola.

She had taken copious notes, in case the maneuver, she told herself, ever might assist a client in securing a mate. And though the need to share "the secret" never presented itself, Hannah had been confident that the information would not go to waste. And she had been right.

Griffin's eyes were wide and dark. He stood above her, looking down with utter astonishment as she wrapped her fingers firmly just beneath his plum-shaped tip. She could smell the light manly scent of him as she lowered her head and began to trace a slick path along its ridge with her wet tongue.

His girth grew in her hand as she spiraled her tongue over his silken head. Blood pulsed beneath her fingers, all along his shaft, and he hardened like a stone.

Hannah eased her lips over him then, until her mouth met her fingers. She pressed downward and brought him deeply into her mouth.

A low growl burst from his lips, and he grabbed her chin and held it in place as she began to move leisurely up and down his velvety length.

She moved slowly at first, then, as her confidence

grew, faster, twisting her hand as her mouth covered him, moistening him as she moved.

"Hannah." His breath came in pants and gasps now. "You have to—"

Hannah raised her free hand and reached between his legs to cup him as her lips rode up and down his hardness. Inside her mouth, he became ever harder, and the width of him seemed to grow.

Griffin's thighs trembled, just a bit. Hannah wondered if this was the moment the maids had mentioned. She wasn't sure, truly sure about anything she was doing, but moved onward and did the last thing the maids had discussed. She stiffened her fingers and lightly dragged her nails across his tightening sack.

Griffin sucked in a deep gulp of air and grabbed Hannah's wrist. "You have to stop—*now*."

She stopped then, and without releasing her grasp, leaned back. He pulsed in her hand, and a single pearl droplet glistened at his tip. Her gaze traveled up his muscled body. His chest rose and fell heavily.

Hannah slowly opened her hand, feeling a wash of crimson overtake her cheeks. "Did I . . . do something wrong?"

A huff of laughter was her reply. "You did everything right. 'Tis just . . . I am not yet finished, Hannah. Far from it, in fact."

She peered deeply into his eyes, and he met her gaze intently as he reached down and pulled at the closure at the throat of her fur-lined pelisse. He released it and let it spread out behind her, then he eased her down upon it.

Impatiently, Griffin tossed up the blue silk and silver mesh of her gown and the layers beneath it, skimming the profusion of skirts over her silk stockings, bare thighs, and finally her hips.

Hannah struggled to pull her gown down again, but Griffin brushed her hands back.

Cupping his hands behind her knees, he opened her thighs and settled his knees between them. He leaned back on his heels then and devoured her with his gaze. "I believe it is my rotation now."

Hannah shook her head and lifted her hand to catch him up and draw him to her. He allowed this, in part, and kissed her deep and hard. But then he pulled back and leaned over her to taste her breasts, giving each their proper time, until Hannah was writhing, and both pink nipples were teased into tight, aching buds.

Griffin's hand moved between her legs, and he stroked her gently, masterfully. He looked into her eyes as he eased his finger up and spiraled, just there, making her whimper, and buck against his hand.

Her heart pounded madly in her ears. She was wet, and swollen with urgent want of him. And she didn't want to wait anymore.

Griffin bent over her then and began to stroke her wetness with his tip. Hannah squeezed her eyes tightly. For certain, she would go mad from the sensation. She needed him inside her. With a groan, she tried to push down atop him, forcing him to take her. But he only leaned back to look at her . . . to be sure.

But when her gaze met his dark, oh-so-purposeful eyes, she knew he needed her as frantically as she needed him.

Now.

Hannah held her breath as the thickness of him pressed slowly into her, silken and solid, filling the aching void within her. Her every fiber seemed attuned to their joining. Every sense heightened. Every touch, burning.

She ran her fingers through the thick locks of his hair as he thrust into her. Griffin looked down into her eyes.

Cupping her hand to his cheek, she gazed deep into his eyes. "I love you, Griffin." In the pale of the moon, she could see his eyes glistening with deep emotion as he kissed her mouth.

Hannah wrapped her arms tightly around him and held him, but it was not enough. She wanted to be closer still, and so, she lifted her legs and hooked her ankles at Griffin's back, holding him tightly against her.

Griffin groaned, thrusting powerfully into her, causing her body to tighten unbearably, making her muscles pulse and constrict around him.

Then, with a look of sheer determination in his eyes, he pushed up on his hands, breaking the embrace of both her arms and legs.

He rammed hard into her, thick and deep. His breathing matched his increasing power, and she lifted her hips, meeting each thrust. Her muscles began to convulse, and she clenched down on his hardness.

He slowed slightly then. Griffin lifted his head and looked into Hannah's eyes. "I love you more than you will ever know. Marry me, Hannah, and make me the happiest man in the universe."

As she clung to his body, tears seeped into Hannah's eyes, wetting her lashes. "Yes, my love, I will marry you. I want nothing more than to be with you forever."

Griffin kissed her again. "Forever," he echoed, his

voice breaking. With a groan, he slammed deep into her one final time, as though sealing their vow.

Hannah grasped his arms. Her fingers dug into his muscles and squeezed uncontrollably as he pumped his heat deep within her, sending them both tumbling into throbbing ecstasy.

Suddenly a great bright ball of light roared up over the horizon and streaked directly overhead above them, followed by an ear-shattering roar unlike anything Hannah had ever heard before.

The ground began to rumble slightly. Hannah's eyes went wide.

She felt tiny stones vibrating beneath her bottom, and for a brief second she wondered if this is what the maids had meant by great lovemaking making the earth move.

And then she heard the sound of a hundred cannons firing at once somewhere in the narrow field near the cliff.

Startled, Hannah gasped and clutched Griffin to her.

"Amazing! Do not fret, 'tis just a fireball. Watch now, for you will likely never see this again in your lifetime." He leaned his head on her shoulder and together they stared up in amazement at the vast shower of floating sparks drifting slowly down from the heavens like thousands of tiny fireflies.

Griffin's face lit up, and he kissed the whole of Hannah's face excitedly. "Brilliant, wasn't it?"

"Brilliant?" Hannah knit her brows. "Griffin, we might have been killed!"

Griffin shook his head. "That outcome would have been highly unlikely. The earth passed through the Bath Comet's orbit. That's all."

"That was the comet then?"

"Good lord, no." Griffin withdrew from Hannah's body, rolled over onto his back, and pulled her against his side. He pointed up into the heavens at a wide smudge of teardrop-shaped light far off to the right. "That is the Bath Comet. What you just saw was a meteor."

Hannah smiled and snuggled close to Griffin. It pleased her that he was so passionate about the stars and how much it excited him to speak about his science. "What is the difference?"

"Meteors, some call them shooting stars, are tiny specks of dust that burn up in our atmosphere. Some rare meteors, like the one that passed over us just now, are much larger, and can produce spectacular fireballs . . . and even strike the earth and explode."

"That was the sound we heard."

"Yes. There's likely nothing left of it."

"But there may be." Hannah sat upright.

"Possibly. Shall we go have a look?"

Hannah nodded excitedly.

Griffin kissed her again as he hurriedly helped her adjust her underpinnings and gown, then wrapped her pelisse around her.

He fastened his breeches and threw his shirt over his head. Snatching up the lantern, he left everything else lying on the ground. "We have to be quick about it. If we are very lucky, we'll see something amazing."

Twenty minutes later, with Griffin's sense of the fireball's trajectory as a guide, the two had made their way by lanternlight down to the western boundary of Prior Park. They stood before a hole perhaps the depth and width of a carriage. In the center, was a black rock the size of a large portmanteau.

"That's it?" Hannah peered quizzically at Griffin. "Somehow it seemed so much larger."

"The ice that surrounded it likely evaporated in the explosion." Griffin climbed down into the shallow crater and studied the rock in the center. He bent to observe its base, and when he did, he set down the lantern and noticed a small field of shards from the meteorite skirting the larger rock. At once, he excitedly began to collect them.

"Ought you to touch those?" Hannah nervously called down to him.

"How else am I to study them?" Griffin removed his shirt and used it as a collection net for his prizes. When he had retrieved every broken piece and shard, he tied his shirt closed and grinned up at Hannah, as happy as a boy with a handful of sugar sweets. "Do you hear that—that buzz?" Griffin hurriedly tried to climb from the hole, but the walls were wet with a black slick mud. "What is it? Can you see?"

Hannah looked up to see the field behind her awash in lanternlight. Scores of people emerged from the woods, and the road, and were bearing down on Hannah and Griffin.

"People. At least a hundred of them!"

"Can you help me climb out?"

Hannah knelt and extended a hand to him, but she could not reach him.

Just then, a pair of gentlemen approached the lip of the crater.

" 'Ere, miss, just get up and stand aside. We've got 'im." The two men reached in and pulled Griffin up by his wrists. By now twenty or so people stood around the crater, murmuring and whispering to one another.

At first, Hannah could not discern what they were saying, until the woman next to her spoke. "That's the comet?" she asked Hannah. " 'Tis so small . . . well, for a comet, that is."

Hannah shook her head. "No, no." She pointed into the sky, as the comet's tail of light was just beginning to disappear in the west. "*That* is the Bath Comet. *This* is a meteorite."

The woman screwed up her face. "I saw the comet swoop right over the Crescent Field. It was huge, and gold . . . with a tail of iridescent sparkles. We saw it come right this way. This *has* to be the Bath Comet. My husband and I followed its path, and it led us to Prior Park."

People around Hannah agreed with the woman in a wave of excited voices.

"No, it's not. *That* is the comet." Hannah jabbed her finger into the air for effect, but when she looked up again, it was gone. "Well, you will just have to believe me. This is not the comet. Just ask Mr. St. Albans here. He is an astronomer, who was studying the comet from Beechen Cliff, when the fireball passed over." Then, Hannah realized what she had just said.

He was studying the Bath Comet . . .

An icy cold hand suddenly seemed to grip Hannah's throat.

Oh, God. Griffin had been viewing the comet, making his calculations, cataloging the heavens, when . . .

she interrupted his work. The work he needed to be perfect.

Needed to secure a royal appointment.

A whimper escaped Hannah. She had ruined everything for him.

Hannah rushed to Griffin and threw her arms around him. "I am so sorry, Griffin. Can you ever forgive me?"

Griffin caught her upper arms and drew her away from the crowd encircling the crater. With a confused expression, he gazed into her eyes. "What are you going on about? Forgive you for what, Hannah?"

She peered up at him for the briefest of moments, but her shame could not let her hold her gaze for long. "On the cliff, I-I . . . made you miss the comet. And now, 'tis . . . gone."

Griffin tilted his head back and looked to the west. He smiled then and laughed. He whirled Hannah around and leaned in close to her ear as he pointed into the sky. "The comet is not gone, Hannah. It's right *there*. Just as my calculations predicted."

Hannah's gaze followed his finger. She squinted her eyes, and . . . she saw it. A pale round light with a wisp of a tail.

"*That* is the comet I have been cataloging. Oh, the Bath Comet all but obscured it from view, being a much grander spectacle, but I've observed it twice, though no other astronomer seemed to, and I vowed not to rest until I proved its existence."

Griffin offered Hannah his arm and urged her forward, away from the gathering crowd. "Come with me, and you may see it properly through my telescope."

Hannah was silent for a few breaths, but her mind could not stop attempting to link together her own observations. She stopped walking just as they reached the near vertical trail to the cliff's top. "But . . . Miss Herschel—"

"Ah, my mentor." Griffin smiled and coaxed Hannah forward again. "Not long after I arrived in Bath, I begged her indulgence in reviewing my calculations and maps. Within a week, her keen eyes had observed my comet as well. She did not believe the comet had been seen before and took my observations under her protection. Together, we sent a letter detailing my observations to the Royal Observatory at Greenwich. I only await acknowledgment of my discovery."

Hannah whirled around, nearly toppling Griffin backward as she hugged him to her. "So tonight . . . was not so all important to you after all?"

"No, Hannah, you are wrong about that." Griffin took her chin in his hand and made her look at him. "Tonight has been the most important of my entire life. Not because my comet became visible for the first time to the naked eye, but rather because you, my darling, made my grandest dream come true when you agreed to become my wife."

Chapter Twenty

Daybreak, Number One Royal Crescent

Hannah slapped one hand then the other to the windowsill and raised the sash as quietly as she could manage. The muscles of her arms were shaking from exhaustion, but still she stepped off the latticework running up the back of the house, pulled herself up, and crawled into her bedchamber.

She didn't notice at first how warm and toasty the chamber was, or that Annie was sitting in the rocking chair before the fire in the hearth awaiting her arrival. She was too distracted by Griffin, who stood on the ground below to be sure his betrothed was returned to her bed safely.

She leaned out the window and threw her love a kiss before easing the sash closed again.

"She's *back*!" came a shrill voice from behind her.

Hannah whirled around and saw Annie running across the chamber, waving her arms excitedly. "Miss Hannah is here!"

She could hear the pounding of footsteps on the staircase, then Mrs. Penny murmuring something unintelligible in the passage. But Annie's voice was plain and clear.

"I told you she would come in through the window. That's what she always does. I've seen her do it. Scampers right up the side of the house like she was a great spider or somethin'."

Mrs. Penny looked dreadful when she entered the bedchamber. Her eyes were ringed with gray as if she hadn't slept all night.

Oh, dear.

Perhaps she hadn't. Perhaps no one had. Perhaps they stayed up all night long when Hannah had not returned.

Mrs. Penny breathed out a long sigh. "You had us so worried, miss. The ladies were beside themselves. They actually had each other convinced that you and Mr. St. Albans had been killed when the comet exploded on Beechen Cliff."

"What a *silly* thought." Hannah shook her head, and both she and Mrs. Penny chuckled together for a moment. When the mirth at last faded from their mouths, Hannah continued. "No, it missed us by nearly a furlong. At least that. Probably more. And it wasn't the Bath Comet at all—it was a fireball . . . and it struck on the edge of Prior Park, not Beechen Cliff at all."

Hannah could not seem to stop her chattering. She was tired beyond words but also exhilarated from the night's events. "Oh, it was *terrifying*! The whole cliff shook when the fireball passed right over us and exploded, but—" Hannah looked up and noticed that the

Feathertons were now standing in the passage, listening. "But . . . as I said . . . it missed us *completely*."

Lady Letitia folded her arms over her ample bosom and narrowed her eyes disappointedly at Hannah.

"So, you see . . . there was naught to fret about." Hannah feigned a smile. "I am quite unharmed."

"Well, I am pleased to hear it, gel." Lady Letitia cast a quick look at her sister then turned her attention back to Hannah. "It seems your Mr. St. Albans survived the spectacle as well. Mr. Edgar encountered the gentleman standing in the back, just staring up into the sky, or perhaps . . . *a window*. We've invited him inside, naturally. In truth, he is taking his ease in the drawing room at this very moment."

Hannah could see that the ladies awaited her reaction. But what was she to do? And so, she raised her lips in a weak smile. "Oh, is he?"

Lady Viola pulled a lavender-lace handkerchief from her sleeve and dabbed her brow. "Yes, he—*and the others*—are awaiting us in the drawing room. You included, child."

"*Others?*" Hannah swallowed deeply.

"Yes, gel." Lady Letitia and her sister began to turn back toward the passage, but they paused first before leaving.

"Hurry yourself now, then do come and join us at once—" Lady Viola advised, before her words were interrupted by her sister.

"Do see to your toilette first, gel. Why, your dress is muddied and has bits of grass sticking out from the mesh . . . and good heavens, your hair looks like a bird's nest after a storm. Just *what* were you doing on the cliffs?"

Lady Letitia looked suspiciously at Hannah, then threw up her hands and resignedly shook her head. "I am too deep in my years for this sort of excitement, Viola," she admitted softly. "Too deep in my years."

"But we are the same age, Letitia."

"Yes, I know, sister. You are too old for this nonsense, too." The two ladies started for the staircase.

"I don't *feel* too old—," Lady Viola began.

"You *are*. We both are. Trust me on this."

"But—" Hannah called out to the ladies, causing them to still their feet and turn back to her. "But 'tis barely morn. We should all still be abed."

"Yes, Hannah, we know." Lady Viola gave Hannah an exhausted smile. "We all have been sitting up for you for some time—since the comet watch on the field concluded. You were so determined to set things to rights with Mr. St. Albans when you left the house, and had stayed away so long, that we were fairly confident that you and Mr. Griffin would have some glorious news to share when you returned."

The two old women leaned forward, as if this prod might glean from Hannah an answer to their surmising.

When it did not, Lady Viola prattled on. "We decided to wait for you. We even asked the earl and Mr. Garnet St. Albans and his miss inside to join us after the comet watch. We were hoping to make a party of it. Who could have guessed you would have gone missing until daybreak?"

Hannah shrugged sheepishly.

Lady Letitia cupped her hand over her mouth as she let out a long yawn. "Please hurry, Hannah. Do not keep our guests waiting any longer, dear. Though you mightn't hint at it, I do believe Mr. Griffin St. Albans *does* have some news to share with us, and I for one wish to hear it."

When Hannah warily entered the drawing room, she had expected nothing less than a good dressing-down. Instead, she found every seat in the room filled with worn-out guests, trying their best to clink their crystals together in celebration . . . of something. But of what, Hannah wasn't certain.

Surely Griffin would not have shared their joyous news without her.

Edgar sidled up to Hannah and moved a sterling salver before her, offering a glass of the Featherton contraband wine from Champagne, France.

She lifted the goblet and glanced around the room. Upon the settee were the Feathertons and none other than the Earl of Devonsfield.

In the chairs nearest the hearth were Mr. Garnet St. Albans and Miss Howard. Hannah tried not to glower, though that was her instinct. For indeed, the misunderstanding had not been the beauty's fault in any way. Truth to tell, Miss Howard had been a victim of the St. Albans ruse just as she had been.

What in blazes was everyone doing here at such an hour?

Griffin came to stand beside her. "Before we celebrate anything, there is something I must confess to you, Hannah—and indeed to every woman in this drawing room."

Nervously, Garnet cast his gaze to the hearth, then belatedly turned his eyes to Griffin. "No, brother, I will not allow you to do this alone." He strode across the carpet and came to stand beside Griffin.

Then Hannah noticed a curious thing. Both of the St. Albans twins silently glanced, for the briefest of instances, at the earl. They paused for several seconds, as if waiting for him to speak. Griffin finally opened his mouth to confess.

"As you are all aware by now, my brother and I are identical twins, and that at one time or another in your presence, we posed as the same man."

The two Featherton ladies exchanged quick glances, then peered across the room where Hannah stood beside the St. Albans brothers.

Garnet laid his hand on Griffin's shoulder, quieting him, then took a step forward. "What you do not know is why we did this."

"Oh, very well." The earl rose slowly, and all attention focused on him. "I should confess it, since it was I who bade the lads to accept this charade."

Lady Letitia was properly gobsmacked. "You, my lord? Why would you do such a thing?"

The earl lowered his head. "When both of my sons were killed, I was forced to trace my family tree to determine my heir. What I found complicated matters greatly, for you see, my search led me to my only male heir—Mr. St. Albans."

Hannah cinched her brows. "Um, which one, my lord?"

Griffin gave Hannah a sad smile. "That was the quandary—we did not know. We still do not know, for there is no record of which of us is firstborn."

"Oh, my." Lady Viola gasped. "When you do pass away"—Lady Viola cringed at her choice of words and sought to amend them—"which will not be for many years yet, I am certain . . . there will be no *clear* heir."

The earl nodded slowly. "Exactly. If it cannot be agreed upon which of these young men is firstborn, the Committee of Privileges has leave to recommend withdrawal of the patent . . . and the Earldom of Devonsfield, my family's ancient legacy, will be no more."

Lady Letitia's brows started for the bridge of her nose. "My lord, if it cannot be established which Mr. St. Albans is the eldest, you have no recourse."

The earl's face reddened. "You are correct, though I was not about to allow the dissolution of the earldom. So I made a pact with the lads. The first to marry a woman of quality, thus ensuring the continuance of the line, would be named firstborn . . . and therefore heir."

The ladies in the drawing room all gasped at his revelation.

"But of course, this all had to be kept completely confidential," the earl added. "Even the existence of the two identical St. Albans brothers put the earldom at risk. Members of the House of Lords often visit Bath. People talk. Until the firstborn was established, the twins could not been seen in public together. As far as Bath society knew, there was only one Mr. St. Albans. It had to appear that way."

"But, with Garnet's penchant for diversion," Griffin interjected, cocking a dark eyebrow at his brother, "we did not always maintain the illusion . . . as well as we might have."

Hannah looked up at Griffin and exhaled. She was quiet for several seconds before she burst into laughter. "Of all the wild explanations that passed through my mind for why you both posed as one, I would have never have guessed this."

Lady Viola impatiently clapped her hands together. "Well, now that the mystery has been solved, let us speak of it no more this morn . . . for I believe Hannah and Mr. St. Albans have something to share with us." She looked up at Hannah and grinned. "You *do* have something to tell us, do you not?"

Hannah looked up at Griffin, and had opened her mouth to speak, when Griffin took her elbow with one hand and raised his glass with the other. "To our wedding," he said.

"You see, I knew it, Letitia," Lady Viola twittered happily. "Oh, this is delightful. Simply the best of news!"

The gathering raised their glasses in the air cheerfully as Griffin leaned in to press a chaste kiss onto Hannah's cheek.

The couple had just lifted their goblets to drink, when Garnet waved a hand in the air. "Just one moment. There is more. To *our* wedding." He tipped his head at Miss Howard, who blushed becomingly.

"Oh, jolly good." Lady Letitia clapped her hands excitedly. "We have two reasons to make merry this morn!"

Glasses were raised again, but before anyone would take that much anticipated sip, Lady Viola came to her feet and cleared her throat. The goblets held, poised before everyone's mouths.

The frail old woman took the tray from Mr. Edgar and set it on the table. She reached down and lifted a glass of wine and handed it to the wrinkled, ancient manservant. Warily he took it from her, appearing almost embarrassed.

Lady Viola could not have had a prouder expression on her face when she raised her own glass. "And to *our* wedding."

"Hear, hear!" Hannah cheered, a sentiment echoed by everyone in the room—except, curiously, the earl.

Hannah saw his eyes shifting this way and that . . . as though he was deep in consideration. "This is a grand celebration to be sure," she began. "Let us toast, now, to *three* weddings."

The earl's eyes began to bulge in his head. "N-no-o. *Four!*"

Lady Letitia slapped her hand to her chest. "What ever do you mean, my lord?" She edged herself forward on the settee. Anticipation and excitement were bright in her eyes.

"F-four weddings. Did everyone not hear me? I am sure I spoke loudly enough, and I do not mumble." Then he tried to bend down onto one knee, but he staggered and could not accomplish it no matter how hard he tried. "Pinkerton! Assistance, please."

The earl's man, in his jet-black attire, hurried into the room from the shadows of the passage where he had waited and took the earl's arm as the rotund old man lowered his knee to the floor. The earl reached his free hand outward and took Lady Letitia's plump hand into his.

"My time left on this earth, my dear lady, is short," he began somberly.

Pinkerton cleared his throat, and Hannah doubted she was the only one who saw him roll his dark eyes after the earl's comment.

"What I mean is that I wish to spend those days with *you*, Lady Letitia. Not a minute has passed since we met that I have not mused about how happy I would be were you at my side. I dream of walking along the lake at Devonsfield together, entertaining in the grand style in which you are clearly accustomed, planning my funeral . . ."

Lady Letitia, whose round face had been beaming with happiness, pulled a sudden sour expression.

Pinkerton nudged the earl's back with his knee.

"Oh, forgive me. I said *funeral.* I meant *wedding,* of course." The earl gazed up into Lady Letitia's pale blue eyes. "Will you marry me, Lady Letitia? Say you will."

Tears trickled down Lady Letitia's face, cutting deep tracks through her bounteous powder. "I will, my lord. I will!" She leaned her substantial weight forward on the settee, making the back legs buck up, and kissed the earl's cheek.

"Now we will truly have something to celebrate," Griffin announced. "*Four* weddings!"

". . . and a funeral," Pinkerton intoned quietly beneath his breath. "Mustn't forget that."

Hannah chuckled into her palm, when suddenly Miss Howard meekly spoke up, shifting everyone in the drawing rooms attention.

"So, my lord," she began quietly, "now that both Messrs. St. Albans are to be married . . . which is to be the heir?"

The earl's gaze fixed on Griffin at once, who shook his head so little that his message was nearly imperceptible.

"I believe I shall have to give this a bit of thought, Miss Howard, for I had not foreseen such an improbable outcome to my challenge. *Both* Messrs. St. Albans betrothed on the same day. Who would have thought it possible. Rest assured though, my dear lady, I shall announce my decision very soon. Perhaps even on the morrow."

Hannah heard Griffin exhale disappointedly, which seemed quite an odd reaction for someone who might soon be named heir.

The earl's decision did not come on the morrow. Or with the week. In truth, it was a full sennight later when he invited both of the St. Albans brothers, the Featherton sisters, Miss Howard, Mr. Edgar, and Hannah to Devonsfield for the much-anticipated announcement of the earl's heir.

Devonsfield was perhaps one of the largest mansions Hannah had ever seen. While the main house must have been at least two hundred years in age, a columned facade had been added of late, adding to the grandeur of the stately home. Two waterways crossed the parklike grounds, littered with follies, and falls of water, and a magnificent boxwood maze.

Annie busied herself with hanging gowns in the ancient wardrobe in the chamber Hannah had been assigned for her stay.

"Well, if you don't mind my sayin', I hope Mr. Griffin don't win this little contest of the earl's. I couldn't bear to think of you livin' here all secluded-like in this musty old place. You should go to London. That's what I would do. I'd go to the theater, and maybe to Almack's. I bet those old patroness dragons would let you in, seein' as how you are practically kin to the Featherton ladies and all."

Hannah gazed out the expansive window and across the endless lawn. "That would be just fine with Griffin. He wants nothing more than to study the stars." She turned around and looked at Annie.

Annie paused and stared blankly up. "What was that, Miss Hannah?"

Hannah realized the lady's maid had not paid any heed to what she had said.

"You know, Miss Hannah, it likely doesn't matter a lick what Mr. Griffin wants. It's Fate, I say. Every time the Feathertons get it fixed in their heads that someone should marry, they end up a peeress of some sort." She sighed deeply. "Maybe I should I ask for another wardrobe. There is no way this one will hold all your frocks when the earl meets his maker and you are forced to come and live in this old place."

"This one will be sufficient, Annie."

Annie handed a pelisse to Hannah. "They are boarding the carriages now. Are you ready for the outing?"

"Indeed. Though I must gather up Cupid first." Hannah took the silk-lined cape from Annie and started for the passage. She cast a parting glance out the window at the bright, sunny day, then turned and manufactured a perfectly suitable smile. "The day could not be more perfect for the earl's announcement."

Hannah saw a wrinkle of concern on Annie's forehead.

"Wish us good favor," Hannah said as she entered the passage. "We can certainly use it."

❧

Hannah settled Cupid on a low branch near the folding table that had been set up for their supper beside the lake. She twined his tether once around the branch, then tugged off her long leather glove and sat down on the coverlet that had been laid across the grass. Griffin lifted a juicy berry from the bowl between them and popped it into Hannah's mouth.

Spring had finally arrived. The air was warm, the sun bright, making this, most certainly, the most comfortable day of the year.

Mr. Edgar sat stiffly beside Lady Viola before the table, clearly uncomfortable in his new role as a lady's betrothed rather than her servant. His critical gaze followed the Devonsfield footmen as they served each course, and Hannah observed him nearly leap from his chair on two occasions to correct the placement of a bowl or to dab away a spot of soup that had dripped from the serving ladle.

Lady Viola, however, was beaming. She simply could not have been happier. For two weeks now, she and her sister had been planning a huge four-couple wedding at Bath Abbey, complete with hothouse lavender bouquets and silken lavender swatches draped from column to column.

They had, not once, bothered to ask Hannah or Miss Howard if a profusion of lavender or a group wedding suited, but honestly, it did not matter in the least to Hannah. All that mattered was that in two weeks' time she would be married to the man she loved.

Lady Letitia noticed Hannah's dreamy gaze. "Hannah, dear, did I tell you I received a letter from your brother, Arthur? Now, I know you mother's condition prevents her from leaving her home, and therefore she cannot attend the wedding. That's why you will be ever so excited to hear Arthur's news!"

Hannah straightened. "Arthur wrote to you? What did the letter say?"

A huge smile crossed Lady Letitia's plump face as she prepared to divulge the information.

"*Sister,*" Lady Viola admonished, "you were supposed to keep the contents of his letter a surprise!"

"*Oh, dear.* You are correct, sister." Lady Letitia's brows arched sadly. "Never mind, Hannah."

"You can't simply tell me my brother has written with some wonderful news, then refuse to tell me all about it!" Hannah narrowed her eyes playfully at the two old women. "You are being most wicked, you know."

Lady Letitia looked to her sister, and they had one of those silent twin discussions. "Very well. Arthur is no longer in India. He is in Glasgow at the moment, and plans to arrive in Bath for a visit not two days before the wedding celebration. Two!"

"So . . . he would not have received the letter I posted to India." Hannah's brows rose. "He could not know of my wedding."

"You have the right of things." Lady Viola grinned. "He will be ever so surprised!"

A spiked chill raced up Hannah's spine. "But what if he doesn't approve of my marrying Mr. St. Albans? He is the head of our family now. He could ruin everything!"

The earl loudly swallowed a wedge of cold beef, then sipped from his teacup. "I've already taken precautions, my dear. He will not refuse Mr. St. Albans."

"Precautions?" Griffin asked. "What sort of precautions?"

"Monetary, if you must know," the earl said matter-of-factly. "Upon your marriage—both yours and Garnet's—you will both become rather wealthy." The earl slapped the table and laughed. "Oh, let us call it correctly, shall we? You will be—*rich* men."

"W-what do you mean?" Garnet leaned over the table toward the earl. "How rich?"

"Rich enough. I have arranged for each of you to be bestowed fifteen thousand per annum, until my passing. Then you shall receive twenty-two thousand per annum . . . indefinitely."

Cupid screeched and Pinkerton, who likely had been poking at the bird, stumbled from beside the tree, muttering a string of oaths.

"Tell them, Pinkerton. Tell the lads of my financial state," the earl demanded. "You know it better than I, after all."

"Yes, my lord. The earl is certainly one of the wealthiest gentlemen in the realm. His family has long been involved with the production and distribution of brandy. You needn't fret about your income, ever again."

The earl snorted. "There you have it."

Hannah and Griffin turned and stared at each other in utter amazement. The earl had always lived so frugally, dressed so simply, that Hannah had always assumed he was guinea poor, though title and property rich.

By the stunned looks on Garnet's and Griffin's faces, they had obviously made the same assumption.

Likely hearing the word "brandy," Mrs. Hopshire,

the St. Albans brothers' longtime housekeeper, appeared at the head of the table with a decanter of amber spirits. "Would you be wanting some brandy, Garn—, I mean, Mr. St. Albans?"

"Thank you, Mrs. Hopshire." Garnet winked at her.

The old housekeeper smiled excitedly, happy, as always, to make herself useful. She had admitted to Annie, back at the house, that today was a special treat for her. Not only had she been asked to accompany the brothers to Devonsfield, but she'd been asked to join them at the outing, where she would be witness to the naming of the heir.

But Griffin and Garnet would have had it no other way. She had practically raised the twins after their mother's death, and Griffin had admitted to Hannah that both he and his brother thought of Mrs. Hopshire as a dear member of the family rather than their lone servant.

Just then, a bee began to circle Hannah's straw bonnet, seemingly drawn to the two flowers Annie had pinned upon its satin band. Hannah raised her hand into the air and swatted and waved at the marauder until she just brushed it.

Cupid, noting the movement of his mistress's hand bent forward, readied for flight. He began to screech and tug at his tether.

"No, Cupid!" Hannah called out as the bee circled her head one last time, then lit off for the table. Hannah watched as it landed on the silken hollyhock adornment on Lady Letitia's new Cambridge dress hat.

Hannah leaped to her feet, pointing her finger in warning at the old woman's hat. "There's a bee! Lady Letitia—on your hat!"

"Oh, goodness!" Lady Letitia jumped out of her chair and hurriedly untied the bonnet and tore it off her head. She shook the bonnet in the air, but the bee clung to it. "Someone get it off—get it off, please!"

Cupid launched from the branch, and the tether slipped loose. The bird's keen eyes focused on Hannah's pointing finger, then the bonnet waving in the air. He gave a piercing scream, then swooped for the bonnet.

Cupid's sharp talons snatched up Lady Letitia's hat on the first pass, then the falcon flew out over the lake.

"My new bonnet!" Lady Letitia shrieked, looking pleadingly at Hannah. "Do something, *please*. Tell your falcon to bring it back."

The earl stumbled from his folding chair, knocking it backward and causing it to snap shut. "Here now, you blasted bird." He trotted down to the water's edge and waved his short arms at Cupid. "Bring it back. Bring it back at once, or I shall have Pinkerton shoot you down!"

"My lord," Pinkerton said, quick on the earl's heels, "I have no rifle."

The earl turned and gave his man a most annoyed look. "But the *bird* doesn't know that, you fool!"

"Quite right, my lord." Pinkerton gave the earl an obligatory bow, no doubt, Hannah decided, to hide the rolling of eyes, then walked back up the gentle slope to the table.

Hannah waved her arm as Cupid made a low run over the lake's muddy shore, then cut her hand through the air like a knife through butter as he neared the earl.

Cupid let out a screech, and as he passed by the earl,

dropped the bonnet into the water not a yard from shore.

"There it is!" Lady Letitia called out to the earl. "Please, retrieve it, my dear, before it is ruined!"

"Yes, my sweet!" The earl high-stepped into the cold water and snatched up the bonnet, yelping his displeasure as his boots sank deep into the mud.

The earl stomped his feet as he emerged from the lake, splattering mud in wide-reaching sprays. When he reached the table, he offered Lady Letitia a gallant, sweeping bow as he bequeathed the hollyhock-topped confection. "Here you are, Lady Letitia . . . your bonnet."

Lady Letitia took the hat from the earl and gave him a quick peck on the cheek in appreciation.

"It will dry in no time at all, Letitia," Lady Viola told her sister. "Perhaps we ought to lay it on the blanket to catch the sun."

Her sister agreed, but when she turned the hat in her hands, she saw the spatter of mud on its lining. "'Tis . . . ruined. Do you see the mud, Viola? 'Tis ruined!"

The earl's eyes riveted on the brown speckles of mud inside the hat. Dark circles of red burst upon his puffed cheeks. "I shall buy you a new bonnet, dear. A better one. You'll see."

"Thank you, my lord. You are too kind." Lady Letitia slipped him a placating smile. "Though you ought to remove those sodden boots and stockings before you catch your"—her eyes rounded as she realized her next word—"before you catch *yourself* a sniffle."

The earl appeared startled. She did not need to say the word. He knew the truth of it. His wet feet could earn him an early demise!

Throwing himself into Lady Letitia's empty chair, he yanked off his boots and stockings and toweled his sopping feet with a linen serviette. "Pinkerton, bring me some dry stockings, and boots. Hurry now. My health is at risk!"

"Yes, my lord. At once!" Pinkerton ran off in the direction of the carriages.

Mrs. Hopshire made her way slowly beside the earl and picked up his discarded boots and stockings. But instead of taking them and packing them in the remaining carriage, she just held them in her wrinkled hands and stared at the earl's left foot. Her eyes grew as round as the supper plates.

Hannah followed the housekeeper's gaze and saw she was looking at a guinea-sized plum-colored birthmark on the earl's bare ankle.

Hannah laid her hand on the housekeeper's shoulder. "Mrs. Hopshire, what is it? Is something amiss?"

"I was just remembering the day the twins were born." The old woman looked up at Hannah. "It was something their mother said before she died."

Garnet and Griffin walked up and stood on either side of Mrs. Hopshire.

"What did she say?" Garnet asked softly.

The housekeeper peered up him and moisture welled in her eyes. "She said we'd always know which of the boys was older, because of the mark on his ankle."

The earl stood up slowly. His eyes were wild as he charged forward, reaching Garnet first and knocking him to the ground.

"What are you doing?" Garnet cried out, as the earl slapped away the younger man's flailing hands and tugged off Garnet's right boot and stocking. He grabbed Garnet's foot and held it before his eyes and examined. Then, evidently not finding what he was searching for, he tore off the remaining boot and stocking. He held his breath as he raised the foot level with his eyes and turned it.

A collective gasp rose up from everyone present. There was no denying what they saw.

There, on Garnet's ankle, was dark, wine-hued mark.

Chapter Twenty-one

Great arches of sunlight beamed through the soaring windows of Bath Abbey, illuminating the floor inside with almost blinding light. The abbey was already filled to near-breathless capacity, with every member of upper Society, as well as representatives of the bridal party's serving staff, standing shoulder to shoulder in the nave.

As the minute hand neared the hour of nine, the groomsmen collected in the south choir aisle, waiting for the grand wedding to commence with the ladies' entrance.

"Are you certain this was where **the** ladies truly wished to be married—or was it simply **the** most convenient?" The earl edged along the wall so as not to step upon the final resting place of Beau Nash, who, like many other Bath luminaries, had been buried beneath the abbey floor.

"It is, my lord," Mr. Edgar replied. "The ladies have spoken of little else since the eve of their betrothals."

Garnet nodded in agreement. "It is the grandest house of worship in all of Bath. No other site would suffice."

"I do not know if I agree with you, brother." Griffin settled his gloved hand on Garnet's shoulder. "The view from Beechen Cliff is glorious, and there is no point in the region closer to heaven."

The earl raised his bulbous nose and sniffed. Then sniffed again. "W-what is that scent in the air?" He pulled a handkerchief out from inside his coat and held it over his nose. "'Tis the putrid scent of rotting bodies, isn't it? Good heavens, it is!"

"Ah, no, my lord," Pinkerton told him. "'Tis the lavender bouquets securing the swatches." He gestured with his chin to the flowers secured to a nearby column.

The earl glanced at swatches of lavender stretching from column to column and cringed at the garish effect. "Yes, yes, I smell the lavender now, but I detect something else as well in the air—burial candles, I think."

Griffin gestured to the candles burning brightly before the sanctuary.

"Oh, I see," the earl murmured. "Still, 'tis rather like being married in a great mausoleum, is it not? And for goodness' sake, a wedding is supposed to mark the beginning of life together—not the end of life!"

The earl screwed up his nose and tiptoed past Nash's grave, suddenly noticing the wall tablets and memorial plaques partially obscured by the lavender silk ringing every column.

Pinkerton suddenly grabbed the earl's coatsleeve. His black eyes rounded with excitement.

"Pinkerton!" the earl snarled. "What are you doing? You shall wrinkle my coat and have to return to the house to press it again."

"My lord—'tis your solution." He tapped his boot on the floor.

"Solution? What do you go on about? Stop making nonsense, can you not see that I am a bundle of split nerves?"

"The solution to our capacity problem in the Devonsfield mausoleum." Pinkerton waited for the earl to think about what he was saying and understand his meaning. "*The floor* . . . instead of expanding outward, which is an impossibility at this moment anyway, given the Anatole family's reluctance to unearth and move their family for you. We simply—"

"Lay me into the mausoleum floor!" The earl's whole demeanor seemed to brighten, and he rubbed his hands together eagerly. "I am ever so thankful the wedding is here at Bath Abbey, else I might never have come up with such a grand idea."

"Indeed, my lord." Pinkerton rolled his eyes.

Inspired, the earl glanced up at an ornate memorial on the wall. "Why, my epitaph would not be limited to a square set into the wall, as the rest of Devonsfields' were—no, the entire floor could be used if I so desired . . . and I think I do. I think I *do* desire it."

"Shall we begin, my lord, sirs?" The vicar, already resplendently robed, already held the Book of Common Prayer in his hands. He gestured toward the sanctuary, and the four gentlemen followed him.

The earl gave a nod to Pinkerton, who in response walked to the west front of the abbey and opened the doors for the four ladies.

❧

When Hannah entered the abbey, walking next to Miss Howard and behind the two Featherton sisters, her stomach fluttered as if Cupid had swooped down her throat and settled in her belly.

As the women began to pass through the aisleway left for them through the nave, the abbey choir rose up in song. The choir had been Lady Letitia's idea completely, and Hannah thought the old woman might burst from pride when their song rose up clear to the heights of the fan-vaulted ceiling.

Even from behind, the two Featherton ladies were a sight to behold. They wore identical gowns of yards of lavender silk over hoops, with bounteous flounces edged with rows of blond lace. A half dozen ostrich plumes, dyed deepest amethyst, were stuffed into each of their mountainous white coiffures. Had Hannah not known better, she would think they were headed off to St. James's Palace for presentation.

As Hannah and Miss Howard proceeded slowly up the aisle, she saw the other woman's eyes were fixed on Garnet's. Unlike Hannah, Miss Howard was the picture of serenity. She wore a high-waisted pale rose gown that brought out the color of her cheeks and lips, with short capped sleeves trimmed with tiny pink and gray water pearls.

In her excitement to reach the sanctuary, Hannah walked too quickly, and the sweep of her short train slipped around in front of her, causing her to stumble. Lord above, how could everyone else be so calm, when she herself doubted even her ability to cross from the west end of the abbey to the east! She didn't dare look forward and meet Griffin's gaze. She would fall for certain and be forever known as the woman who made a cake of herself on her wedding day. And so, she focused on her slippers, carefully placing one foot in front of the other.

"Miss Chillton," came a whisper from the crowd.

Hannah looked up and her gaze met with Mr. Hercule Lestrange. She could not guess at why he would interupt her wedding, but as she neared, she heard the little man whisper again.

"Your secret is safe."

"My s-secret?"

Mr. Lestrange nodded and redirected his gaze toward the front of the abbey.

She started forward again, scanning the sea of faces, until her eyes met with her brother's. *"Arthur."* Hannah stopped. She did not care if the other ladies proceeded without her, for standing beside Arthur was . . . her mother.

Tears welled in Hannah's eyes. "Mother? How . . . ?" She looked to Arthur for an answer, for this could not be possible.

Arthur looked at their mother and whispered softly to her. "This is Hannah, Mother. Your daughter."

Her mother looked blankly at Arthur, then turned her eyes to study Hannah. She gazed upon her for several moments, then smiled warmly at her, the same smile Hannah remembered from her childhood—before everything changed.

It was only for the briefest of seconds, but in that time, Hannah thought her mother might have known her. A tear of happiness rolled down Hannah's cheek.

"She cannot stay for long, Hannah." Arthur gave her

a sad smile. "But when I visited her last eve, she was having a good day, so I brought her with me . . . to see her daughter on the happiest day of her life."

Hannah leaned close and softly kissed her brother's cheek. "Thank you, dear brother. You cannot know what this means to me."

Arthur reached out and, taking her shoulder into his grasp, turned Hannah forward and gave her a slight nudge back down the aisle. "Go now, little sister. Your betrothed awaits."

Hannah nodded. Happiness like she'd never known filled her every fiber as she proceeded, alone, through the aisle between the choir boxes and to the sanctuary.

She turned and looked up at Griffin then and smiled at him.

"I love you, Hannah," he said so softly that she was sure only she could hear him.

"I love you, too."

True to form, the Feathertons had carried off a grand, glittering carnival of a wedding, to which there had been no equal.

Everyone agreed. To wit, Mr. Hercule Lestrange's *on dit* column in the very next release of the *Bath Herald* touted the group wedding as a "majestic spectacle eclipsing even the passing of the Bath Comet and indeed, the explosion of a fireball in Prior Park."

Hannah, though, was much relieved that the wedding was in her past . . . and wedded bliss was the only future she saw before her.

She was a bride of two full days now. Only two. So

short an amount of time, but at this moment, somehow, she felt as though she'd known Griffin, at least in her heart, forever.

She smiled across the tea table in the parlor of Griffin's Queen Square house at the handsome, brilliant gentleman sitting across from her—her husband. *Husband!* Oh, it tickled her so to even think the word.

"What are you grinning about, my love?" Griffin reached across the table and squeezed her hand. "Could it be that my brother is leaving this evening for Devonsfield with his new wife—and the earl . . . and the countess."

"*And* Pinkerton. I should be most disappointed if they should leave the poor man here."

Griffin laughed. "No doubt. But by this eve, we shall be alone—except for Mrs. Hopshire, of course."

Hannah grimaced. "Yes, Mrs. Hopshire . . . how dear Garnet was to agree to leave her here to see to our needs. He always was so considerate."

"Still, for the most part, we will be alone. Whatever will we do to occupy ourselves?"

Hannah cocked her head to the side and slid Griffin a mischievous grin. "A walk might be in order. Yes, I think a stroll would be lovely, don't you? In fact, the sky is so clear—and ought to remain so this eve, do you agree?—that perhaps we should venture to Beechen Cliff . . . to view the stars. Mayhap we will see your comet, hmm?"

The earl stalked into the room and plopped down at the table. "I, for one, have had my fill of comets. Comets, comets . . . why, I am positively exhausted from comets—the Bath Comet in particular. Why is everyone so agog over a bit of light in the night sky? Why must it be celebrated with soirees, routs, balls,

and viewing parties? I for one hope that I never have
the misfortune of seeing a comet again!" He lifted the
lid from the teapot and grimaced. "The tea is cold. Mrs.
Hopshire, do see to your business and ensure that a
fresh pot of hot tea is served at once."

Mrs. Hopshire bobbed a rigid curtsy. "Yes, my lord.
Right away, my lord. Beggin' your pardon, my lord."

"Stop your babbling, woman, and fetch the tea, will
you?"

Griffin stiffened at the earl's outburst. "My lord, I
will not have Mrs. Hopshire spoken to in such a manner. When she returns, I trust you will show the respect
due a woman of her years and position within my
household."

The earl just shook his head. "I just asked for my tea
to be hot, that is all. I daresay, that is not too much to
ask," he snapped in retort.

There was a thud in the passage, and Hannah
glanced up from her own, suitably heated, tea to see
Pinkerton enter the room.

"My lord, your portmanteau is packed and ready for
the journey."

The earl flicked his fingers in the air dismissively.
"Very well, very well. See that it is lashed atop the carriage within the hour, for I do not wish to keep my
bride waiting. I wish to depart for Devonsfield the very
moment she is prepared to leave. I have waited long
enough." The earl glanced up to see everyone staring at
him. His cheeks colored. "Well, we've been married for
two days—but it is no secret we have yet to reside in
the same household! I am a newly married man, I'll
have you know, but still she puts me off—until I can
carry her over the threshold of Devonsfield. Well, I do

not have to tell you, I am not a well man. How am I supposed to carry her over the threshold? How, I ask you?"

Hannah pinned Griffin with her gaze and inclined her chin toward the earl in silent communication.

Garnet strolled into the parlor with his wife at his elbow. "All of the documents are signed, my lord, and a barrister has been dispatched to see that all are filed with the correct authorities." He smiled as broadly as the heir of an earldom possibly could. "As far as anyone is concerned, I am firstborn."

"And heir." Griffin grinned at his brother.

Garnet turned and smiled at his bride, then at his brother. "Well, yes, there is that, too."

Then, Hannah noticed the most peculiar thing— Garnet winked at Griffin, who, like a reflection in a mirror, winked at his brother at the very same moment. What in blazes? Hannah narrowed her eyes suspiciously. There was something she wasn't being told.

She was all set to quiz her husband about it when Mrs. Hopshire entered the room. Without delay, she poured the earl a steaming cup of tea, then pulled a card from her apron and turned to Griffin. "Begging your pardon, but *this* was just left for you, sir."

"Another card of wedding congratulations, I am sure. Thank you, Mrs. Hopshire." Griffin reached out his hand and took the card she handed him. He looked twice at it, reading the few words written upon it, then set it back down on the table, pushing it toward Hannah.

Hannah glanced down at the cream-colored card. She had to admit to herself, she was ever so anxious to read it, and wondered if, as Griffin's wife, she could simply snatch it up and do so. Or if she should wait until she was given leave to do so, which, sadly, she knew was likely the appropriate course. *Blast.*

Griffin persisted in staring at the card, not speaking a word.

Finally, Hannah intervened, for she could not bear not knowing the meaning of the card any longer! "Dear, who . . . um . . . sent us thoughts of congratulations? Shall I read the card?"

"No one." His gaze was blank, as if he were off gathering wool.

"No one? Griffin, someone sent a card. I can see it on the table between us." She laughed, trying to make light, but heavens, she could not endure the suspense even a moment longer!

Griffin poked his index finger to the card, then pushed it across the surface of the table to Hannah. He raised his eyes to hers and waited as she lifted the card in her hand and read it.

Miss Caroline Herschel,
Twenty-six Brock Street, Bath

She flipped the card over and read the slanted inked words.

A letter arrived from the Royal Observatory at
Greenwich. Should you like to read it, please call
at your earliest convenience.
CH

One hour later, Griffin and Hannah sat across from Miss Herschel in the library of Twenty-six Brock

Street. In the older woman's tiny hand was a letter, the wax wafer having already been broken. She raised it to Griffin, and he hesitantly accepted it from her.

"You should read it. No sense in my reiterating what it says." There was no emotion on her face. No disappointment. No joyfulness. Her expression was as flat as the plaster ceiling above. "You can read well enough." She flicked her fingers at Griffin, urging him to begin.

Hannah could see that his fingers were shaking as he unfolded the foolscap. Her first inclination was to reach out and take it—to read aloud for him. But she knew, favorable or foul, Griffin had to read the news for himself.

He sat very still, staring at the letter, though Hannah knew he had to have finished reading it already. "Griffin, what does it say?" He said nothing, but handed it to Hannah, then fixed his gaze on Miss Herschel. Now, the old woman's expression was dancing.

Dear Miss Herschel—

I wish to thank you for your letter detailing your protégé's account of a possible new comet. I do hope you did not think low of me for not replying before this day, but you must know that we at the Royal Observatory at Greenwich had to judge the merits of the calculation and observational accounts independently to either accept or deny its validity.

Having completed our own study, I wish Mr. St. Albans sincere joy and our fondest congratulations on his discovery. It is not so often that one so young as he is able to immortalize his name. I also wish to commend you on your assiduity in

astronomy and for encouraging such a bright
young stargazer as your Mr. St. Albans.

Per your request, I requested for Mr. St. Albans a royal appointment and immediate mem-
bership in the Royal Astronomical Society. To my
utter delight, and I am sure yours as well, I am
pleased to tell you that the request has been ap-
proved this morning. Mr. St. Albans will be expected in London on the 14th of April to accept
this great honor he is so deserving to receive.

> Your most obedient and obliged
> humble servant,
> Alexander Aubert, Esq.

"Griffin! This is the best of all possible news!" Hannah sprang from her chair and threw herself into Griffin's arms, heedless of possibly embarrassing the old
woman sitting across from him.

It seemed that Hannah had nothing to fret about
anyway, for Miss Herschel threw back her head and
laughed aloud. "Now, my dears, you must excuse me. I
have a caller due at any moment." And then the tiny astronomer threw them both a mischievous wink.

The day was sunny and bright, a good day for a
walk, as Hannah had predicted. They had just stepped
from the steps of Twenty-six Brock Street, when who
should stop in front of Miss Herschel's home but Mr.
Hercule Lestrange.

He removed his gleaming beaver hat from his oddly
shaped head and gave a neat bow to Hannah. "Fine day
we are having, Mrs. St. Albans, Mr. St. Albans."

"The best," Hannah replied.

"I wholeheartedly agree. Good day!" With that, Mr. Lestrange replaced his hat on head and bounded up the steps of Twenty-six Brock Street.

At precisely five minutes before five o'clock, the earl waved his walking stick in the air and quite literally herded the St. Albans brothers and their brides into the town carriage, and they started up Gay Street toward Number One Royal Crescent.

The earl impatiently thrummed his fingers on his knee as the sturdy team of horses huffed and strained up the steep incline.

Pinkerton, who had already seen that the earl's portmanteau and trunk were lashed atop the conveyance, had been required to walk up the hill in the direction of Royal Crescent, as there had been no room for him inside the cab. But Pinkerton did not truly mind this inconvenience in the least, for he was not at all convinced that the carriage would make its way to the top of Gay Street.

At the earl's request, or rather because the testy, squat earl demanded it, Pinkerton had not only carefully loaded the carriage with the earl's belongings. He had also prepared for the first leg of the long journey to Devonsfield by packing three large baskets of breads, cheeses, sweets, an assortment of dried fruits, and a generous selection of brandy and wine.

The carriage was heavily weighted, even without the new Lady Devonsfield's travel trunk, despite his protestations to the earl that another carriage be secured for stowage.

From the steps of the St. Albanses lodgings, Pinkerton watched with a wicked sense of pleasure as the carriage slowed to a stop and, indeed, rolled back a few feet, despite the driver's best efforts to spur his team up the hill.

When the cab door was angrily kicked open from the inside of the carriage, Pinkerton disappeared back inside the St. Albanses house, deciding that this was the most opportune time to share a parting cup of tea with dear old Mrs. Hopshire.

Having been unable to locate a pair of chairmen, or even a hackney to convey the party up the incline, then on to Royal Crescent, the earl arrived in the Featherton ladies' elegant drawing room near dripping from the exertion.

"Oh, my dear husband, come in, do come in." Lady Devonsfield rushed forward and kissed her husband's damp cheek. "My things are folded and packed, and I am ever so eager to be on our way to Devonsfield just as soon as we all toast our good-byes." She reached out and squeezed his hand twice, then whispered, a little too loudly, "I am *very* eager, my lord, if you grasp my meaning."

Hannah swallowed and bit the inside of her lips to quiet the amusement that otherwise would have flown from her mouth. "Where is Lady Viola Edgar?" she asked the countess.

"She and Mr. Edgar shall be down presently. They are . . . dressing, I believe." Lady Devonsfield caught

Hannah's arm and drew her close. "Dear, might I have a word or two with you privately, in the study?"

Hannah looked quizzically at the elderly woman. "Why . . . certainly, if you wish it."

"I do, Hannah. I wish immensely." Her faded blue eyes grew wide with some meaning Hannah could not fathom.

Hannah turned to her husband and the others who had hiked Gay Street so that the carriage might progress up the rise. "Please take your ease in the drawing room. I shall only be a moment."

Lady Devonsfield seemed to exhale her relief the moment the quartet retreated from the passage. She grabbed Hannah's wrist and hauled her down the passage and into the study.

"Oh, Hannah, I am in such a quandary, I know not what to do or where to turn. You must assist me. Please."

"I will help you in any way I might, Lady Devonsfield." It was then that Hannah noticed the old woman was trembling. Trembling! How strange. Why, she could not recall a single instance when Lady Devonsfield seemed the least but fearful—but now, it was clear, she was terrified. "Tell me what troubles you."

Her powdered cheeks glowed red like ash-covered embers in a hearth. "I admit, what I am about to say is most . . . most embarrassing." She pulled Hannah to a settee near the window and looked, with all seriousness, into her eyes. "'Tis about the wedding night."

"Your wedding night?" Hannah searched Lady Devonsfield's eyes until she thought she saw something. "Oh, I see. The earl was simply overwrought, 'tis all. I am sure next time, all will be well with . . . the earldom." She patted Lady Devonsfield's hand comfortingly.

"What?" It took some seconds for the old woman to gather Hannah's meaning. "No, no. The problem is not the earl—I am the problem."

"I do not understand."

"There has been no wedding night." She widened her eyes twice. "We haven't . . . well, we simply haven't."

"But you are married. Why haven't you . . . been close?"

"Hannah, I am an old woman. Unlike my sister, I haven't . . . I haven't—oh, perdition—I am still *a maid*."

"So this is why you and the earl have not slept in the same house since the wedding. It had naught to do with the tradition of a husband carrying his wife over their home's threshold."

"Oh, please, Hannah. I am not daft. I know the earl cannot support my weight. He is not a well man, you know."

Hannah fought the urge to smile. "Sadly, you are right."

"But what else could I say? I have not the faintest notion what truly happens between a man and a woman on their wedding night. I have some notions, but I do not know what to do. He is a widower. He has experience in these matters. I do not. I do not wish, after waiting all these years for the man of my dreams to marry me, for my husband to be . . . disappointed in me."

Tears budded in her eyes, and for the first time Lady Devonsfield appeared completely lost and vulnerable.

"Dear, dear. Have you not spoken to your sister about this?"

Lady Devonsfield seemed startled by the question. "Ask Viola about lovemaking? Heaven forbid. I am her older sister, after all. She looks to *me* for guidance. Can you not, secretly, educate me?"

Hannah donned a confident smile. "I will do my best, but truly, there is naught to worry about. As you said, the earl has been married before." She drew in a deep breath, then played her fingers across her lips. "Now then, where shall I begin?"

Twenty minutes later, Hannah and Lady Devonsfield emerged from the study. Hannah wiped her brow with a handkerchief, the old woman's probing questions having quite exhausted her.

But it seemed she had been successful in quelling Lady Devonsfield's fears, for as they quit the study, they passed a glowing Lady Viola Edgar and Mr. Edgar, wearing a saucy grin on his lips of a sort Hannah had never before observed.

Lady Devonsfield didn't even seem to notice her sister and Mr. Edgar. Instead she caned her way into the drawing room and straightaway poured two crystals of cordial.

She handed one to the earl and kept the other for herself. "My lord, it seems . . . er . . . the lock on my portmanteau will not latch."

"Is that all? When Pinkerton arrives I shall just send him up to manage it for you." The earl sipped his cordial slowly.

"My lord, I do not think Pinkerton can fix it. Come, let me show you."

"Well, if Pinkerton cannot mend it, I certainly cannot." The earl continued nursing his glass of cordial, clearly not taking her meaning.

Garnet finally interceded. "My lord, you have the key to the lock. In your pocket, sir."

"I do? But I don't recall putting a key—*oh!*" The earl slammed his cordial to the table and took Lady Devonsfield's hand. Together, they raced, as best they could given their ages and infirmities, out into the passage, then above stairs for a bit of privacy.

It was an hour later, and the earl and his countess still had not descended from the bedchambers above, when there was a knock at the door.

Mr. Edgar rose from the settee where he sat beside his doting wife and answered the door. This, Hannah surmised, was done strictly out of habit, for a most efficient replacement manservant had just been employed at Number One Royal Crescent.

Everyone in the drawing room looked up as a veritable crowd of visitors entered the room.

Hannah jumped up. "Good heavens! Look, 'tis Meredith and Lord Lansing." Hannah ran forward and hugged her old friend Meredith.

Lady Viola Edgar rose and started for Meredith when the girl's sisters, Eliza and Grace, swept into the room, trailed by two toddling children, and their handsome husbands, Magnus MacKinnon and Lord Hawksmoor. The old woman clapped her hands with joy. "All of you here at once. Only one pair missing—"

"No, no." Mrs. Penny entered from the passageway, leading her daughter Jenny, and Lady Viola Edgar's grandson Callum, and in his arms, her great-grandson James. "We've got them all now, my lady."

Lady Viola Edgar was so completely overcome that she did not know whether to laugh . . . or cry. And so she did the next best thing. She hurried to the staircase.

"Letitia, come at once, Sister! We have visitors— the whole family is here at once."

When she reentered the room, Eliza approached her first. "We are all dreadfully sorry we were unable to attend the wedding, for it sounded the event of the Bath season to be sure."

"Darling, the wedding plans were drawn together so quickly, we didn't anticipate that you would be able to come. But how lovely that you came now!" She gave her grandniece a tight hug.

There was a sound, not unlike two draft horses taking the stair treads; then, a quite disheveled Lady Devonsfield followed by the earl, entered the drawing room to greet the family and to introduce her new husband.

The ladies' plans were announced. Both women and their husbands would live together at Hanover Square for six months of the year—during the season obviously. Then, Lady Viola and Edgar would reside at Royal Crescent for the other half of the year, while Lady Devonsfield and the earl lived at Devonsfield. It was the perfect solution, for the sisters, who could not bear to be apart, and for their husbands, who needed a modicum of marital independence.

Mrs. Penny set aside the tray of cordial crystals, for this was a true celebration after all, and brought out the cut-crystal glasses from Ireland and filled them with the Feathertons' last two bottles of contraband French wine from Champagne.

She circled around the room, passing every adult a glass, then boldly took up the last one herself.

Hannah raised her glass in the air and turned a soft eye to her husband, Griffin. "To everlasting love."

"Hear, hear! To love!" the party cheered as one.

The elderly sisters joined hands and beamed. Here they stood in the bosom of their family. Their hearts were full, and now their lives were complete, for never before had they felt such love and happiness.

Epilogue

Hannah rubbed her eyes against the morning light streaming in the cottage window and snuggled closer to her sleeping husband. With a pleased sigh, she ran her fingertips lightly over the crisp mat of hair on his bare chest as she nestled closer still to kiss him.

Though they were pronounced husband and wife a full month hence, Griffin had been summoned to Greenwich, as a royal appointee, to present his findings on the discovery of a new comet. Only now had he been able to whisk his bride away from the city for a few days before having to return to Greenwich and to begin his work cataloging nebulae.

Surprisingly enough, they had not been truly alone until last eve.

Hannah's heart had been so full, she had not believed it was possible to feel such happiness—until last night.

Had Griffin not sworn to the contrary, Hannah

would have believed another fireball had passed overhead.

With that thought burned into her mind, Hannah ran her hand down over Griffin's chest and beneath the coverlet.

Griffin grinned before opening his eyes. "Good morning, my love," he whispered to her.

"Will it be? Do you promise? Will it be as good as your 'good evening' was?" Hannah widened her eyes with feigned innocence, as she pressed herself against him and twined her leg around his.

Griffin laughed softly and pulled her atop him.

Hannah braced her feet against his, then pushed up to cup his face between her palms and kiss him deeply. Then she stopped and lifted her mouth from his. She felt something at the end of the bed and wriggled her toes beneath the covers.

There was a sizable bump on his ankle.

"What is that, Griffin?"

"Oh, that." He sought to distract her with another kiss. "'Tis nothing."

"Have you been injured?" Hannah stared with all concern into Griffin's eyes, but he merely arched his eyebrows, in a close approximation of her earlier expression of innocence.

Hannah pushed off Griffin and tore back the coverlet from their naked bodies. She crawled down the mattress and touched a white-mottled raised bit of skin. "Griffin?" She turned her gaze upward at him.

"Yes, darling?"

"Griffin, my love, this looks suspiciously like . . . a birthmark."

"Does it?"

Hannah pounced atop his body and pinned him. "Do not toy with me, sir. You know what I am speaking of. You do!"

Griffin chuckled at her persistence. "That's because it is—or rather was. I had it from birth. Faded though, as I grew older. Barely noticeable now."

Hannah widened her eyes. "So you *were* firstborn!"

"If Mrs. Hopshire is correct in her memory, I would have to say . . . yes."

"Why didn't you say anything? Why didn't Garnet for that matter?"

"Garnet wanted the earldom badly." Griffin exhaled slowly. "And, I, well, I had no desire to become an earl, spending my days and evenings in pursuit of amusement. I wanted nothing more than to study the stars . . . and you." He laid his hands behind her neck and back and rolled her to the mattress and moved over her. He kissed her deeply, and a sigh fell from her lips.

"Now, let me observe that heavenly body of yours."

About the Author

KATHRYN CASKIE has long been a devotee of history and things of old. So it came as no surprise to her family when she took a career detour off the online superhighway and began writing historical romances full-time.

With a degree in communications and a background in marketing, advertising and journalism, she has written professionally for television, radio, magazines, and newspapers in and around the Washington, D.C., metropolitan area.

She lives in Virginia in a two-hundred-year-old Quaker home nestled in the foothills of the Blue Ridge Mountains with her greatest sources of inspiration, her husband and two young daughters.

Readers may contact Kathryn at her Web site:
www.kathryncaskie.com.

THE DISH

Where authors give you the inside scoop!

♥ ♥ ♥ ♥ ♥ ♥ ♥ ♥ ♥ ♥ ♥ ♥ ♥ ♥ ♥ ♥ ♥

What could an author of historical romances and an author of contemporary vampire fiction possibly have in common? We find out when authors Kathryn Caskie and Robin T. Popp chat online about their books.

Robin T. Popp: Do you know that the hero of *Seduced by the Night*, Dirk Adams, was never intended to be a long-term character and end up with his own story? When I first created him in *Out of the Night*, he was supposed to be like one of the extras on *Star Trek*—killed off in the first fifteen minutes of the show.

Kathryn Caskie: You mean the guy in the red shirt with the landing party, right? Don't tell anyone, but I grew up watching *Star Trek*.

Robin T. Popp: Me, too. I loved that show. So, what about in *Love is in the Heir* (on sale now)? Any "red shirts" turned heroes?

Kathryn Caskie: No red shirts, but over the course of the book my hero did split into two characters. You see, my heroes are usually bad boys, but Griffin, the hero of *Love is in the Heir,* couldn't be. Problem was, no matter how hard I tried to keep him in line, his wicked side kept showing up, making my heroine hate him. Then my heroine thought, it was almost like he was two different men. And that is exactly what he became: two separate people. The good twin, Griffin, and the rakish twin, Garnet, who are both pretending to be the same man.

Robin T. Popp: I foresee many interesting situations.

Kathryn Caskie: It's especially bad when Griffin tells her he loves her and wants to marry her, and they make love. Then the next day, she runs into the rakish twin who acts like it never happened. She thinks she's fallen for the oldest trick in a rake's book.

Robin T. Popp: Why are Griffin and Garnet pretending to be the same man?

Kathryn Caskie: There is this law called primogeniture. The eldest inherits everything—titles, houses, money—but if no one knows which twin was born first, meaning no clear heir, the Crown can reclaim it all. The ailing earl in my story doesn't want that to happen when he dies so he makes a deal with the twins. The twin to marry a woman of quality first will be named "firstborn." This is all pretty illegal, so the bride hunt has to remain a secret.

Robin T. Popp: Ah, secrets, lies, and deceptions. In *Seduced by the Night,* I have a similar situation when Beth (the heroine) believes Dirk is something he isn't. She's a biochemist and vampires are trying to kidnap her because they want her to duplicate the chupacabra venom that turns humans into vampires—they plan to sell "immortality" on the black market. So Dirk, as her bodyguard, is trying to protect her without her knowing that he, himself, is a changeling—half-human and half-vampire.

Kathryn Caskie: Griffin's dilemma is that he wants to tell the heroine everything, but he can't because he doesn't want to betray his brother's trust. It's a case of honor and integrity versus love.

Robin T. Popp: Dirk faces a similar choice. If Beth discovered the truth, she'd be terrified of him. This is further complicated because Beth is engaged to another man and while honor dictates that Dirk keep his emotional distance from her, his heart demands otherwise.

Kathryn Caskie: I wouldn't have thought our stories could be so different and yet share so much common ground—two books about deception and dual identities.

Robin T. Popp: Tough issues to overcome, especially in a romance story.

Kathryn Caskie: But as you say, our books are romances, so our characters will live happily ever after.

Kathryn Caskie   *Robin Popp*

www.kathryncaskie.com   www.robintpopp.com